Libidinous Variations

Volume Two:
Chillaxin'

Libidinous Variations

Volume Two:
Chillaxin'

by

J. Laux Perren

Duclerc Press
Wichita, Kansas & Santa Barbara, California

Duclerc Press

An imprint of
Saint Gaudens Press
Post Office Box 405
Solvang, CA 93464-0405

Preface

———

This is the Second volume of a compilation of short stories written over many years. A few of these stories are fictionalized autobiographical in nature; some are just fantasies; and most are just stories I found interesting and worth writing about.

A word of caution or forewarning might seem appropriate with respect to works of erotica. I tried to create a spread of sexual experiences; thus, some will undoubtedly not be to your liking. Rather than cast this modest compendium aside in disgust, I urge you to skip the offending story and read on. Let your imagination wonder about what might have been, or what could be. The human experience remains a vast spectrum of colors, shades and nuance.

If you find these stories entertaining and engaging, please let the publisher know, so they will demand more stories from me. I will write as long as you wish to read.

Enjoy!

J. Laux Perren

———

Dedication

—

To my lovers and friends,
who never cease to inspire me.

—

Acknowledgments

———

I was pleasantly surprised and gratified to hear from family and friends, but I suppose that is to be expected since they know me and appreciate the substance behind the words.

I am especially appreciative of strangers whom I have not yet enjoyed the opportunity of meeting in person and communicated with me after the publication of my first volume of erotic stories (2015). I have been overwhelmed by the generosity and candor of so many people who freely shared their stories with me. Sexuality has never been an easy or open topic of discussion. Perhaps these little glimpses into the vast spectrum of human sexuality will help us all become more comfortable with talking about sex and the importance of sex in our relationships.

I received so many stories from citizens I do not know that several trends began to emerge, so much so, they have stimulated me to seriously consider graduate and doctoral studies into the genesis of our sexual phobias, into societal strictures, and perhaps into the forces that constrain and restrict our sexual expression and how they might change.

I would be quite remiss if I failed to acknowledge the courage and resoluteness of the publisher – Saint Gaudens Press – and especially my editor, Jeremy Hawking. Thank you for allowing my voice to be heard.

J. Laux Perren

———

Michael

—

Everything about this day needed to be forgotten. Not one thing had gone right from the failure of the electrical power during the night that reset my alarm-clock radio, to the absence of my assistant due to a sick child, to the constant stream of crisis after crisis all day long. These days happened, but this one had to be the worst in recent memory. Of course, things would eventually improve although sometimes that rationalization became particularly difficult to digest.

The damp, chill of the night air tightened my neck even further. The inevitable headache lurked just a few more minutes in the cold. The thought of returning my meager apartment especially in my current mood brought a pseudo-nauseous sensation.

I stepped into a local bar between the Underground exit and my apartment. A straight-up Jack Daniels took some of the chill away, but the conversation and clientele remained distant and not particularly engaging. There was no question this approach would not remedy my melancholy. I needed something else. The solution had to be a good workout and maybe the extra expense of a good full body massage to eliminate all the kinks.

The additional five-block walk in the cold air did not seem so bad with the prospect of some good sweat and a hot shower. The sting of accumulating automobile exhaust mixed adversely with the incessant din of tires, brakes, shouting of obscenities, engines and shuffling humanity trying to be oblivious to the clutter. The dimensions of my surroundings wore though the last vestiges of warm from the alcohol.

Fortunately for me, the gym was nearly empty, an oddity for such a poor night, but I was inwardly grateful. I changed quickly into my shorts, T-shirt and running shoes. The stretching did little to loosen my tension. The calisthenics followed by weight work brought a modest sweat. The run around the monotonous, short, mezzanine track added a thorough dampness to my clothes, but without some reasonable scenery, just did not provide satisfaction. Now, there was no choice; the extra expense of a massage remained my only hope for relaxation.

"Do you have any openings?" I asked the rather plain, young woman behind the desk.

She consulted her appointment book. "Were you needing a rub down or something else?"

They offered a full range of massage therapies. My first impression seemed the best. "I'd like a full body massage, if there are any openings."

"Helen is open now. She's fully certified."

"I haven't met her before."

"She's fairly new, but comes highly recommended."

"That should do. I just need something to work these knots out – a good sweat didn't do it."

"All right, then. Why don't you take a good shower, and she'll meet you in Room 7 in ten minutes."

"OK."

I hung my damp clothes in my locker to dry, then walked to the shower room. The ten shower-head, tiled room was completely empty and a bit chilly, which did not help my body. I started my shower with the water temperature as hot as I could initially stand it. I washed down twice just to give my still achy muscles an added push. I knew I did not have much time to dally, but I decided to take the water temperature up a couple of steps. The heat felt good, as it soaked into my body. My shoulders, chest and back had a reddish tint when I turned off the water. The hot water had done the trick. I felt much better. The tension was gone. I could easily just climb into bed and drift off the sleep.

I considered canceling my appointment. The need just did not seem to be as prominent as it had been five or ten minutes earlier. This massage was an extra expense I did not need, but it was also an implied commitment. In the end, I decided to go ahead with the treatment. It would not hurt anything other than my wallet, and I would not be jerking anyone around with indecision.

"Oh, what the hell," I said to myself, as I wrapped a large towel around my waist and donned a large, thick, Terry-cloth, robe.

Room 7 was the fourth door on the right side of the common corridor between the male and female dressing rooms. There were ten rooms altogether, five per side. I knocked softly on the door with the large seven painted on it. There was no answer. I entered. It was a comparatively good sized room. The large massage table or maybe it was a bench stood in the middle of the room. Several chairs as well as a workbench containing the various items used by a masseuse or masseur sat along the far wall. The gym employed an equal number of both. The assignment appeared to be sequential . . . who was up next. Unless you specifically requested one person or another, the assignment was random to the occasional patron. The white tile room was fairly warm for an all tile room. A simple, peripheral, fluorescent lighting bar brightened the room quite well.

A double knock at the door interrupted my reexamination of the room. I did not answer simply because there was probably only one person it could be. The door opened. A moderately attractive woman probably in her late thirties or early forties entered the room wearing a white, work dress that buttoned up the front.

"You must be Michael?" she asked in a warm and friendly voice that hinted of an unusual mixture of French and English accent.

"Yes."

"I'm Helen," she said extending her right hand to shake mine.

Her hand was warm and dry as well as noticeably firm – a woman with strength and confidence.

"I haven't seen you before."

"I'm rather new here, I should say . . . less than a month, actually."

"You have such a delightful accent. Where are you from?"

"Boston."

I knew that answer was not complete. "Yeah, but where did you grow up?"

"The South of England . . . Dorset, actually."

"But, it seems like you've a smear of French in your voice."

She smiled. "I did have some schooling in France."

"Nice to have you with us."

"Thank you. Now, shall we get to it?"

"Sure."

"A full body massage . . . is that correct?"

"If you don't mind."

She laughed as she placed her hands on her hips in a mock gesture of authority. "You are the customer. I'm here to make you feel better. Simply put, I will do what you need me to do."

"A full body massage would be great."

"Then, so it shall be. Would you like a towel or not?"

"A towel?"

"Covering you."

I was not sure if she was asking for me or for her. Every previous session left the towel wrapped around my waist. If she was asking, then she probably did not care. "It's up to you."

"Well, as long as you're not embarrassed, it does make my job easier without a towel."

"There you go," I said, as I dropped my robe and towel. I felt a twinge of 'is-this-really-what-you-want.' She moved to the equipment workbench to prepare for her work. Without fanfare, I climbed on the table and lay face down placing my face into the conformal, donut hole that supported my head.

"Are there any special spots I need to be aware of?"

Most of the professionals did not bother to ask. A few did. They wanted to know if there were bruises, cuts, particularly sore muscles, et cetera, to make sure they were appropriately sensitive to those spots. "None I know of."

"Excellent. Then, shall we get started?"

"Fine by me."

"Would you like me dressed or undressed?"

"Excuse me?"

"Would you like me dressed or undressed?"

The thought of having a naked woman working whatever knots were left in my muscles did have a certain appeal to it. However, it also raised many more questions. *Was this a setup? Was she some kinda cop trying to catch a decency law violator? Was she a hooker in some cheap, thin disguise?* The magnetic attraction of the flame captured my thoughts.

"I heard the question. I just wondered what you really meant."

"It's a normal question I ask out of courtesy. I have always figured, if my clients are naked, it is only appropriate that I share the exposure."

More questions. My heart jumped up several notches. *What was she after?* The old adage: if it sounds to good to be true, it probably is. *Did her simple question send me down one of two vastly different paths? What would I encounter on either path? Was there some type of secret, hidden camera? What did all this mean?* I struggled with my thoughts. The flame flared brighter. "Whatever you prefer," I finally answered.

"Right, then." She started unbuttoning her work dress. "I find clothes particularly restrictive."

I returned my head to the donut and fought the urge to assess her body. I wanted this to appear at least in some fraction as a normal situation.

"This is something you do for both men and women?"

"Certainly. There is nothing lascivious in nudity."

"I suppose."

"If you are uneasy with this, Michael, I will gladly put my dress back on."

"Not necessary. I was just curious."

"Right then. Shall we begin?"

I nodded my head.

Helen started by moving to my head. I could see her bare feet and lower legs through the hole in the table . . . nice shape; smooth, tight skin; delicate feet without nail polish. She began by massaging my scalp. Her touch sent chills through my body. It was nearly perfect; the right combination of pressure, movement and feel. Just her scalp massage acted like a pressure relief valve venting any residual tension.

Helen moved with effortless precision from her position at the top of my head to straddling my waist without missing a stroke of my head. The character of her movements provided enough wonderment. Her hands drifted from my head to my neck to my shoulders, back and arms. I could feel the occasional brush of her smooth, warm skin. The exquisite blend of hard and soft, firm and gentle, worked its magic on my muscles. She moved gracefully down my body pausing only to apply the requisite amount of warm oil to lubricate the contact of our skin. A light scent of pine filled the room.

It was her treatment of my buttocks, legs and feet that produced a state of excitement I began to worry about. I did not know whether I should pretend it did not exist or wait for its passing.

"You can flip over, now," she said as she touched my thigh.

"Give me a few minutes."

"So, my magic hands have affected you, have they? Not to worry, Michael. I take it as a compliment. Your choice, but you won't offend me."

I thought for a moment. *What the hell . . . nothing has seemed to bother her yet.* I gradually turned over to lie flat on my back.

Helen stood next to me looking into my eyes. I wanted to look at her body directly, but fought the urge as I concentrated on her eyes and remained content with the less detail of my peripheral vision.

"Well, now a fine specimen you have here," she said as she diverted her eyes to my state of excitement. I glanced at the object of her attention.

"I'm sorry. That doesn't usually happen."

"Quite all right, Michael. We'll have to let it pass before I can proceed, or it will get in the way."

"I'm sorry." I squirmed a little, as if my movement would help it go.

She chuckled. "You've nothing to apologize for. We have a choice here. We can wait for it to pass, or if you'll allow me to be so bold, I can take care of it for you."

"Take care of it?" I asked, knowing exactly what I thought she meant, but not believing it.

Without the slightest hesitation, she reached for me. As her fingertips began to move gently up and down, an additional urge of inflation teetered me on the edge of pain and pleasure. I resisted my urge to groan as I shut my eyes to fight the mounting pressure to react.

"Is this OK?"

"Yes, yes . . . oh sweet Jesus, yes."

"Good."

She applied some warm oil that enhanced the sensations on my skin. Her touch transitioned from finger tips to hand as she grasped me with just the right pressure. Her strokes were perfect . . . not too long and not too short . . . not too low and not too high . . . perfect.

"I enjoy this part of my job," she said so casually. I really did not feel like talking. I just wanted to enjoy the exquisite sensations. Helen apparently wanted to talk. "If I can bring a little more pleasure or relaxation, I think it's worth the extra effort." She continued her stroking and replenishing the oil as required to keep the silky connection fresh. "I always find the physiology of excitement and climax so fascinating." Helen must have felt my changing state as my entire universe collapsed down to one single point and the sensations surrounding that point. Her pace picked up in harmony with my approach to the peak.

The surge to the peak came quickly. Every muscle in my body tensed and shook as the waves engulfed me. I squeezed hard to choke off any sound. I could feel my hot fluid hit my chest to my belly button. Her motions changed according to my state. When the majority was out, her hand began a more milking like action. I collapsed back to the table.

"Now, I would say that was pretty good."

I could only nod my head. That was the most fantastic hand job I had ever experienced.

"Thank you for allowing me to do that and sharing your pleasure with me."

I looked at her with incredulity. I was the one who derived the pleasure. I wanted to reciprocate . . . to give her pleasure . . . but, in the end, I decided that would be the wrong thing to do. It would imply the event was something other than what I thought it was and would probably offend her sense of propriety.

Helen cleaned me up as she talked about her fascination with the subtleties of the human body. Her matter-of-fact actions made the event all the more innocent like a cough or a sneeze. It was just part of nature.

She returned to the massage in the normal flow of things applying oil to my chest, then climbing up to straddle me. This time I did not try to avert my eyes. I absorbed every inch of her.

Her eyes remained primarily focused on the spot of her kneading motion with an occasional glance to my eyes. She knew I was now looking at her with focused interest, but again, she seemed to accept my attention as a natural activity.

Her breasts hung naturally. They bore the changes of maturity well. The swing of her breasts as she moved possessed an almost magnetic quality. Her nipples were prominent, but did not appear to be fully erect, but they were nice, large, round nipples . . . the kind I just loved to suck on and play with using my fingers, lips, tongue and teeth. Even more attractive was the junction of her legs. Her skin was so smooth and hairless, not even the slightest sign that hair ever existed there. I ached for her to allow her lips to touch me, but she expertly avoided contact of our more intimate parts. I could she her lips part and join as she adjusted her position. The hooded point of flesh poked out from between the folds. Helen had an exquisitely toned body that showed little of the rigors of life. I could see no evidence that she might have had children. My eyes invariably kept returning to the pendulous swing of her breasts.

I decided to interrupt her chatter. "Is this something you do for everyone?" I asked, not really sure why I asked it.

"What . . . massages?"

"No."

"Massages without clothes?"

"That wasn't what I was thinking of, but maybe we should start there."

Helen continued her expert work, as she moved down my body.

"It depends, actually. Generally, if a patron doesn't want a towel, I will make the offer. For the most part, I won't disrobe if my customer is covered. Just seems rather odd, to me, maybe even sordid, don't you think?"

"I see what you mean. So, no one objects?"

"No complaints, as far as I'm aware."

"I can't imagine why," I mumbled.

"Now, now, let's keep this on the up and up."

"Women as well?"

"Yes. In fact, my being in the same state they are seems to relax women more than men. I suppose it's our puritanical heritage . . . you know . . . the human body is sexual and therefore should be covered up. I don't happen to agree with that, but it does seem the way."

"What about the other?"

"You mean my manual relief of your erection?"

"Well yes."

"Again, no one has objected, yet. Most folks are quite complimentary, if you must know."

"Women?"

She chuckled. "Now, aren't you the inquisitive one? To answer your question, yes, there are women who appreciate some manual relief of their excitement."

"Wow."

"What?"

"That's impressive."

"How so?"

"You are so casual about it, almost like you're wiping a child's nose, or something more elegant."

"I hadn't thought of it like that, but I suppose you are correct. It is something I happen to believe is perfectly natural. There is nothing wrong with the extraordinary body human. I remain in awe of the depth of Mother Nature and what she provides. We have the capacity for pleasure. It is not something to be ashamed of or hide."

Helen had worked her way down to my feet. She found some magical spots that as she pressed and rubbed shot the softest, most sensual, sensations up my legs into my body. The feelings were incredible like some machine that knew precisely what steps to take. The combination of her stimulation of my feet and her touch on my legs especially my inner thighs returned me to a state of physical excitement.

She moved up and tended to it, again, as though it was the most common and ordinary response, and not the least bit sexual which seemed like such a contradiction.

I allowed the sensations of her stroking to fill me while I watched her breasts swing in rhythm with her motions. The magnetism proved too much. Without the slightest thought of consequences, I slowly reach for her breast as though my lack of haste would allow her time to object. She did not miss a stroke nor stop her running commentary about her fascination and appreciation of the human body, both male and female.

Her breast was quite soft and pillowy. I could feel her nipple rise against the palm of my hand. I closed on the protruding mound of flesh. I squeezed it gently at first, rolling it between my fingers. She hardened against my touch. Her body began to betray her excitement. Helen continued her effort to relieve me, as I took the opening to move down her body.

I could not tell whether she intentionally spread her legs slightly or just shifted position to better manipulate me, but nonetheless, I touched her lips. The soft, smooth folds possessed an intoxicating quality. I could feel her erection although I did not dwell on it. I probed into the folds. She was incredibly wet. Her hot, slippery interior broke down the last of my control, as she took me over the top in another glorious climax. She completed the task, then expertly disengaged from my touch to perform her clean up of the product of my pleasure.

"Let me give back what you have given me," I said.

"That would not be appropriate, Michael."

"Isn't it natural for you to have pleasure as well."

"It does not seem proper."

"Why?"

"I suppose if I were to give in to those urges, it would be confirmation that what I did was sexual rather than an innocent service function."

"Perhaps, but I won't tell, and I certainly won't think less of you. If anything, you will be more human."

"I don't know."

"Helen, please, it is the least you can let me do after all the pleasure you've given me."

I could tell by her hesitation that she was considering my offer. I decided to let her arrive at her own decision without further influence from me.

She smiled. She was going to do it. "I suppose it wouldn't hurt."

"There you go. How do you want it?" I asked, as I sat up.

She smiled, again. "I'll make a deal with you."

"OK."

"Let me sit on your face . . . I suspect you have a magnificent tongue . . . and, I'll do you one more time."

"That's a hell of a deal, but OK, let's do it."

Once more, Helen climbed up on the table, but this time she turned as she straddled my chest, and then inched back. I guided her to the correct position. I could now admire up close the folds I had only felt at arm's length. Her spread legs fanned the petals of her flower. The shades of pink mixed so perfectly with the deep, rich, flesh tone of her skin. The soft, tight skin of her groin was devoid of any signs that hair ever existed there.

I extended my tongue to touch her ever so slightly. She squirmed, and then took me into her mouth. Her tongue raced around me, as she sucked as I thought I might be completely swallowed. Her salty, warm, musty taste came to me in waves as I probed progressively deeper into the magnificent folds of passionate flesh. I found the button of hard flesh at the top of the folds. I teased it with my tongue causing more squirms of pleasure. The tempo of her pleasure produced associated change in her attention to me. Her swelling attracted me to a singular focus.

Drawing her into my mouth, I sealed my lips around her. With a pulsating sucking action, my tongue danced over the head of her button, using alternating flicks of the coarse and smooth sides of my tongue. Her squirms became more pronounced. Her hips began to move in an undulating male rhythm, as though she was the penetrator. Her efforts on me became more sporadic and less frequent, broadcasting the approaching peak. Her diversion redoubled my efforts on her. My finger found her sphincter and pressed gently against the tight muscle.

Helen groaned loudly ending any further effort on me. Her climb excited me. Her muscles began to relax, as she pressed back against me.

The peak came quickly as her body shook under the waves of her climax. Her voice quivered in a prolonged groan of ecstasy that lasted as long as her convulsions of pleasure. A warm fluid gushed from her covering my face. It was slippery and sweet to the taste.

Eventually, her body relaxed. She made several random strokes on me as though she was having some trouble concentrating on her task. Then, without the slightest indication, Helen nearly jumped up, spun around, squatted over me and grabbed me to guide me to the spot she wanted.

Her incredible wetness made entry effortless, as she took me completely into her. She continued to look down as though she needed to see what she was doing. Helen ground her hips probably trying to satisfy that peculiar itch of pleasure. She leaned forward to place her hands on my chest, and then went back to moving her hips up and down.

Helen adjusted her angles several times to get just the right sensations as though there were dials or instruments on my chest that told her exactly how to tune her motions. The hot, velvet grip slid smoothly over me. The rhythm changed as she felt my swelling. Her entire body disappeared, suspended in space beyond our single connection. Once more, my world coalesced into a finite, narrow point as the sensation grew rapidly in intensity until I exploded into convulsions and semi-consciousness. The waves continued for the longest time, then almost instantly switched to a coarse, abrasive pain.

I grabbed her hips to stop the motion. I held her tight until the last vestiges of my climax passed into memory.

She collapsed onto me. Her slippery, cool body conveyed the extent of her exertion. Her chest heaved as she struggled for air and recovery. The groan associated with Helen's straitening of her legs also told of her efforts. I wrapped my arms around her to hold her in place. We lay together without worlds, both of us probably lost in our thoughts and recollection of what happened, until her breathing returned to normal.

Without pronouncement, she slowly rose from the table and me. Helen found the necessary items and cleaned my entire body. When she completed the task, she stood back a step, placed her hands on her hips and said, "I think that should do the trick."

I laughed hard as I picked myself up onto one elbow and rolled toward her. "That may be the biggest understatement ever made."

"I hope you enjoyed it. That is most definitely not something I do. I'm not sure what possessed me to do that, but I, for one, am very grateful for your indulgence."

"My indulgence! My God, woman, that was without a doubt one of the most extraordinary events in my life. I shall never forget this."

"Nor I."

"Thank you, Helen."

"No, thank you, Michael."

She quickly wiped off her body and donned her simple work dress, as I began to gather up my towel and robe. She thanked me once more, gave me a hug and an intimate kiss, and then left the room. My legs were weak and shaky, as I walked back to the dressing room. Several men were into themselves as I started to get dressed. I thought about a shower but decided to hold whatever fragrance remained. Walking proved difficult. The residual warmth within me blocked the chill of the night air, as I returned to my apartment. I would sleep well tonight with dreams of my moment in heaven.

———

Michelle

—

The slow rhythm of the van responding to the joints in the concrete road made for a soothing action against the night's activities. It had been a good night so far, but I knew it was only the beginning.

One of the Marine battalions returned from a long, difficult overseas deployment earlier in the day. The 600 or so, young, horny men had pockets of money and weeks aboard ship with only their right hand for relief. These were always the times I loved the best. The night's business usually went on in a seemingly endless stream, sometimes until dawn. The cool foggy night made the mood nearly perfect.

"Looks like we might have a couple more for you, hon'," said Bob, my husband, business agent of sorts, and also a Marine -- a staff sergeant to be precise.

"Great. I'm ready."

I sat up slightly to look out the front window. Two absolutely gorgeous young men in their perfect Levi's and T-shirts were waving for Bob. They recognized the van and knew what awaited them inside.

I quickly took a dab of KY Jelly from the dispenser behind the seat and rubbed on my already swollen lips. Always better to be safe although I was probably naturally wet enough. The easier they slid in even if they were not quite ready for entry, the easier the session went. It had become part of my ritual. As Bob slowed the van to pick up the two young bulls, I squeezed my nipples, rolling them between my fingers to make them nice and erect. I could feel the sensation I wanted in my groin. I then leaned back on my elbows, raised and spread my knees to give the boys a proper welcoming view.

Bob stopped the van and got out to take care of business. "What's your pleasure, Marines?"

"We're lookin' for a good poke."

"Then, you've come to the right place. Michelle is waiting for you inside. Now, do you want this together or separate?"

"Jesus, man . . . separate."

"Who's first?"

"I am," said the shorter one.

"That'll be $20 for one off."

"Hurry up, man. Get with it. My fuckin' dick's hurtin' already," said the taller one.

Bob collected the $20 as the gatekeeper, and then opened the rear door. Both looked in. I smiled back at them.

"Oh, Jesus," they said in unison.

The shorter man climbed in kneeling in front of me. As soon as Bob closed the door, the young man fumbled with his belt and zipper fighting his own frustration with his hands not moving as fast as his mind. The bulge in his pants foretold of his readiness. I was afraid he might make it to entry. His respectable organ nearly sprang from the confines of his jeans.

"Easy now, sport. Slow down. I want you to get your money's worth here," I said, although I was really more concerned about getting what I wanted. The strokes of hard flesh deep into me were more important than a deposit of semen. I needed him to get some good strokes in before he let go.

He seemed to take a deep breath with his eyes riveted on his target. I motioned with my hands for him to move closer. I touched him, at first with only two fingers. After a few strokes, my hand encompassed his rigid organ. This was going to feel so good . . . good size and girth . . . and, hard as a rock . . . if I could just keep him going for a while. He knelt patiently as I played with him, but I needed more. I guided the tip of his spear to its target.

I could feel his body tense without the minutest sound, as he pushed into me. As he reached full insertion, I grasped his hips to hold him in place for a moment, as I moved my hips. His presence felt so good. When I released him, he instantly began his stroking.

"Ooooo," I cooed. "That's it, baby . . . slow and deep. Stay with me," I said, as he started to pick up his anxious pace. He responded properly. I could feel his tension. This one would go in an instant, if I let him. He stopped several times probably in his struggle to maintain control and keep going. When the stops became longer than the strokes, I knew I had to let him go. When he returned to his stroking, I constricted my key muscles as well as touched him at the base of his sack. The result was immediate. I could feel his body twitching in orgasm although he barely moved, and he choked back any sound.

As his tension subsided, I said, "Give me a couple of hard strokes to get the last of you into me."

He performed as he was asked. His energy felt so invigorating; I just wanted him to keep going, but I knew I had another one outside.

"Very nicely done, sweetie," I added, as he withdrew. He could only nod his head without looking me in the eyes.

I cleaned him up first, and then helped him back into his clothes. As he completed arranging his clothes the way he wanted them, I quickly cleaned up to ready myself for his friend. The door opened.

"Come on in, friend."

One young man got out, and the other, taller man got in. The door closed behind him. The young man's expression of anticipation turned instantly to apprehension as the door latched behind him. I knew in an instant . . . I had a virgin, a first timer.

"Are you OK?" I asked.

"Sure, it's just . . . ," he voiced tailed off so quickly I could not hear if he said anything more or not.

I whispered to him as I touch his arm. "It's OK, sweetie. There is a first time for everything. I'm glad you've come to Michelle for your first time."

"I know what to do," he said so softly. "I've just never done it. I really don't want to do something wrong. I just don't know how this is going to happen."

"Let me teach you. Just do what I tell you. You'll do just fine."

I knew I had to move precisely. Unless this kid had been tossing off regularly, he might not make it home. I reached to the bulge in his jeans. He was not ready. I needed a distraction.

I took his hand and placed it on my breast. He cupped my flesh but did not move. "Have you felt a woman's breast before?"

"Not really."

"Feel the curves. Knead it kinda like bread dough. That's it, gently. Feel my nipple. Squeeze it between your fingers." The electricity coursed through my body to my groin. I took his other hand and placed it on my wet spot.

"Oh God," he gushed. His hand did not move, not even a twitch.

"It's OK. I want you to be familiar with places I'm going to take you."

"Oh God."

"What's wrong?"

"I don't think I'm supposed to touch you there."

"It's quite all right, sweetie. It's just flesh like all others."

"But . . ."

"No, buts. Just feel it. Feel the texture." His fingers began to move. His timidity produced a strange excitement within me. "That's it. Feel the wetness. Feel how smooth. That's my clit, my magic button. Rub it gently." The electric charge began to build up. "Feel in the folds. There," I said, as he reach to correct point, "push in. That's it." His finger wiggled inside me. "Feel how hot and wet it is in there. You feel it."

He grinned broadly as he looked into my eyes, and then he nodded his head.

I reached for his bulge. It was much more pronounced. When I started to unzip his jeans, he stopped his manual manipulation of my body. "No, no. Don't stop. You keep exploring my body. Feel all of it. Go wherever you want to go. Let me worry about this."

He did as he was requested. His fingers and hands moved into new areas and touches as I unzipped him. I pulled his pants down. He fell out like an ironing board falling from a wall cabinet. He was ready, and I knew I did not want to waste time. If I stroked him manually, he could release before he entered.

His body followed, as I guided him to the proper spot rubbing his cock-head among my lips to moisten him and to make sure he was at precisely the right spot.

"Push gently into me," I whispered to him.

The slowness of his penetration sent jolting shocks to every limb from the point of our union. I felt the tickling urge building. Somehow I was going to have to use this young man for my own satisfaction. He pressed against me to the fullest reach he could achieve and held it there. I could feel the pulsing of his organ within me. I contracted my muscles in concert. I did the wrong thing.

His body shook. He groaned and bent over me, as he erupted into me. "I'm sorry," he said.

"Not to worry. Stroke for me."

He began to move his hips as Nature's instincts took over. Maybe if I kept him going, he might be able to hold it. He grimaced, verging on the thin boundary between pleasure and pain, but he did as he was told. He began stroking with long, deep thrusts. I rolled my hips into him to get a better angle for my purposes. He tried to stop several times, but I immediately coaxed him to continue. He remained hard enough for my purpose. I found the right position and held my hips there, as he stroked. His shaft rubbed against my clit. The friction worked its magic taking me up the mountain the rest of the way. It only took a few minutes and the peak came.

"Oh, yes, there it is," I growled as the waves began to break over me. He missed a beat in his uncertainty. "No, keep going. Yes, harder. Harder . . . deeper . . . that's it. Ohhh . . . awwww," I growled some more as my back arched against the ecstasy. My descent came quickly. It was not the best orgasm I had ever had, but it was quite unusual for me to go in these circumstances.

"Feel my cunt pulsing around you?"

He nodded his head.

"That's what a woman's orgasm feels like."

"Wow."

"I'd say," I added with a slight chuck of discovered pleasure.

He withdrew. I found his right hand and the index finger of that hand. I placed it at the base of my clit. "Feel that?"

"Yeah. It's really slippery."

I smiled at him. "Yes, it is. That's my cum, very much like yours."

"Wow."

I smiled more broadly, as he absorbed the sensations. He retained his gentle touch. This one will make a good lover, I told myself.

As I had done for his friend, I cleaned him up. Before I returned him to his jeans, I decided to take him in my mouth. He froze like a statue. The taste of our mixed fluids filled my head; the salty, almost musty, flavor added to the moment. He began to respond to my attention. As much as I might like to demonstrate my appreciation, I stopped and returned him to his jeans.

"Maybe next time," I said. He smiled and nodded. I returned the smile. "I just needed to thank you for helping me, and now you've got something to remember me by."

"Thank you, ma'am. This has been the best moment of my life." He turned and opened the door. I cleaned up to prepare for the next event, as Bob returned to the driver's seat.

"What took you so long with that last one?" he asked as he drove away.

"The kid was a virgin. I gave him a little extra time and attention to make sure he made it. Damned if the excitement of teaching him didn't get me off."

"The hell you say," Bob said, as he drove away.

"Damnedest thing that's happened to me in some time."

"Well, glad you're having fun, but let's stick to business."

"What? I can't have a little fun with my work?"

He thought about things before he answered. "Sure, you can. I was thinking too much about the cash register. With all these young bucks comin' off cruise, we stand to make a bunch over the next few days."

I knew Bob was right. "I'm ready for the next comer, so find me a stiff dick."

"Yes ma'am. Comin' up." His search process took less than a block. "You lookin' for some nookie, young man."

"You got some? You the pussy man?" asked the man. I sat up to see an attractive man with smooth, chocolate brown skin and short-cropped hair.

"You got it."

"How much?"

"Depends on what you want."

"Look man, I don't mind tellin' ya, I'm pretty big, so I need the back door."

"That's $50 for a pop in the back door."

"You gotta deal."

Bob opened the door and jumped out. While he was collecting our money, I quickly grabbed the KY Jelly to lubricate my sphincter. *I just hope this guy was appropriately patient to let me accommodate him.* I had not run into a man I could not take vaginally, yet, but maybe this was a first. Regardless, if he paid for anal intercourse, that is what he would get. Bob let him in the rear entrance.

The man had started to unzip his pants before the door was closed behind him. As Bob returned to the driver's seat and started to move, my partner was undressed and ready. He did not look any bigger than many other men just darker than most.

"You want to try it the regular way?" I asked.

"I'm too big. You won't be able to handle me, lady."

"We can give it a try."

"Naw, I'd just as soon get my off the way I want it."

"OK by me." I moved quickly to position myself on my knees ready to accept him. I felt him find his spot. The van continuing to move. "Let me press on to you."

"Do it," he commanded.

I pressed back relaxing my muscles. He entered without a problem or pain. I groaned as I felt him filling me. He waited for my muscles to complete relaxing. He had done this before; he knew what he was doing.

I signaled my readiness by moving on him. He began stroking slowly giving me time to adjust. He was able to reach forward to cup my hanging breasts and squeeze my nipples, as he continued to stroke into me. His full strokes brought the persistent sensation of being filled then emptied. I could feel him grow. The van's movement over the pavement along with a few turns caused him to miss a few beats and me a little pain.

He kept pumping into me without a break, other than a few misses Bob's turns caused. I was beginning to feel soreness developing among the accumulating drips of sweat from his exertion. I needed to finish him off.

I reach through my legs to caress his testicles. That just gave him more energy. I pressed on the ridge of skin between his sack and sphincter. That made him grow even more. I knew there was only one choice left. I pressed a finger gently against his tight gate. My pain began to grow steadily. He finally relaxed enough to let me in as I began to wiggle my finger. The extra stimulation did the trick.

His strokes shortened and increased in frequency until I felt the convulsions of his release. He fought to remain silent although a deep groan, choked off within him, reverberated between us. When he was done, he leaned forward pressing me down. We lay there motionless except for the sway of the van's movement. The wetness of his body made him almost slippery. We waited for him to deflate to ease the disengagement, which I was quite thankful for, although I remained silent and motionless. His weight made my breathing more labored, but after a few minutes, he began a slow withdrawal.

Once separated, he sat back leaning against the rear doors. I performed a few contraction exercises to return my muscles to their normal state, as I reached for my cleaning materials. He sat there like a lump as I tended to him first. I did not wait for him to leave before I cleaned myself. It did not appear he was going to move.

"OK Bob," I said loudly, "we're done."

"I'll pull up over here," he answered as if we would know what he was talking about.

"Sorry it took me so long," the man said finally.

"I thought you were going to tear me up."

"Sorry. I guess it was just the van or something, but you were great. Thank ya for hangin' wit me."

"You're welcome. At least you got your money's worth."

He chuckled slightly, as he began to pull on his clothes. "You can say that again. It oughta last me for a week. I hope I didn't hurt ya."

"I'll be OK. Next time, I like to take you in the front door."

"Ladies have problems with me that way."

"Let me take a shot at it."

"Ya gotta it."

Bob had stopped and opened the rear door, as the man completed refastening everything.

"Thanks again."

"You're welcome."

He disappeared into the night. Bob found a secluded portion of the city street with some amount of light, but not a lot of traffic.

"Are you all right?" he asked.

"That one was tough, hon'. I thought he was going to rip me a new one."

"You want me to check you?"

"Sure," I answered, as I leaned back and spread my legs to give him the best view possible. He had a small, focused flashlight he used to examine me.

"You're a little red, but you've closed up and no bleeding or tears." He gave me a few licks on my clitoris that felt so good in contrast to the pain of the last session. "Should I finish you off?"

"It'll take too long. Let's get on with things."

He did as he was requested. I applied some more KY Jelly that seemed to soothe my abused flesh. Bob had only turned the corner when he stopped again. *Damn, so soon*, I said to myself. For the first time tonight, I began to feel the weight of too much.

"Hey, man," the new one said to Bob, "can I have some of what you got in there?" *A repeat customer, no doubt.*

"What do you want?"

"A good fuck, but I only got $5. Can you spot me some 'til next payday?"

"Do I look like a bank? Five bucks gets you a hand job."

The pause meant the young man was thinking about it. *At least, he was not another back door man*, I said to myself. I don't think I could take it.

"I really need the full deal, man."

"Five bucks gets ya a hand job . . . better than doin' it yourself. You want it or not?"

More thinking.

"I'll take it."

Bob hopped out, collected the fee and open the door.

"So, you're a bit short of funds, Ay?"

"Yeah, but he said you could take care of me."

"I sure can."

"Damn, I've dreamed about your body for months. Can I touch you?"

The van started moving, as I extracted his stiff organ from his pants. "Sure," I said. He gently caressed my breasts. "Lay here," I added patting the spot next to me. He did as he was requested.

I sat at his hip cross-legged. He continued to fondle my breasts in object fascination like a baby would focus on a rattle. I found the lubricant I needed, applying it adequately over him, and then I started my task. His eyes and attention did not leave my breasts as I stroked him. The end did not take long.

"Oh, shit," he said as his hand stopped, but remained attached to my breasts. "Too soon." He swelled in my hand as I picked up the pace. "Ahh-hhhh . . . ooooohh . . . Jesus," he said as he erupted.

The stream of white, milky fluid shot up a foot or two and arced over to his chest. Several more, lesser spurts jumped out as I continued to pump him. He nearly double over as his release finished.

I quickly cleaned him up. I let him continue to fondle me as I completed my task and let him shrink before returning him to the confines of his trousers.

"OK, hon', we're done."

"That was quick."

Bob opened the rear door. "You were right, man. It was a lot better than doin' it myself." He stood in the door opening to look back at me. "One last look to keep me going 'til payday. I'll be back for the whole enchilada."

"I'll be waitin'," I said adding a broad smile, and then spread my legs wide for him to see what would be waiting for him.

"My God, I've never seen such a smooth pussy. God, I can't wait," he said, starting to get back in.

Bob grabbed his shoulder as I closed my legs. "Not so fast, junior. You gotta have the money before you get to enjoy the flesh."

"I'll be back."

"I'm sure you will," I said, as the young man turn to leave.

Bob waited for the last one to be a reasonable distance away before he turned to fill the rear door. "What do you want to do?"

"To be honest, I like a real good pussy fucking before we call it a night."

A smile washed across his face. "You want me to handle that request, or you want more money."

I knew what I wanted, but I considered whether I might hurt his feelings. Maybe all this sex had made him horny, although it usually had the opposite effect on Bob. I decided to take the chance.

"We could use the extra money, hon'."

"OK, let me see what I can find for you."

Bob returned to cruising as I busied myself freshening up the interior of the van. It was beginning to smell of sex, not always the best aroma for a young buck with the image of sweetness and purity in his head.

Once again, the hunting was great. It did not take long for Bob to find a prospect.

"Great to see you, Jimmy. How are you doin' tonight?"

"Not as great as I'm going to be. Good to see you, sergeant."

"What do you have in mind?"

"I just like one of those great blow jobs your wife gives."

"Actually, Jimmy, she's in need of a regular fucking. Can you handle it?"

"I'm a little thin on funds 'til next payday."

"Maybe next time, then."

"Wait, I didn't say I didn't have the money. I just said I was thin. If she wants a fucking, I can handle it."

I readied myself. Jimmy was always a good lover; he was a regular customer and one I enjoyed. He would be perfect for what I needed. Money changed hands, then the young, well built, man appeared in the rear doorway practically naked already, as he stepped into the van. I lay back on my elbows with the knees so my feet nearly touch my buttocks and spread wide for a perfect view. The door closed him. He finished undressing himself completely, even down to his socks.

"Good to see you again, Jimmy. You are just what I was looking for."

His eyes flashed from my eyes, to my breasts, and then froze on my exposed, rosy pink, lips waiting for him. "Good to see you again, Michelle. I know as many times as I've seen your pussy, it never ceases to amaze me." He touched the periphery, then the folds and the rigid organ protruding from its hood. "You've got the smoothest, Best lookin' pussy I've ever seen, maybe that exists in the whole wide world. How do you keep it so pretty?"

"Well, thank, Jimmy. I just treat her real nice and pay her a lot of attention to keep her so smooth and ready for you."

He needed no preparation. He was ready as he usually was. "Can I take my time? This is going to have to last me for a while."

I smiled. "Take all the time you need. I'm in need of a good, slow fuck right now."

He moved between my legs. He allowed the tip to barely touch me. My muscles contracted wanting to pull him inside. He moved himself among the folds to pick up my wetness, and then he rubbed my exposed, protruding and sensitive organ. The electricity was incredible. He kept at it stopping only briefly to pick up more wetness. As my excitement and anticipation began to grow, he would insert himself only a little bit without any strokes, and then return to rubbing me. *This kid is good.* He had learned his lessons well. An ache began to build in my groin. The very agonized want he tried to create in me, demanded to feel him satisfy me and made me try to force him in several times; but, he fought to resist me as he chuckled, smiled and shook his head. *Yes, indeed, this kid is good.* He remembered everything I taught him.

As my mounting hunger demanded all of him, my actions became more pronounced. I moved my hips and constricted my muscles to grab him, to hold him even partially in, and each time he fought me off. I was getting too close to my pinnacle. I forgot about him, to focus on the incredible sensation of his soft flesh rubbing so exquisitely where I now wanted him to stay.

The approaching waves caused me to draw my knees back farther and wider to tighten the skin of my groin even further. He recognized my withdrawal into my sensations, my pleasure, and my focus. He did his part increasing the frequency and pressure to just the right levels.

"Oh, yes. Oh, yes," I gushed. "That's it. Oh, ye . . ." My voice tailed off as the enormous wave took me to the top. "Uuuuhhhh," I groaned, as lesser waves washed over me from behind the great peak. Then, at just the right moment, he stopped his rubbing and plunged into me to the hilt. The feeling of his entry sent another few waves over me as he began stroking. He kept thrusting until my climax subsided and my eyes opened again to see his smiling face above me.

"You like that, did you now?" he said with virtually all his teeth showing.

"Yes, Jimmy," I cooed softly, "that was great. Now, how do you want yours?"

Without words, he turned me over, and then lifted me at the waist to my knees. He entered me from behind. My natural wetness made the joining so smooth, slippery and easy. He felt good, filling me up. He leaned forward to fondle my breasts a little before he placed his hands on my hips and began his own purposeful stroking. He did not waste any time nor did he try to protract the union. He needed no other assistance from me, as he reached his own peak within a few minutes. I did not need to encourage him, as he must have sensed my yearning for his deep, hard strokes. His convulsions of pleasure took him into his own ecstasy. I squeezed him with my muscles, giving him just a few extra small peaks as he finished. He was so hard; I did not want to separate.

I motioned for him to follow me as we rolled slightly onto our left sides. We lay joined like spoons. He caressed and played with my breasts until he shrunk to the point of separation.

Rather than rush things, I took my time cleaning him up. In an unusual move, I leaned forward to kiss him passionately allowing my tongue to dance around his tongue. I hugged him.

"OK hon'. He's done."

As the van pulled up, he cupped my left breast, leaned forward to take my nipple in his mouth, and then sucked like a baby as he swirled his tongue around erect flesh. The exquisite sensations made me squirm with delight.

"I thought I'd leave you something in return," he said.

"Thanks Jimmy. You were great tonight." The van door opened. "Come back anytime."

"I will."

Bob waited for Jimmy to leave. "I hope you enjoyed yourself."

"It did the trick, hon'. I can take on some more, if you want to make some more money."

"The streets are overflowing with horny Marines with pockets full of money. I'd say we should keep going as long as you can or 'til the business runs out."

"No problem. Bring 'em on."

The night's activities dispensing pleasure continued until dawn. It was our largest one-night haul since we started this business. The rarity of my pleasure added to the success of the night.

—

Sheila

—

"**D**eary, you'll like workin' here. This is the easiest job on earth," said the matronly charge nurse.

"But, this is a nursing home full of old people who need a lot of extra attention."

"No, really. Oh yeah, they're here, but they don't need that much help. They pretty much take care of themselves."

"Yes, well, that is what we are all about, but we will find these are good people who just want some extra attention, to feel good about their last years, to feel alive."

"I can understand that."

"Don't get me wrong, there are a few who have been sent here by un-grateful children or have lost a loved one and are here just to die . . . a few will say as quickly as possible."

"That's sad."

"Yes, it is, but we still try to make them happy, or at least as comfortable as we can make them."

"I think I can do that."

"I know you can."

Sheila's training progressed more rapidly than other young people near her age. The nurse enjoyed her absorbent mind, always wanting to learn about things beyond her immediate reach. The residents took to her quickly as well. Her buoyant and effervescent personality most often brought smiles to the faces of those who found little joy in the waning years of life.

She took a unique pleasure in helping others who were not as able to help themselves. Sheila also found herself working extra hours for the smile or kind word offered by the residents. The young woman was becoming a fixture at the institution for staff and residents. She liked the attention she gave and received.

The buzzer rang on room 177, Mr. Strong's room -- a relative new resident of only three days. "I'll take it," Sheila said much to the relief of the night nurse.

The young assistant walked down the darkened and quiet corridor to Mr. Strong's room. She knocked twice and waited for a reply as she always did. "Come in."

Sheila pushed the large door open only to find Mr. Strong completely naked on his bed. A frustration and perhaps a bit aggravated expression greeted her. It was not particularly uncommon for the staff to find residents in various stages of undress, often unintentional due to forgetfulness or complacency, and occasionally intentionally out of defiance or rebellion. As she was trained, Sheila pretended not to notice.

"Can I help you, Mr. Strong?"

"Yes, I know you can."

She waited for the request. She gestured with her eyes for him to speak.

"This is a bit embarrassing, but it's my arthritis," she said, holding up his disfigured hands.

"Yes, do you need some pain medication?"

"No, I am quite accustomed to the pain, but I need your help."

"OK. What do you need?"

He averted his eyes for several seconds, and then looked directly and deeply into her eyes. "I need to get off." Sheila started to leave. "Wait. Please," he said with a strain of desperation. He waited for her to turn around and catch his eyes. "Listen, I know this is quite irregular and perhaps a bit peculiar, but my missus used to take care of me until her stroke." He lowered his head and ran the back of his right hand across both eyes. "I'm sorry."

"No problem, Mr. Strong. I understand your loss."

"Yes, well, she would do me every night whether I needed it or not."

"Mr. Strong, really," she protested. "This is kinda personal."

"Not really. If I wet the bed, would you not change the sheets? If my nose was dripping, would you not wipe it for me."

"Yes, certainly."

"Then, what is different with this," he said looking and nodding his head toward his groin.

Sheila considered his logic for a moment, and then looked over her shoulder wishing she had left the door open. "Your request is sexual."

"Yes, and isn't sex part of life, just as breathing is?"

"At your age?"

"Do I stop breathing or eating at my age? No. So, why should it be any different? My wife and I had a great relationship for over fifty years. We remained sexually active even when my arthritis became crippling. I just need some help."

Sheila again considered his thinking. It did make sense, but she wanted to go ask the nurse. She instinctively knew what the nurse would probably say. The older woman did not have much humor or compassion. What would it hurt? She could feel his sincerity and genuine need. He could barely walk, so it was not likely to progress to anything else.

Sheila smiled softly, lowered her head, but did not take her eyes off his. He smiled cautiously in return. "What do you want me to do?"

He grinned more broadly and looked to the ceiling. "Thank you, God, for answering my prayers. He looked back to her. "Hand manipulation will probably do the trick."

"A hand job?"

"Yes," he said with caution returning this voice, as if he might have offended her. "To put it in the colloquial, yes, a hand job should be sufficient. That's what the missus did most often, unless she wanted one, and we did each other orally."

"OK," Sheila barked to stop the vivid images flashing through her mind.

He lowered his hands to his side and spread his legs slightly to give her sufficient access. Sheila told herself that what she was about to do was simply a humanitarian act, no different from a sponge bath or any other task of care and comfort.

Sheila took him in her hand and began to gently pull on him and rhythmically squeeze him.

"You have done this before."

She thought about the late night sessions with her younger brother when the urges for experimentation had been strong. She had learned the basic mechanics with him. "My boyfriend taught me. We used to manually pleasure each other for several years before we decided to have sex."

"So, a hand job is not sex?" he asked playfully.

"Well, yes it is, I suppose, but I think you know what I mean."

"Yes, my dear, I do know what you mean."

Sheila looked at the extremity she held in her hand. He was not responding, as she was accustomed to feeling.

"Patience, my dear," he said. "At my age, things like this take a little longer." She nodded her head. "The best thing to do with older men, or any man who is slow to respond, is to do exactly as you are doing. You have a perfect touch, a perfect feel for this. But, it is best to talk to him, to help him get his mind off the slowness of his response."

"OK, so what do you want to talk about?"

"Do you like sex?"

"That's kinda a personal question."

"Yes, but I suppose this is kinda a personal moment."

She could feel him beginning to respond, so sex talk was what he needed. "Yes, I do." She used her fingers to gently squeeze him as he expanded.

"Do you have a brother?"

"A younger brother, yes."

"Did you do it with him?"

Sheila stared at him, but did not stop her manual task. He was beginning to stiffen. His eyes had an innocentness to him, an almost child-like inquisitiveness. "I have done this with him when we were much younger."

"And?"

"And, we have done some oral experimentation, but no intercourse."

He smiled. "Thank you for confiding in me. I know that wasn't easy." He closed his eyes as he hardened to her touch.

Sheila absorbed the sensations. He was bigger than any man she had ever been with. It was a fine, straight, rather large specimen that nearly filled her hand. She gripped a little tighter so she could feel the skin move over his rigid shaft. It was amazing that a 77-year-old man could become so hard and large. She had always thought this part of a man's life past at middle age.

"I had an older sister," he said with his eyes still closed, "and we experimented too, as you say."

"Really."

He chuckled, and then opened his eyes. "Young people always think they were the first to invent sex. Dear God Almighty, you have such an exquisite touch. You are a natural with a dick. Yes, she was 14 and I was 12. We experimented with many things, and I unlike you, we went all the way a few times."

"Isn't that illegal?"

"Yes, it is, but we were just kids, and we wanted to know. Our parents occasionally left their door open, and we would naturally watch them out of curiosity. Our parents were very loving."

"That's sweet."

"Yes, yes," he said closing his eyes again. "Yesssss, sweet Jesus, don't stop."

Sheila could feel him swelling even more within her hand. She recognized the anatomical response of his approaching climax. She quickened her pace even though her arm was beginning to hurt from the exertion.

An odd growl came from deep within him. He felt like his organ was going to explode. His stomach muscles flexed pulling his head off the pillow. His eyes remained closed, as if his chin was glued to his chest. "Oh . . . my . . . ," he grunted, "Ohhhhh . . . ahhhh." A long, white, milky stream erupted from him and arced toward the foot of the bed. He could only growl deeply, as his body shook. Several more, lesser spurts issued forth from him before the usual pain of male hypersensitivity caused him to withdraw.

She gently milked him to produce a few residual shudders before the rest of his body went totally limp. Sheila stayed with him and held him until the last of his rigidness disappeared. Without saying anything, she released him and began the process of cleaning up the product of his pleasure.

He lay so quietly, she wondered if he was all right. The movement of his chest with each breath confirmed he was alive. The amount and distance of his ejaculation impressed her. It was amazing a man so old could produce so much. It took her several minutes to clean up.

Sheila tiptoed to the door to let him rest quietly. She looked back at his frail and limp body. She decided to cover him up. As she pulled the sheet over him, he opened his eyes.

"Thank you, Sheila. I know this was not exactly what you signed up to do, but I cannot tell you how happy you have made me. I hope I have not offended you."

"No, Mr. Strong, you did not offend me." She smiled. "In fact, I am glad you could share that with me."

"How so?"

"Well, I didn't know men your age could still get an erection."

He chuckled. "Sometimes it doesn't work as fast as it used to."

"And, I have never been with a man as big as you."

"Then, I suppose I was good for something."

"Nor came as much as you."

"Well, sometimes it causes more problems than it's worth."

"So, thank you for sharing yourself with me."

"You are a true angel sent from heaven, Sheila. Thank you for taking care of an old man."

"You are most welcome."

"I hope you can find it in your heart to help me out every so often."

"Every night?"

He laughed hard this time, as he raised himself on his right elbow. He winced with the pain but did not stop. "No, every night might be a bit much for you," he winked at her, "although I certainly wouldn't complain."

"I will see what I can do."

"Thank you, dear woman. You are a true saint."

He lay back down and closed his eyes. She turned out the light and left.

The experience made an impression on Sheila. She returned to Mr. Strong each night when things quieted down. They talked and learned from each other as she tended to him. Oddly, Sheila began to look forward to the nightly encounters. There was no threat to her, and no voiced expectations from him. He was kind and generous with her. He also taught her more about the pleasure side of life. Several weeks passed before their physical exchanges changed.

"Good evening, Mr. Strong."

"Don't you think you can call me, Bob."

"I suppose so. Then, Bob it is. Are you ready for your nightly release?" She really did not need an answer since for the last week, he had at least a semi-erection when she approached.

"May I ask something more of you tonight."

"Sure," she said without hesitation although she wondered what it might be.

"Would you mind letting me see you naked?"

Sheila instinctively looked at the door. Ever since the first night, she had locked the door to prevent intrusions even though they were not likely with only one other not particularly energetic nurse on duty.

"I suppose so."

Sheila watched him as she disrobed. His eyes continued to have that innocent curiosity she had seen that first night. She felt a bit awkward, but surprisingly comfortable standing in front of a man her grandfather's age. She turned several times to allow him to see each angle, and then curtsied for him as though he was a king.

"You have a very impressive figure, my dear."

"Thank you."

He continued to absorb the vision of her. She felt a flush warmth wash over her, and even more surprising, she felt a growing wetness between her legs. There was something seductive about him and a growing attraction to the crippled man.

"Shall we get started?" she said, as she moved toward him and reached for him.

He pulled his hips down slightly as if to signal his reluctance. She stopped and looked into his eyes. His eyes danced back and forth from one of her eyes to the other.

"You have been so generous and kind to me, and you have asked for nothing in return."

"I just enjoy giving you pleasure and seeing you happy."

"Yes, well, for that I am most definitely grateful, but what would give me the most pleasure now, would be to give you pleasure."

Sheila thought about the possibilities. "What exactly do you have in mind?"

"There is not much this feeble body can do, but there is something I am very good at and still capable of doing." She nodded her head but did not speak. The serious expression on her face did not intimidate him. "I can give you a great deal of pleasure."

"Yes. I'm listening."

"I would like to lick you off."

Sheila stepped back several paces, and then turned for her clothes.

"Wait."

She turned to him.

"It is about the only way I have left to give a woman pleasure." She stared at him. "I am very good at it. I know you will like it." She could not speak. "Please give me a chance to pleasure you. It would truly give me a great deal of pleasure. I feel the need to taste you."

The urges she felt earlier returned. The noticeable throbbing between her legs was now undeniable.

"OK."

"Good."

"What do you want me to do?"

"Well, you will need to help me a little. My hands and fingers are no longer useful, and I need something inside you that I can move. The best thing I can think of is my toothbrush holder." She found it at the sink and snapped the two halves together. "Excellent. Now, if you will hand me the holder and be so kind to straddle my face, I will take you to heaven on earth."

Sheila gracefully and slowly did as he instructed until her genitals hovered over his face. He stared at her for the longest time. She wondered what could be so fascinating for him. Surely, he had seen many other women in his life.

"Shaved clean like a baby."

"My boyfriend likes me like this, and I found that it makes me more sensitive."

"You have the most lovely flower I have ever seen. Your petals are so smooth, and full and delicate. And, you are already swollen in anticipation. Just this sight of you excites me."

Sheila looked over her shoulder and sure enough he was fully erect and in his full glory.

His tongue touched the folds of her soft flesh sending an electric shock through her body. She remained in place, closed her eyes and concentrated on the sensations, as his tongue probed and caressed each fold. He had to have a very long tongue as she felt him enter her. It was almost like a curious snake trying to find the warmest, softest place to hide.

He stopped for only a moment to say, "You have the most exquisite taste."

The soft but strong raspiness of his tongue returned to her. Soon, the snake found the velvet soft sheath covering the rigid, throbbing and now prominently protruding finger. He circled it several times before he took it into his mouth. He sucked on it slowly and gently at first. It was a sensation she had never felt, and her body quaked in response. The tip of his tongue danced across her clit-head as he maintained the suckling rhythm.

As the sensations intensified, Sheila could feel her hips pressing toward him. He sensed her need and increased the pace of his licking and sucking. The snake was becoming quite focused and intent, as he devoured her. As he felt the tension mounting, he began to hum or growl into her. The vibration of his guttural sounds pushed her quickly to the mountain.

The electric pulses of her approaching climax caused every muscle in her body to twitch uncontrollably. "Woowwww," she heard herself groan, as the white-hot waves emanated from the point of his attention and shot to every extremity of her body. She moaned deeply as the waves kept coming in a strange violence that caused her to lean forward to support her torso with her weakened and barely controllable arms.

He knew exactly when to ease up on the pressure, bringing her down slowly. Her chest heaved as the ripples of her fatigue followed the waves of her orgasm. The energy of her release made her muscles quiver with exhaustion.

When he finally stopped, she leaned back sitting partially on his chest. She looked down at this face only to find his long tongue sweeping large arcs around his lips. "Your cum tastes divine."

"Mr. Strong," she protested.

"It has been a very long time since I've tasted a woman's cum. It is the frosting on the wonderful cake."

When he was finished, he pushed on her buttocks for her to return to him.

"You are ready for another."

"I don't think so."

"I can tell, my dear. You have another one just under the surface ready to burst forth."

"I've never done that," she said, as she responded to his urging.

Before he returned to her, he said, "Then, you are about to experience the power of your womanhood."

This time the tip of his tongue flicked across her in a fast, almost vibrating manner. The return to the mountain was so quick it surprised her. The pinnacle was not quite as high, nor as broad, as her first rise, but it brought the same pulsing pleasure that made it all worth it.

"See. I knew I was right."

"I've never had two in a row like that."

"Yes, well, my dear, I suspect you could pop off another couple or perhaps a long string."

"I don't think I could handle that."

"Now, you have an idea of what your body can do for your mind."

"Yes, yes, I do."

For some reason she could not identify, she lowered her left nipple to his lips. He did not hesitate as he drew her into his mouth. He suckled like a baby, although without the reward. She alternated her breasts in his lips. He kept at her. Like someone winding up a hand generator, the pulses of current spread to other parts of her body. She had felt other guys sucking on her nipples and fondling her breasts, but all of them combined could not approach the skill he brought to the task.

The urge quickly changed. Sheila inched her hips down his body. He lay perfectly still as she reached for his bone hard member. She wiggled several times to find the position she wanted, and then she rubbed his cock-head among her folds to gather some of her accumulated wetness. Finally, she placed him precisely where she wanted him and pushed back with her hips. He was much bigger in girth than anyone or anything she had ever taken into her. Sheila pushed slowly allow her muscles to relax to accommodate him. Before she reached the bottom, she could feel his size filling her, almost choking her. He was truly the biggest man she had ever joined with, and the full sensation of his rigidness within her brought its own form of pleasure.

"Oh, my God, I have surely died and gone to heaven," he said with his eyes closed, and his hands oddly raised above his elbows.

Sheila began to move on him. It took several minutes for her body to adjust to his size. As the minor shots of pain disappeared, she began to occasionally flicker across her own rigidness. She ground her hips until she found the extra angles she wanted. She quickly found that she could not quite get the rhythm and stroke she wanted. She experimented with several variations of her dominant position until she found the perfect one.

He continued to lay completely still except for the motion of his chest and the occasional soft groan from his belly.

She now had her feet under her so she was on all fours. The angle of her hips was perfect, every stroke of her hips, up or down, produced a delightful rubbing on her.

She lost the sense of his approach as the waves of another orgasm shook her body, disturbing her stroking of him. Sheila fought for air as she tried to continue through her fatigue. As her waves of pleasure subsided and she returned to her stroking, she could feel an almost burning heat within her. She almost felt him swell to an even greater size and hardness.

Then, with his eyes still closed, his head arched so far back she could no longer see his eyes. She thrust rapidly on him until the convulsions shook every inch of his body. Oddly, he made no sounds until his body went limp.

Sheila returned to her knees but remained joined with him, and then lowered her heaving chest onto his heaving chest. He wrapped his arms around her and held her close. They remain in that position until their breathing returned to normal and his flaccid member naturally withdrew from her.

Slowly, she moved off of him. The creaking in her knees was painful. Sheila eventually stood beside the bed. She could feel rivulets of liquid descending along the insides of her thighs. His body was wet from the pleasure they enjoyed. She cleaned herself but did not dress as she cleaned him up. He appeared to be resting peacefully throughout the process. When she finished, she pulled the sheet, covering him and up to his chest.

Without opening his eyes or moving, he said, "If I die tonight, you shall know that you made me a very happy man."

"And, you made me a happy woman."

"Excellent. Have a good night, Sheila. I shall see you tomorrow."

Sheila dressed, and then checked on him before she left his room. No one would ever believe her story, she thought, as she closed the door behind her.

—

Cary

—

"That was a delightful dinner," pronounced Cary.

"I don't think I have ever had such an incredible combination of steak and seafood," added Julie -- Cary's blond, blue-eyed wife.

"Glad you liked it," replied Virginia, otherwise known as Ginny, as she began clearing the table. "We thought it only reasonable since Cary is leaving next weekend."

"It is kind of a neat touch barbecuing shrimp, crab and salmon isn't?" Micka said.

"The best," responded Julie.

Lifting his half full glass of Cabernet, Cary said, "And, the wine is not bad either."

"Nothing but the best for our friends," chimed in Ginny from the kitchen.

The other three joined in to clear the table. There were few leftovers. What remained that was worth saving was covered and refrigerated. The wine glasses were refreshed, as they followed Ginny through the dining room to the outside picnic table. The cooling evening air in the country added to the refreshment of good company. The discussion between friends as is so often the case turned to children and their growing pains, as well as the good life of country living. The disappearance of the evening twilight allowed the array of stars known as the Milky Way to brighten the darkening sky.

"It's getting a little chilly," observed Ginny.

"Hey, great idea," chimed Micka. "Let's warm up in the hot tub."

"Micka, not tonight," Ginny answered.

I was not about to enter into the middle of what might become a spat. Julie and I took a quick glance at each other without expression.

"What do you guys say?" Micka asked Julie and me.

"Please, Micka, not tonight."

"Come on. It will feel good. It is the perfect night for a nice warm dip." He looked again to us.

"I'm not getting in the middle of any disagreement."

"No disagreement. Come on, Ginny."

"No."

Not wanting to press things any farther, Micka got up and went in the house. "Well, then, I will enjoy it myself," Micka said as he opened the door.

"He just wants us all to get naked."

"Fine by me," I quickly added.

"I'm just not in the mood for that tonight," Ginny added.

"Whatever," said Julie.

A few minutes later Micka returned wearing a boxer-type swimsuit and carrying a couple of towels. He said nothing, walked over to the hot tub, took the cover off and laid it aside. He then lowered himself slowly into the warm water and groaned with pleasure.

"Why don't you want to go in?" Julie asked her best friend.

"I just don't feel like getting my swim suit on."

"Then go without it."

"No, that's just what he wants us to do."

"Come on guys. Sure feels great," Micka added from the steam rising around him.

"You guys can go if you'd like," said Ginny. "I know we've got some extra suits in the house."

"I want to," Julie said as she stood up and began undressing, "and, I don't need a suit." She was naked in short order, and I watched walk across the patio and settle into the hot tub. Micka's swim trunks soon flew on the adjacent bricks.

"You can go," Ginny said quietly to me.

"No," I answered with a self-deprecating tone. The giggles and sloshing of water from the hot tub changed her mind. "I'll stay here with you. We can talk while they play."

"Oh, what the hell," Ginny said as she got up and went inside.

I thought she was going to change clothes to join in the hot tub. I shucked my clothes. Micka was in one corner. Julie was sitting next to him. They were probably playing with each other under the bubbles. I lowered myself into the warm water in the corner opposite Micka.

"This is nice, isn't it?" Micka suggested.

"I'm sure it is."

"I could do this every night."

"Yeah, I know. Very relaxing."

Ginny returned in a white, one-piece suit.

"Come on, Gin. We're all naked. Take that off and join the fun."

She did not respond until after she lowered herself in the water and slid next to me. "That's OK. I'm just fine."

I reached over to touch her left about mid-thigh. She did not return the touch or withdraw. Without some sign, I did not want to pressure her. The chitchat was of the water temperature and the great night.

"Do you mind if we play?" asked Micka to Ginny and me.

"Doesn't bother me. Julie's wanted to do you for a long time."

"It's OK with me," added Ginny.

"But, I don't want to do this alone," Julie said.

"It's OK."

"Come on, Gin. Let's have some fun."

"I am having fun. You guys can do what you want."

"At least show us your tits," Micka prodded.

Ginny rose up and sat on the edge of the tub. "You want to see 'em?"

"Sure."

"Sure," added Julie.

Ginny reached up, pulled both shoulder straps and peeled the top of her suit to her waist. She was proud of her enhanced breasts. They were nice, round and her nipple stood out.

I could not resist the temptation. Her breasts were firm and yet soft. She looked into my eyes and winked, as though she was thinking, do you like them. I smiled and leaned across her to take her erect left nipple in my mouth. I suckled.

Ginny gently pushed me back and said, "they're too sensitive."

I wanted to continue perhaps more softly, but I did not want to press her. She re-covered her chest. The short scene must of have been sufficient. By the time I looked around, Micka was sitting on the edge of the tub and Julie's head was bobbing above his groin. His eyes were closed with his head tilted back. He was clearly enjoying the sensations coming from Julie's mouth.

Ginny touched my shoulder suggesting I sit on the edge. She moved smoothly between my legs and took me in her mouth. The soft, rhythmic pulsed and sucking were exquisite. I watched Ginny's head move over me and Julie's head move over Micka. The scene was delightful and irresistible. Now I figured out why Micka had his eyes closed. The combination of Ginny's exceptional skills and the visual stimulation from the opposite corner of the tub were overwhelming. I wanted the sensations to last, to continue, perhaps to be perpetual. But, alas, the overwhelming stimulation was too much for me to resist. The rush of orgasmic heat flooded my body and my groans of pleasure broadcast Ginny's success.

She hugged my chest and rose for a kiss. I could taste the cum on her lips. The kiss was short, hot and passionate, filled with sex.

Ginny whispered, "thank you."

"My God, Ginny. Thank you. That was fantastic."

"I do enjoy it."

"You are very good."

"Thanks."

"Now, let me return the favor." I started to move toward her, but she stopped me.

"No, Cary. I don't want that."

"I would be honored to give you a good licking and a delightful orgasm."

"I know, and I would like that, but not now."

"OK." I did not know why she did not want her own pleasure, but it was not fair or reasonable for me to press her. I sat back down next to her and put my arm around her shoulder. We watched Julie and Micka.

The sounds of my pleasure must have inspired Micka, or he wanted more. He stopped Julie and guided her to lean on the edge. He moved behind her and entered Julie producing an "oh yes" from her. He stroked into her slowly and deeply. Julie's breasts swayed gently with each movement. The attraction pulled me toward her. As I move beneath her, she looked at me and smiled as she realized what I was going to do. Like a newborn calf, I took her nipple and began suckling at her breast. I could feel the groans from her chest. To my surprise, Ginny joined me on Julie's other breast.

"Oh my God," Julie gushed.

One hand enjoyed the softness of Julie's breast in my mouth, while my other hand found its way to the swollen and protruding sensitive organ just forward of Micka's stroking cock. I could feel Julie's hips press against me, as my fingers began to work her pleasure spot. She groaned loudly.

As Ginny and I sucked, she winked at me, again. I felt her hand reach for me and begin playing with me. I continued to rhythmically stroke Julie gauging my frequency to her response. Ginny's hand was gentle but purposeful. I reached with my other into Ginny's loose swimsuit to fondle her breast and feel her hard nipple in the middle of my palm. Ginny repositioned herself to continue her attention on Julie's other breast, but communicated with me. She wanted something more.

I reached down to the bottom of her suit. I saw her nod slightly. I move the suit material aside and found her swollen pleasure source. What a rush! I had never stroked two women at the same time. Ginny stopped her sucking and leaned back against the tub to give me a better angle. She pulled her suit farther away, so the material did not interfere.

Micka's pace quickened, as he began to pound into Julie. He was getting close. I move quicker on Julie. To my surprise, the telltale grunts of Julie's approaching orgasm brought the usual focus and enjoyment for me. I tried hard to concentrate. She liked her nipple squeezed before her climax.

With both hands busy, I kept my lips over my teeth and squeezed her nipple, not hard but firmly. The added stimulation worked. The convulsions of her orgasmic waves shook her body, as her groans became nearly cries of pleasure. The pulses of Julie's orgasm sent Micka over the top. There were no sounds from him other than the slap of his flesh against Julie's rump. Micka tried to continue his stroking, but found it difficult. Micka rested and then pulled out. Julie stood up.

"That was great," she said.

"Oh God yes," added Micka.

Ginny rose up of out the water to sit on the tub edge with her legs still spread. Her desire was now quite apparent. I slid over to her, adjusted my position, and took her in my lips. She moved her hips to give me better access. My tongue flicked over her swollen flesh. I alternated with gentle sucking. As I licked Ginny, I watched Julie and Micka peel her top down again to fondle her breasts and tweak her nipples. I inserted two fingers, sliding them easily into her hot flesh and stroking into her as my tongue and lips continued my efforts for her pleasure. Her pelvis began to twitch as a prelude to the more dramatic shudders of her body as she climaxed. Ginny tried to stifle the sounds of her pleasure, but the rumble came from deep inside her. Her hips pressed forward into me urging me to continue my efforts. I could not disappoint her.

Ginny's convulsions of pleasure lasted for the longest time until we heard her say, "No, no, enough," and she grabbed my head. She slid down into the water.

"Now, wasn't that fun," Micka said.

"Oh yes," responded Ginny.

"The best," added Julie.

All four of us hugged and kissed as we touched and fondled until it was time to go home. Julie and I could only partially dress, as we walked to our car for the drive into town. What a night, and a great time was had by all!

———

Clark

—

The evening meal with friends proved enjoyable as always. The comfort we enjoyed with Gloria and Mike remained at an elevated level. We shared so much in common and truly embraced them as good friends . . . for the long haul of life. With the bill paid, we sat in the booth for a few, slow, moments of relaxation.

"So, what are we going to do now?" asked Mike.

"Movie?" suggested Gloria.

"What's playing?" Mike asked.

I knew this was a lull period in the Hollywood releases. "Nothing much."

"We got some movies at home," offered Jennifer.

I was not exactly sure what she had in mind, but we did have numerous DVDs and videotapes of movies – old and new. I wondered.

"OK. Let's do it," Mike declared.

The cool night air refreshed us. The umbrella of stars overpowered the city lights.

"Why don't you come with me," Mike said to Jennifer.

"Why?"

"I want you to see how our new BMW compares to your RX8."

Jennifer looked to me. I shrugged and motioned for her to try it.

"Would you like to drive the RX8?" I asked Gloria.

She chuckled. "Not necessary."

I opened the passenger door for her, let her settle into the seat, and we set out. Jennifer and Mike took a different route to our house.

"What do you think they're doing?" Gloria asked.

"I suppose they are giving the 'Beamer' a little test drive."

"Nothing else?"

"Well, I'm not sure. They could stop for a little touchy-feely time, I guess."

"Do you think they will?"

"Maybe."

As we pulled up the drive and into the garage, the BMW pulled in behind us. If they had done anything, they had been very quick about it.

We gathered up a few drinks and went downstairs to the big screen television to watch a movie. The large 'L' shaped couch always gave us plenty of room. Jennifer and Mike sat on one leg, while Gloria and I sat on the other.

After some banter of which movie to watch, Jennifer volunteered one of our porn tapes. The tape was a little dated but the bodies and sex were good. We watched and chatted over the sounds of the screen couples performing.

The conversation drifted toward the sex before us. Pubic hair, common when the tape was made, was becoming less so as measured by Internet pornographic images.

"I've shave mine," Jennifer volunteered.

"Oh yeah," Mike answered perking up a little. "Let's see."

Jennifer stood up, unzipped her jeans and pulled down her pants and panties exposing her smooth, tanned, front crease.

Mike reached for her and stroked Jennifer's exposed skin a few times. "Nice."

"Clark is shaved, too," Jennifer announced.

"Well, let's see that too," Gloria said.

I did not need any more encouragement. I stood up, unzipped my jeans, pulled down my underwear and took out my cock and balls.

"Go ahead," Jennifer suggested to Gloria. "Touch 'em."

Gloria reached out to cup my testicles in her hand while Jennifer stroked the smooth skin above.

"Soft, huh?"

"Wow, yeah . . . really soft."

The ladies returned to their seats, and I returned my genitals to my pants. The video continued at a point where several couples traded places in a mass of flesh. We quietly watched the images gyrating on the large screen.

Within a few minutes, Mike clearly had an erection bulge. He leaned back making the bulge more pronounced and turned toward Jennifer.

"Are you going to help me?" Mike asked Jennifer.

"Help yourself."

Mike did not wait and released his erection and scooted his hips a little closer to Jennifer, virtually begging for Jennifer's attention. When she did not move to assist, he took his clothes off.

"OK," I said. "Let's get naked." I stripped off all my clothes.

Jennifer and Gloria made no move toward removing their clothes. They watched us and the movie still running before us. Mike spread his legs and scooted even closer to Jennifer. I wanted to tell her to go ahead and help him, but I just watched. Mike was stroking his cock. He was hard and ready.

Oddly, I noticed the Southwest desert sunset painting above the fireplace was not straight. I went to straighten it.

"Nice butt," Gloria pronounced.

I shook my hips a little.

"Yooohooo."

After straightening the painting, I returned to my seat next to Gloria.

Jennifer must have decided Mike was getting too close in his gestures to gain her attention. She moved over to sit between Gloria and me as she leaned back against me and fondled my cock and balls.

I reached around to fondle her left breast, as we watched Mike stroke himself. The clothing did not help. I moved my hand under her sweater and freed her breast from the confines of her bra. I lifted her sweater exposing her breast. The soft curves of her breast contrasted with the hardness of her erect nipple.

"Hello," Gloria exclaimed, when she acknowledged Jennifer's exposed breast under my hand.

Jennifer played with me although my cock had not yet responded. The tactile pleasures added to the scene.

The two women and myself were on one leg of the large couch while Mike remained on the other leg stroking himself. It was his erect cock and stroking that kept my attention. He needed someone to relieve him. The urge to help him amazed me. I wanted to feel the soft flesh move over the hardness beneath. I needed to feel his cock in my mouth and taste his hot, musty cum. The urges and thoughts surprised me. My apprehension regarding offending Mike kept me next to Jennifer and fondling her breast. I suspected that Jennifer and Gloria would accept acting out my urges, but I did not know how Mike would react.

Mike kept stroking oblivious to the audience watching him. His legs went rigid just before a stream of milky white cum shot from his cock head up his belly. He pumped his cock a few more times to get all his cum out and enjoy the last few shudders of his orgasm. Mike made no attempt to clean up and simply put his clothes back on.

I remained nude and continued to play with Jennifer's breast as our attention momentarily returned to the movie and the array of flesh moving on the large screen television.

Gloria kept glancing at my hand on Jennifer's breast.

"You want to feel?" I asked, as I moved my hand away.

"Sure, go ahead."

Without encouragement, Gloria stood up as she lifted her top and bra exposing her larger, round, right breast. "I have two," she giggled.

"Sure," I said as I cupped and jiggled Jennifer's breast, "but, all breasts are different."

Gloria returned her breast to the confines of her bra and top, and sat back down.

"Wait," Jennifer protested, "we didn't get to feel yours."

"Go ahead."

Jennifer put her hand on Gloria's covered right breast and gave it a gentle squeeze. I ran my hand down the top of her shirt and inside her bra to feel the soft flesh. Jennifer joined me against Gloria's skin. We both enjoyed the pleasures of her flesh. I certainly would have appreciated more time with my hand inside her bra or better yet on her exposed flesh. Jennifer withdrew first and I followed.

The remainder of the movie was uneventful and unentertaining.

"OK, time for us to go," Gloria announced.

Jennifer turned off the television as we all stood.

Jennifer looked at me. "Aren't you going to put some clothes on?"

"Naw. Everyone has seen me."

We followed Gloria and Mike up the stairs. We exchanged a hug and kiss on the cheek, and said goodbye. After Gloria and Mike drove away, we let the dogs out, and then back in before securing the house for the night. Preparations for bed did not take long. As was so often the case for me, I watched Jennifer's naked body walk from the bathroom around the bed. Even after 20 years of marriage and countless nights, I reveled in the soft sway of her breasts. She floated into bed and moved to snuggle up – skin to skin. My hands drifted over her curves – still a pleasure after all these years. Her hand moved to my smooth genitalia.

"You are inspired."

"I need a fucking."

"Well, then, let's see what we can do."

My hand moved down her body. "My, my, you are wet."

"Like I said, I need a fucking."

As my fingers went back to work on her pleasure spot, Jennifer rolled her hips and spread her legs slightly. She purred as pleasure blossomed through her body. As she focused on her pleasure, my urges compelled me to move between her legs and taste her. One arm wrapped around her right hip to spread her lips and tighten the skin surrounding her protruding and swollen clitoris. I gently sucked on her hardened magic button, as my tongue flicked across the head. Two fingers slipped into her hot, slippery flesh to find that special spot on the front of her vagina. The tension mounted within her body. Muscles tightened. Her hips began to move in a recognizable rhythm, as her groans became more audible. Two fingers stroked into her and teased her magic spot as my tongue moved faster over her firm and swollen flesh. Her breathing slowly changed to shallow, irregular, almost convulsive panting. She pulled her knees farther back to heighten the pressure. I could feel her cling to the approaching climax. Jennifer reach for her breasts and began twisting her erect nipples, as her head arched back and that magnificent, guttural, groan from deep within her chest mixed with the short choppy panting.

"Ooohhh, Gawd," she growled, "Ooooohhhh."

The peak felt high and wide as the convulsions rolled through her body. Jennifer put both hands on my head to signal me that my continued licking was too intense for her post-orgasmic recovery. My fingers remained inside her and quiet as the convulsions of pleasure confirmed the strength of her climax. I absorbed the taste and smell of her generous release.

We intertwined, as I manipulated the wet folds of her swollen flesh and she stroked my smooth cock and balls. My return to hardness did not take long. She knew how to handle my cock.

"Oh my," she cooed.

Without a word, Jennifer disentangled and raised herself on all fours with her posterior angled toward me. She looked back at me and wagged her hips. She was ready.

I scurried behind her to find that warm, wet spot between the folds of her flesh. Ever so slowly, I slipped into her, relishing the sensation of flesh against flesh and the joining of our bodies. We both softly groaned, as we enjoyed the union.

With my hands on her smooth, round hips, I began to slowly stroke into her. The fascination, sensation and singular focus on the warm, slippery grip of her body brought that unique electricity so seductive to all of us. The selfish side of these sensations gradually gave way to the movements of Jennifer's body as she swayed and pushed into me.

I slowed my stroking. My left hand slid up her body to find her dangling and fluid breast. The curves and softness of her skin heightened my sensations. I gently caressed her breast and intermittently found the rigid, protruding nipple. Each squeeze of her erect nipple offered up a moan and gyration of her hips. As I enjoyed our union and her breast, my right hand reached around her hips to the juncture to find that smooth, swollen, rigid knob under her smooth, wet flesh. My fingers straddled her clit and began to gently vibrate across her button.

As Jennifer began to climb to another peak, I moved my left hand down her side and across her round, swaying buttocks and slid my thumb slowly down the cleavage of her rump. I wetted my thumb generously and found her rosebud almost begging me for attention. I pressed gently, as I stroked fully into her. As I massaged the spot, I could feel her muscles relax. She pushed back into me. My thumb entered her.

The sensations nearly overwhelmed me. I had to stop my stroking.

"Don't cum yet," Jennifer whispered.

I waited for my upturn to subside. I had to stop my thumb action to gain control of my sensations. My hesitation allowed me to concentrate on my right hand.

Jennifer responded to the focus. I tried several times to re-activate my motion with hers, but I was too close.

"Oh yes," she grunted. "Don't stop."

The rapid motion of my right hand picked up with her short panting breathing and shaking of her body. Her peak was approaching. I allowed my thumb to restart first. I waited until I could hear the groans of her climax before I moved my hips again.

"Aaaaahhhhoooommmy gaaawwdd," she cried, as her body convulsed.

The gripping of her muscles on my thumb and cock ended any resistance I had left as the hot waves rushed through every molecule of my body. My growl must have come loud and deep, as I pounded into her hips.

"Yes, Clark. Give it all to me."

My groans continued as I allowed myself to come down slightly. I stroked again with purpose and was rewarded with another peak. I continued until the waves passed. My pace slowed. I began to massage her hips and back, to feel the soft smoothness of her skin. We remained joined as we rolled together to our sides. My hands continued to cover her body including a few gentle squeezes of her breasts.

"We always have great sex after we've been with others," observed Jennifer.

"Indeed, we do."

We remained spooned until our connection was broken. So ended a pleasant evening's enjoyment.

———

Gretchen
(This story is dedicated to Jeanne L.)

—

"Gretchen, we've talked about this a hundred times," Jill protested.

"Not enough, I guess. I still don't think I'm doing it right, and you've always said you are a master, if not the master."

"Yes, well," she said with animated, but sophistic humility, "nonetheless, I don't know what else to tell you. Maybe it's not you. Maybe it's him."

"Maybe, but I don't think so. Everything seems to work just fine."

Jill returned to her milkshake as we watched humanity pass by our corner cafe. The occasional tight set of buns or 'come-to-me' smile made the late spring sunshine and light breeze ladened with the rich aroma of the ocean more humorous, pleasant and relaxing. The afternoon respites with my best friend continued to grow in significance as they decreased in tempo. Although our marriages slowed the process down for several years, the near daily intermission functioned as a touchstone, pressure relief, confessional and idea well.

I always admired her. The soft, smooth skin, subtle facial features and her new breasts just seemed so perfect. My only criticism had to be her incessant need to change her hair color. Jill started the process when we were in college and has kept it up ever since. For this period, it was an odd combination of deep brown verging on auburn with light streaks of highlighting. Jill enjoyed playing with her appearance, and she certainly had enough to play with.

"I've got an idea."

"What's that?" she inquired, as she approached the bottom of her milkshake.

"Why don't you show me?"

"You mean on him," she laughed as she nodded toward an attractive boy walking passed.

I laughed with her. "He'll do."

She returned to the completion of her task. I stopped to reconsider what I was thinking. *Maybe she would be offended or insulted?* I fantasized about this many times, which provided a fertile orgasmic mood, and I seriously considered it as a means of improvement. After all, she was my best friend and best friends shared everything.

"I mean Carl."

Jill coughed and choked on the remnants of her milkshake. The thought was obviously not one Jill shared. "You've got to be joking."

"No, I'm not."

"You're crazy, Gretchen. I can't do that."

"Why not?"

"Because he's your husband and a friend."

"So! You've done guys you didn't want to before. Why not Carl?"

"That's different. He's your husband, Gretchen."

I gave the discussion a moment's respite. She needed the time to think things through. "What if I gave you some money?"

"What . . . like a prostitute?"

"You've accepted money and gifts from other guys."

"Gretchen, this is crazy. You are my best friend from high school days, and I've known Carl for just about as long as I've known you. He's been a good friend even though he hasn't always agreed with the things I do. I don't think I could do this even if I wanted to."

"Sure you can. Just think of him as just another dick."

"Yeah, right . . . just another dick that knows all about me. He's not even attractive to me. I certainly wouldn't go out with him, if he weren't with you, so why would I do him?"

"Because I want you to show me how to give a good blow job."

"I know that, but . . ."

"But, what?"

"I don't think I could do it."

"What if I gave you $100 to give him a blow job and let me watch? Maybe you can tell me what I can't see."

"What does Carl think about all this?"

"He knows about my fantasy, and I've told him several times I want to do this."

"So, what does he think?"

I knew quite well what Carl thought of my idea, but I think he was just telling me he did not want to do it because he thought that is what I wanted to hear. "He says he doesn't want to do it, but I think he's just saying that."

"See! There you go." Jill sucked out the remainder of her milkshake, but still held onto the cup.

"Jill, ever since your boob job, he's wondered what your breasts feel like."

She laughed more to relieve the tension rather than the humorousness of my words. "You mean kinda like you."

The memory of my best friend opening her blouse several years ago to expose her newly augmented and unbridled breasts came back to me in vivid detail. Jill was proud of her breasts and was not particularly embarrassed or self-conscious about them. She allowed me to examine them closely. The incision scars at the side of her breasts were barely detectable even knowing where they were and looking closely. Her breasts were now of moderate size, a little larger than mine, and much firmer. The saline implants were almost undetectable. Her breasts felt like youthful, pre-childbirth breasts. Carl's curiosity was never sufficient to overcome his sense of impropriety even though several opportunities had been presented.

"Yes, kinda like me," I answered.

"Just because he wants to see or feel my tits doesn't mean he would accept a blow job."

"If I ask him to, he will."

"Why don't you just get an anonymous hooker?"

"Too many uncontrollable elements, plus you're a friend I know I can trust."

"Are you sure you really want to do this . . . to see another woman going down on your husband?"

"You're not another woman. You're my best friend and it is for educational purposes."

"What if Carl just doesn't like blow jobs?"

"Every man likes a blow job."

"I don't know. I've had a few hard ones."

"Yeah, I'll bet," I laughed. Jill responded in kind.

"You know what I mean. A few guys who just didn't seem to get into it like most guys."

"Yeah, but you still got them off, didn't you?"

"Sure, but it was hard work."

"Carl, may be one of those, but you've always said there was no man you couldn't get off with your mouth or your pussy. So, I want you to show me."

"What if it leads to more?"

"That's OK. I've always had a fantasy about watching Carl with another woman. Anyway, I've never tried a *ménagé à trois* like you have."

"It's not as simple as that. Don't you think you'll be just a little jealous watching your husband enjoy another woman going down on him, or if it comes to that, fucking another woman?"

"I've thought about that. You're not another woman. You're my best friend, and I know you have no interest in Carl. So, I don't think I'll be jealous."

"That's a big risk, Gretchen. Once the Genie is out of the bottle . . . you know."

"It's just an educational experience. I'm trying to learn how to give good blow-jobs."

"Are you absolutely, no kidding, cross your heart, really sure?"

"Yes."

Jill looked off toward the ocean several blocks away, as she considered my request. "OK, but you've got to promise me neither of you will tell Andy. I don't think he'll mind since we've done three'sies before, but he'd probably want to join in."

"Agreed."

"When do you want to do this?"

"How about tonight? Carl is supposed to get home early. We can do the deed, and then have something to eat and play some more before you need to leave."

"Gretchen, I don't have a problem with this. I've done this kinda thing many times before, but I'm very worried about you. I've shared Andy with several of my other friends. So, it's not a problem for me, but our friendship may never be the same."

"Yeah, you're right. It might be stronger. We'll be sharing someone who is very special to me, and hopefully, I will be learning something about how to give my husband more pleasure. I don't see this as a risk. I see it as a growing opportunity."

"OK. Let me call home to leave a message on the machine for Andy, then let's do it. I imagine Carl is about to have the shock of his life."

This Tuesday evening made the perfect occasion. Carl would be home relatively early and it was after all his birthday. We had planned nothing special. This birthday would undoubtedly be one to remember. if it happened the way I wanted it to. Jill and I arrived home before Carl.

We talked about how to get the event going. In the end, we decided there was no subtle or delicate way. When we heard Carl drive up, Jill would wait in the spare bedroom. My part entailed getting Carl into bed. When I said the password, 'ready,' Jill would enter without clothes, so we would give Carl the minimum time to think about things.

A glass of White Zinfandel helped us both relax. Jill seemed calm although I could tell she was becoming more nervous about what we had agreed to do. I knew I was probably more nervous than she was. Trepidation began to corrode my confidence in this constructed event. Although I did not tell Jill, I did have my doubts about the wisdom of this surprise. I remembered the saying about not trying to live out your fantasies, but I convinced myself this was different. This was partly a sex education lessen for me and partly a birthday surprise for Carl. I never had been able to get Carl off with fellatio and Jill always said she never failed to get a guy off, so it had to be her technique.

This was as much a challenge for me as anything else. This would be fun and just maybe I would learn something. Carl's car moved up the driveway.

"This is it," I said.

Jill looked at me with a very serious expression. "One last time, are you absolutely sure you want to do this?"

"Sure, I'm sure," I lied.

Her answer came as she started to unbutton her blouse. I left the room to execute the next stage of the plan. I tried to change my thoughts away from my naked best friend in our guest bedroom and our wicked plan. I needed to quickly assess his mood and work my part of the plan as quickly as possible. If I was right, Carl would see it as perfectly normal for me to want a good sex session before dinner on his birthday. It was what we usually did anyway. I told myself to think normally and this would not be difficult.

"Evenin', sweetheart," he said as he entered the kitchen from the garage. He appeared to be in good spirits. At least, he had a smile on his face.

"Hi, sweetie. How was your day?"

"The usual crap, I guess. I'm ready for the weekend, and it's not even hump day, yet."

"Well, we'll see if we can make it better before hump day." I walked toward him. "Happy birthday," I purred as I gave him a good, passionate kiss.

He looked at me as if I were some strange person in his wife's body. "Thank you, sweetheart. I ought to have birthday's more often."

I clasped his hand and led him toward the bedroom.

"What's going on?"

"I've got a surprise for you, but first I thought we'd get comfortable."

"Oh, yea, a mid-week poke."

His non-romantic reference to making love did not add to the moment, but at least it said he was willing to proceed. He started to undress until I stopped him. I let him know I wanted to do it. I removed each item of his business attire slowly, purposefully, and with the appropriate caressing. The smile on his face and in his eyes conveyed his appreciation. Once completely nude, I led him to the bed, pulled back the comforter and sheets, and signaled him to lie down.

I walked to the door, turned to face him and performed a little striptease routine without the music. I always felt good standing in full glory for his consuming gaze. Even after ten years, we still liked looking, touching, feeling, tasting and smelling each other.

"Ready," I said rather loudly without turning my head.

"Oh, yeah, I'm ready," Carl said, thinking I was speaking for his benefit.

I just smiled at him until I saw Jill out of the corner of my eye as she approached the door. I stepped to the left, leaving a space for her to enter and stand beside me. "Surprise!"

The shocked expression added to the suction of air filling his lungs. He squirmed slightly, but did not try to cover up or hide himself.

"Happy birthday, Carl," said Jill.

Carl's mouth dropped open. He made no attempt to respond.

"I told you I always wanted to do this, so I finally convinced Jill to help me. This is it."

Carl remained frozen. His expression conveyed an emotion closer to terror than ecstasy. It was impossible to determine whether he was scared stiff, overwhelmed with excitement, or absorbed in trying to sense my true feelings with what was obviously about to happen.

I needed to break the ice. I looked at Jill who returned an inquisitive glance. She needed some direction. I reached over to fondle her left breast that she willingly accepted. "You've wanted to feel these beauties since she got them. Now's your chance."

"Gretchen," he protested, finally showing some sign of life.

"It's OK," Jill added quickly to reassure him.

"This is for your carnal enjoyment," I said. "Just lie back and let us take care of everything."

"I don't know."

"It's OK, sweetie."

"I don't know. Are you sure we should be doing this?

"Just relax, Carl," I said as I moved slowly toward the bed. "Everything is great."

"What does Andy think about this?"

"This must be only between the three of us, Carl," I said looking for an affirmative response. "Do you agree?"

"I guess so."

"No, Carl. Jill thinks it is best between us and we must promise to keep it between us."

"OK. So, what are we going to do?"

"Jill's going to give you the best blow-job you've ever had and she's going to teach me how."

"Jesus, Gretchen."

"Any problem with the plan so far?" I asked.

"No, but don't you think it is a little personal and a little fast?"

"Not really. Sex is sex."

I started by softly touching the inside of his thigh, as I moved onto the bed dragging my breasts across his chest. His whole body shook as if he shivered from the cold. Jill took her cue moving between Carl's legs.

"Oh God," was all he could say.

I needed to distract him or occupy his awareness. I leaned over to kiss him deeply, passionately and thoroughly to convey my acceptance. I turned to watch Jill.

She fondled him and gently stroked him, as if she were conducting an examination or assessment. Apparently satisfied with whatever she was looking for, Jill began her narration as if she were in a surgical amphitheater describing a delicate operation. "First, I lick the entire shaft making sure I use the coarse, top side as well as the smooth, bottom side of my tongue." She moved up and down like she was licking dripping ice cream from a cone in the hot sun. "Make sure you go all around the head. It's the most sensitive." She kept it up. "You want to get the shaft really wet with your saliva, so your lips and fingers can slide easily."

Watching Jill move over Carl's penis gave me a contraction in my groin. Watching her work on him was everything I had dreamed it would be, so far. I wanted to reach down and deal with the growing itch between my legs. I tried to remember to stroke his chest and occasionally kiss him to let him know I was still here.

"When you're ready, you tighten your lips and push onto him like he was entering a vagina." She pulled his skintight and squeezed the base, as she took him into her mouth. Her cheeks sucked in rhythmically as she moved on him.

Jill stopped to allow her hand to grasp the shaft and continue stroking him. "You need to suck as you're pulling off him like you're trying to draw his jism through a straw." She repeated her action several times, and then continued with her hand. "I stroke the bottom of his shaft allowing my fingers to slide over his wet skin while occasionally pulling his skin just tight enough and squeezing the base like this." Jill again demonstrated the specific action. "You keep going like this." This time the cadence of her movements was more purposeful. "You can use your free hand to gently fondle their balls, especially the base, and sometimes you can push 'em over the top by using a wet finger on their rosebud." Jill returned to her task.

It was truly amazing watching Jill perform on Carl. His groans and growing rigidity indicated his absorption into the act. I could feel his muscles turning to stone. Jill stopped.

"He's close," Jill said looking directly into my eyes. "You know how the dick swells before they go?" I nodded my head. "You can walk them along the line sometimes, which really multiplies the intensity of the climax." She held him, squeezing slightly. "You always have the choice of taking the load or not. I've grown to like the taste and texture. Do you mind?" she asked, as if she needed my permission to finish him. The sensations were unbearable. I wanted someone to tend to my agonizing itchy, contractions. I wanted to jump onto him. I smiled and nodded.

Jill returned to her task repeating her earlier actions. The conclusion only took a few minutes to achieve. Carl's body stiffened with every muscle locked against the wave soon to crash down on him. Jill's motions picked up a fevered pace. The convulsion shook his body, as his back arched against the onslaught. She slowed her pace and used her fingers to draw more from him. She withdrew from him and licked the head, as if she needed to catch every drop. Carl's body shook with each touch of her tongue like he was in pain, although he did not protest.

"How was it, sweetie?"

"Oh God," he groaned.

I looked to Jill. "That was amazing."

Jill wiped her mouth dry. "Now, you know all my secrets."

"I can see why you're so good."

"Thanks. That was fun. I can see why you love him, Gretchen. He's a fairly decent specimen."

"Yeah, I think so." A thought came to me like a lightning bolt from a clear sky. "Now, it's your turn." A puzzled expression communicated her confusion. "Carl's got the best tongue I've ever experienced. I want him to do you."

"No. I've done what you asked me. That's enough."

"Oh bull. You know your pussy's askin' for it just like mine is. Come on, lay down here and let Carl do you."

"No."

"Sure," Carl said, as he began to move. "An orgasm for an orgasm, as they say."

Her resistance did not last long. "All right," she said. "This probably won't take long."

She lay down raising her knees as Carl moved into position. The fascination of detached observation of the actions I had come to worship possessed me. Watching Carl, I could feel his tongue exciting me even more. I was swollen hard and dripping wet. I needed some attention. Jill was obviously enjoying Carl's skill.

I moved across the bed raising Carl's hips for access. I wanted him to return to readiness. To my amazement, Carl's hardness returned quite rapidly. Feeling him made my condition worse, but I had other ideas. The convulsive, pulsating squeaks of Jill's climax signaled the moment. I waited until I saw her body start to come down from the peak. I pushed Carl's buttocks toward my best friend. "Enter her, Carl," I commanded. "Fuck her."

He turned to look at me with questioning eyes. I smiled my consent. He turned to look at Jill. She nodded her willingness. Carl moved slowly and delicately, as he always did until he was fully engulfed. Jill drew her knees back to allow deeper penetration.

I stood up, consumed with seductive curiosity. The two bodies moved against each other with the most amazing smoothness and rhythm. I could see them completely, as he drew almost apart, then slid back fully into her. The motions of life before me were more than I could tolerate anymore.

"I need you," I said, as I moved beside them on my hands and knees. My signal did not take long for Carl to respond to.

Just as carefully, I took him into me. He felt bigger than I had ever felt him before. He filled me. I stroked my swollen clitoris, as he rocked me. Finally, I felt some relief to the terrible itch. A desperate sensation drove me toward the inevitable peak, but suddenly I knew I needed my climax in a more complete way.

I pulled away from Carl. "Lay down," I said softly. He did as I asked. I straddled his head, which left no doubt what I wanted. I looked at Jill whose eyes sought guidance. I nodded toward Carl and Jill knew. She straddled his hips taking him back into her.

Carl's magic worked with exquisite precision. To my utter amazement, Jill's breasts moving in front of me became incredible magnets. The combination of watching her hips move, feeling Carl's incredible tongue and lips on me, as I enjoyed Jill's firm roundness sent me into orbit like a huge rocket.

Carl altered his action to enjoy the products of his work, as Jill sent him over the top again. Jill must have been close herself. She reached down to the point where she needed attention. A few minutes of fast motion brought her to the peak as well.

As her body began to relax with Carl and me, Jill leaned forward cupping my left breast in her warm, soft hand and kissed me in the most delightful, gentle, appreciative and passionate manner. I wanted to resist, but I could not. I returned her kiss until we fell together in an entwined mass.

———

Sophia

(This story is dedicated to Cindy M.)

—

A cloudless, whisper-less, baby-blue sky allowed the mid-summer sun to warm my body, as I stepped off the terrace and descended the steps. With my summer lessons complete for the day, the sweet, earthy smell of the expansive garden captured my attention and served as a broad platter offering me the exquisite blend of flowers, blossoms and scents. My mind sorted through the various aromas, as I meandered lazily past the manicured hedges, bordered flowerbeds and modest, dispersed groves of fruit trees ripening their yield.

The day was too magnificent to waste it inside although I tried to ignore the various contestants flittering about inside the château that would be seeking my participation in one project or another. I just could not go inside.

A grizzled and discolored oak bench nicely located under a young oak made a convenient way station for me to absorb the little details in this section of the garden – the bees scurrying from blossom to blossom, the array of birds happily chirping their buoyant songs, and the occasional butterfly dancing on the air. I sat and let the sights, sounds and smells envelop me. The warmth convinced me to pull the ribbon from the neckline of my sun dress and tie my thick, black hair up in a ponytail. The air felt cool on my neck.

The faint gurgling from a distance reminded me of the bountiful stream that bisected my family's land and separated the pasture and crop land from the woods and château. I could feel the coolness of the water and felt the attraction that drew me to it.

I left the garden through a portal in the high hedgerow passing into a small meadow with knee-high grass that tickled my legs as I walked. The stream lay among the trees on the far side of the meadow. I remembered that it had been nearly a year since I was last down this way, and I had to confess an inner heat building like flickering flames rising to life from embers. The water was going to feel so good on my skin. Perhaps I could find a moment for my intimate pleasure.

Eyes! The oddest feeling flushed through me, as if someone was watching me. I stopped as much to listen as to look around the extent of the area I could see. Nothing. The birds continued to sing, and the stream continued to gurgle. None of the vegetation moved in the slightest. I did a slow pirouette in the middle of the meadow to take another full look. Nothing. Just my imagination, I concluded. The boundaries of my family's land were miles away. No one just wandered across our land.

The babbling brook beckoned. I did take quick glances around just to assure myself that I was alone, and I was.

The shade of the leafy trees and other bushes cooled the air, as I gently moved the branches in my way. The bordering tree line was not particularly wide. The stream came into view. I sidestepped over a small group of river rocks to a sandy patch. As I looked up and down the stream as well as to the opposite bank, I chastised myself for not coming down here more often. The picture before me possessed an idyllic, almost magical, quality. The water flowed smoothly and swiftly over the patches of rocks giving me the song of the stream. There were also areas of near mirrored stillness marking the nice pools between the rocks.

I slipped off my sandals to feel the soft, wet sand beneath me. Kneeling down, the hem of my sun dress touching the ground, I swirled my hand in the water – cool, almost cold, but still tempting enough.

Standing, I looked upstream and downstream. The sensation of being watched was not there. I stepped into the water ankle deep. The brief shiver raised the sensitivity of my body, wanting more. This was life.

I dipped both hands into the cool water and patted my cheeks, cooling my face and preparing my body for what was to come.

My nipples tingled, still contained in their constraints. This was going to feel so good. Starting at the top of my light dress, I purposefully undid each large button down my front to the damp hem of my dress, shrugged out of the light dress, and found an appropriate branch behind me to hang the dress. I walked a little deeper into the stream feeling the sand give way to smooth, roundish rocks on the bottom. The cool water seemed to make my skin dance, urging me on. My nipples began to ache as I felt the soft flesh of my breasts under the thin, light cloth. The hardness of my nipples standing out in contrast to the softness of the mounds upon which they stood begged for attention. I took each nipple between my thumb and first finger squeezing them, and then rolling them slightly sending another shiver through my body and producing an audible groan from deep inside me.

As I turned back to the bank, I reached behind my back and unfastened the clasp holding my bra together and again shrugged, allowing my bra to slip off, catching it in my left hand. An urge made me shake my shoulders as if to feel my breasts move and my nipples to cut the air. Once on the bank, I stepped out of my petite panties and placed both undergarments on the branch adjacent to the dress. Then, without thinking, I jumped around, spread my legs and raised both arms high like a victorious athlete on the award stand. I was free.

I needed to feel the cool water all over me. I strode into the water toward the upstream pool until I was nearly waist deep, and dove into the water. The cool clear water swallowed my whole body. Fantastic. I could feel every little inch of my skin. I stroked a couple of times underwater placing me in the middle of the pool.

At the surface, I rolled on my back and floated with my eyes closed. The warm sun beat down on my face and breasts while the rest of my body remained cool. The muffled gurgling in my immersed ears gave this moment a certain fetal sensation. I could stay here forever. Other sensations or perhaps they were urges popped into my consciousness. I touched that spot and was rewarded with the unique electric feeling. The urge was there.

I raised my head out of the water to have a look around for an appropriate spot for what I needed to do. A couple of quick scans found a nearly flat rock in the sun with several other larger rocks around it, almost like a large, over-stuffed chair. I gently swam toward the flat rock.

The surface felt a little too warm from the sun, so I splashed some cool water on the rock until it was cooler to the touch before pushing myself to a seated position on the rock. I slowly leaned back against the adjacent boulder to give my skin time to adjust to the temperature of the warm rock.

I took another look around. I was still alone with only the sounds of the stream and the birds around me. Closing my eyes again and laying my head back against the rock, my hands cupped my breasts and tweaked my erect nipples. Additional warmth flushed through my body. This was the perfect time.

My right hand slid slowly down the cool, wet, soft skin of my abdomen until it found the crease between my legs. As my left hand moved to my right breast, my right hand fingers began to manipulate the soft flesh. The sun's warmth added to the pleasure of the moment. The special wetness came to the folds of skin, as my fingers probed and circled the soft, sensitive bud of flesh growing from its hiding place. When my middle finger finally connected with the now, nearly rigid button of flesh, my chest sucked in a breath and groaned deep inside.

The motion of my hand and finger started the back-and-forth rubbing I knew so well. I raised and opened my knees as my feet came together just below my bum.

"Oh yes," I gushed aloud, as my activity gained intensity.

Images began dancing in my head. The usual fantasies drifted through my consciousness as the exhilarating mixture of hot and cold, wet and dry, soft and hard, brought my senses to a contracting focus. The natural selection did not take many passes.

In my mind's eye, I saw my younger cousin sitting in the chair across my room, just five or so feet from my bed, as I did this for him. His eyes did not blink or move. I had his absolute attention. I wanted to show him what I had learned and what I knew. He did not make a sound. My attention turned from him to the rapidly mounting charge building within my body waiting for the trigger. The rest of the world ceased to exist, as my hand began to move into invisibility. But, it was the peculiar subtle slap of skin that brought back away from the peak for a moment and caused me to open my eyes. There he was, still fully clothed and his eyes staring intently at me, but now his rigid, pinkish, shaft of flesh rose above his pants and guided his hand in its stroking motion. I had seen other boys do this, but not him. I knew precisely what I wanted to see. I slowed my pace and pulled a pillow under my head, so I could watch him more comfortably. Our gaze was very focused, as if nothing else mattered. I worked my sensations allowing them to rise and fall as I walked on that seductive plateau just short of the peak. I knew the ache of spread joints and stretched muscles had to be underneath the exquisite sensation that occupied my awareness. I knew the moment had come when I saw his eyeballs go white as his head slowly fell back. His chest began to heave in convulsive jerks, as the first of several magnificent streamers of milky white fluid shot from his shaft high into the air before falling back down on his pants. He groaned almost like he was in pain, as several more streamers erupted from his shaft. As his body began to relax, I closed my eyes and ran for the peak I knew was close. My reward came quickly as my nerve endings collapsed to that single point, and then shot out like shock waves exploding from a bomb. This was a good one. The waves continued, as if they were never going to stop. Surge after surge shook my body repeatedly and gradually began to subside.

With my eyes still closed, I stretched my legs back out and dangled into the refreshing water. My hands slowly gathered some of the cool water to splash on my flushed, hot chest and face. The coolness felt so refreshing. A nice, deep, cleansing breath concluded my moment of genuine freedom.

My heart leapt in my chest. I was startled as I opened my eyes. A quick flash urge me to cover myself passed into an odd defiance.

An attractive, dark-haired, tanned man sat on his haunches at the bank with his arms wrapped around his knees. His gaze along with an ever so slight grin remained riveted on me. He did not move, not even to blink.

A series of emotions shot through my mind, from offense, to curiosity, and then strength and confidence in myself. I had never seen him before. It was hard to tell how tall he was, but he appeared to be roughly my age. I decided not to let him spoil my moment. I slipped into the cool water, made a little colder by the sun's warmth on my skin. I dunked my head just to cool off my face and wet my hair, and then kept my head above water with my eyes on him, as I breast-stroked gently toward him and the bank where my clothes were.

I told myself I had nothing to be ashamed of or embarrassed about as the water became more shallow. I stood up on the stream-bed rock at about waist deep. I walked slowly toward the bank rising out of the water. His eyes remained continuously connected to mine. I was impressed. He did not allow his eyes to scan my naked body as I approached.

Stopping within arm's length, I looked deeply into his dark brown eyes that remained unblinking. Slowly, he stood. His loose fitting white muslin clothing did not particularly hide his lean but well-muscled body. This was not a boy. He was a young, fit man. We stood looking into each other's eyes trying to see what the other was thinking.

As if of their own free will, my hands reached for him. I could feel the solid roundness of his muscled chest. He still did not move or take his eyes off mine, but I could feel his excitement pounding hard inside his chest underneath my hand.

I wanted to ask him who he was? What was he doing in the middle of our property? Why was he spying on me? But, no words came out.

He touched my cheek ever so gently and traced an imaginary line down to my chin. His eyes possessed a softness that was appreciative and perhaps even grateful. Any concerns I may have had evaporated in his un-blinking gaze.

My mind and body seemed to relax as I unbuttoned his shirt from top to bottom without breaking the eye-to-eye connection between us. I brushed open both sides of his now loose shirt and feeling his smooth, brown skin as if a thin sheath over his rock hard body. He stood stone still locked on my eyes. Only his chest moved with each breath, and a small slight and rapid pumping of his heart. I touched him, feeling the excitement he contained within him. I reminded myself I did not know his name, did not know where he came from, or why he was here. I did not know if he could even speak. And yet, as my mind processed the craziness of me standing naked in front of and touching a strange man along with the mass of flash thoughts, in that instant, I realized what I wanted – what I needed.

I pushed the shirt off his shoulders. The light shirt fluttered to the ground. My hands lightly descended the sides of his torso. He shivered. As my hands touched the top of his thin muslin pants, held on his hips by a simple tie, my eyes broke with his for the first time. The bulge straining against the cloth left no doubt about his arousal and desire.

A smile bloomed broadly on my face as my eyes recaptured his. I could see his readiness, and yet there was a mysterious hint of apprehension or perhaps hesitation in his eyes. What could that clash of emotions be within him? My curiosity vanished instantly as my thoughts jumped to the pleasure I yearned to enjoy.

I untied, unbuttoned and released his pants as his rigid flesh sprang from its confinement. The urge to grab it was strong, but I resisted allowing my fingers to slowly and lightly trace the ridge of his hips toward the center. The smooth, hairless skin slipped beneath my fingertips. I expected the coarse hair of his *mons pubis*, but his skin remained smooth as I reached and lightly touched his shaft. My left hand surrounded the rigid protuberance as my right hand gathered the two orbs contained in the surprisingly smooth, incredibly soft sac of flesh beneath his shaft. My hands and fingers explored every inch of his manhood. The urge to know more coaxed me along my chosen path of pleasure.

I quickly scanned the area, touched his shoulder turning him slightly, and then lightly pushed down indicating I wanted him to lay down. He lowered himself without taking his eyes off mine. He shifted his position ever so slightly to find a comfortable spot in the sand and grass.

I focused my attention on the rigid shaft now standing straight up in all its glory – a marvelous specimen, despite my limited sampling. I stroked him a few times just to feel the thin, delicate skin move so easily over the hardness beneath. Magnificent was the only word that occupied my mind as I stood and bent over, continuing to stroke him. I straddled him with my feet at the top of his hips and lowered my hips toward his. I felt him against me. Moving his shaft back and forth, the bountiful wetness made the folds of my eager flesh slippery and ready. I felt him at the sweet spot I needed him. I slowly took him inside me savoring that unique sensation of entry. I rose off him just to repeat the pleasure of that initial union. This time I took all of him and rejoiced in the deep sensation of him filling me seemingly to my throat. I remained motionless for just a few moments to absorb every little nuance of this most unique of human connections.

His eyes were closed and his head arched slightly back. I shifted my hands to his chest to balance myself on him. My hips began to rhythmically pulse him. To my amazement, the preparation and anticipation had moved me well up the slope of the peak I sought. The tingling, almost electric feeling emanating from my magic spot validated the extent of my climb. I kept my hips moving, as I thoroughly enjoyed that special slippery friction that was the essence of female-male union. I could feel him swelling inside me. I gripped his chest and noticed the rapid heaving that told me of his approaching summit. The awareness heightened my sensations and urged me to pick up the pace of my efforts. The little rivulets of perspiration descending the skin of my torso acted like streamers of electricity pushing me rapidly up the massive mountain I was now swiftly ascending.

His moment came as his head arched farther back and his lips parted showing his clenched teeth. A deep, rumbling groan marked the spasmodic shaking of his body. I could feel the head of his shaft swell substantially, as if to prevent separation although that was the last of my wishes. I continued to stroke rapidly on him as I closed my eyes and concentrated on my peak now rushing toward me. His spasms of pleasure began to subside as my climax shook my body, taking control of my muscles. The hot waves of my pleasured pulsed through my entire body. I commanded my hips to move up and down a few more times sending more powerful waves shooting through every nerve.

The peak lasted for an unusually long time for me, but did not last forever. I lowered myself to his chest. The wet slipperiness between our skin felt good. His arms enveloped me as if to secure me in place and did not move to explore the curves of my body.

Our breathing began to subside to a normal pace. I waited for him to deflate and fall from me before I rose from him. As I stood above him, he kept his arms outstretched beckoning for me to return to his embrace, and his eyes now sparkled with a playful brilliance I had not seen before. His body was indeed magnificent – quite chiseled, devoid of any body hair, and brown all over. I could not tell whether it was his natural skin color or the baking of the sun's rays.

I turned and stepped quickly into the water and dove the remaining way into the now chilly pool. After making several strokes nearly to the other side and feeling the water glide so sensually over my hot skin, I surfaced and turned back to my origin. He was gone.

I scanned the entire area. I could not see a trace of his presence or departure. I shook my head, as if to confirm I was not dreaming. He just left. I did not know his name and did not know if I would ever see him again.

I slowly moved toward the stream bank. A clear imprint of his body remained in the sand and grass. Even my footprints on either side could be readily seen. My experience was not a dream. My thoughts reveled in the afternoon's activity, as I dressed and continued during my walk back to the château. I stopped at irregular intervals to see if his eyes might still be on me, but I could see nothing. I knew I would have the sweetest dreams tonight.

———

Adam

(This story is dedicated to Stewart K.)

—

"**I**'m glad you could make it."

"No problem," John answered. "I always enjoy watching a movie with a friend."

"I'm glad you call me a friend."

"Cuz you are."

"Thanks."

I motioned toward the living room and the couch. "I'm going to make some popcorn. Would you like a soda?"

"Sure. Dr. Pepper, if you have it?"

"Yep'a'do."

John followed me into the kitchen. I retrieved a can of Dr. Pepper and Diet Coke from the refrigerator, put them into insulator sleeves, hand the Dr. Pepper to John, popped the top on mine and took a short sip. He popped the top on his and took a longer swallow. I removed the popcorn bag from its protective cover, placed it properly into the microwave and hit the correct button.

I wanted to test the water quickly, to see if my impression of John was even close to the mark. "Would you mind if I take my clothes off?"

He looked into my eyes, as if to determine if I was serious, and decided quickly. "If you wish."

I did not hesitate and removed my shorts and T-shirt. I truly preferred being naked, and I had long suspected John and his wife had seen me in the backyard a few times, although they never said anything. He did not appear even the slightest bit uncomfortable with a naked man in front of him. As soon as the popcorn was finished, I dumped the contents into a large bowl, grabbed my soda and led him back into the living room.

"How long have you been shaving?" he asked.

He noticed, I said to myself.

"Probably ten years or so."

"Isn't it a pain in the ass?"

"Not really. The feeling is worth it."

"What do you mean?"

"I don't think there is a smoother, softer skin on any human being. Would you like to feel?" I asked, as I fondled my scrotum.

"Sure, if you wouldn't mind."

"Who could ever mind being touched?"

I stood in front of him with my legs spread slightly. His warm, dry hand tentatively touched my balls, and then he grasped them gently, moving my testicles in his hand. John was clearly enjoying himself. The touching of my scrotum had the usual effect . . . my cock soon stiffened, standing straight out.

"Looks like you enjoy this," John said.

"What is not to enjoy? You handle balls well."

"I do have my own," he laughed. "Perhaps I should get naked, too."

"Your choice, John. No pressure. I just prefer being naked and I'm thankful you do not object."

John removed his clothes, laying them on the back of an adjacent chair. He had a fine body for his age and a modest package. I wanted to reach out and touch him, but I knew I could not, at least not yet. I did not want to risk scaring him off. He joined me on the couch.

"What is showing today?"

"What do you think about the 1999 movie, *Notting Hill*, with Julia Roberts and Hugh Grant?"

"That should work."

We finished the popcorn by about the 30-minute mark – William (Hugh) arrived at her Ritz hotel room to interview Anna (Julia).

John looked at me, and then at my lap. "May I?"

I smiled. "By all means."

John took my cock in his hand. His eyes returned to the movie. His fingers and hand gently and gracefully worked my cock, an erection did not take long arriving. The stiff cock in his hand clearly did not bother him, and it felt so good to be touched, to be stroked, and to be appreciated. I wanted his cock, but as far as I knew or was aware, he was a straight, married man, although that assumption was obviously questionable with my cock in his hand. It was not until the dinner scene at Max and Bella's kitchen before my erection exceeded expectations.

I looked at John, and he looked back at me. "Would you mind?" I asked, as I glanced at his partially inflated but not yet erect cock.

He smiled, "If you wish."

John kept stroking me, as I worked his cock to rigidity. Then, at the appropriate and opportune moment, Max asked William, 'Do you ever mas-turbate?' I started laughing. A moment later, John collected the irony.

"Do you think you can give me a dose of your man-milk?" I asked.

"If you keep doing what you are doing, I would say, definitely."

My stroking took on more purpose, which did not take long to attain success. John groans softly, stiffened and gave a good squirt. I did not wait or ask for permission, as I leaned toward him and took his cock in my mouth. The last few, little squirts and drippings gave me a reasonable taste of his man-milk. Damn, I just loved that taste – warm, salty and musty – great stuff. I gained sufficient confidence to move between his legs. His cock softened, as would be expected after ejaculation, but that did not deter me from sucking on him. In admirable form, John responded by my skills, eagerness and enthusiasm. I caressed, stroked and sucked on his cock until he climaxed again, although the product of his orgasm was barely enough to taste.

After a minute of afterglow and recovery, John pronounced, "You are good."

"Thank you. I do enjoy what I do."

"Indeed. That was more orgasms than I've had in the last two weeks."

"I'm sorry you have been deprived."

"My wife has long claimed that blow-jobs are overrated."

I laughed and continued to play with his cock and balls.

"My reaction precisely. She's never experienced one, and she clearly does not have the enthusiasm you do."

"I suppose it is an acquired taste, so to speak," I said, and then added, "I didn't know you were into guys."

"Well, to be blunt . . . I've not played with another man's dick since I was a boy."

"What brought you back, not that I am complaining you did."

He chuckled and answered, "You have always been very open about your sexuality, and the urge struck me to find out if my boyhood dalliances were a brief, youthful passing, or perhaps more of a reflection of my true sexuality."

"So, what have you learned, if I may ask?"

John chuckled, again. "Well, for one, a good blowjob is a good blow-job, no matter who gives it to you."

I smiled. "Thank you, again."

"And, I will not know for sure unless I can suck on your dick and taste your cum."

"Is that so?"

"Yes, so if you will permit me, I would like to return the pleasure."

I smiled, again, and responded, "Who am I to stand in the way of a man's enlightenment?"

We traded places. I lay back on the couch, closed my eyes, and spread my legs for John. He took up his position, gently ran his hands along the inside of my thighs, and took my cock and balls in his hands. John seemed a little tentative when he put his lips to my cock, as though he was having a quick taste to make sure it was OK. Whatever his concerns or hesitation, he quickly passed that point and took to the task before him. Surprisingly, for a man supposedly unaccustomed to playing with another man's cock, John was quite adept at it. He mixed sucking and stroking my cock like an experienced and accomplished professional. I could feel his enjoyment. I did not have to see him to know. The unique sensations of the approaching climax told me I needed to warn him. I did not want to surprise him with more than he wanted to encounter.

"I'm going to cum," I announced.

John did not miss a beat. He pressed his efforts. Forewarned is forearmed. He did not wait long for the reward he now sought. It was a good and worthy orgasm, and John kept our connection sealed up, taking and savoring every drop I could produce for him. When I was done and my deflation commenced, he looked up at me, withdrew, licked my cock head and slit a few more times, as if to capture any residual drops, and then smiled at me.

"Yummy yummy," he said. "You are every bit as good as I remember from my childhood. Sucking your cock and tasting your cum makes me feel like a boy again."

"I'm glad to be of service, John."

"It was everything I remembered."

"So, have I made you gay?"

John offered a muffled, almost nervous laugh. "Well, I don't think so. I still enjoy pussy . . . when I can get it." He gave a hearty laugh, this time. "We shall see."

"The important thing is, you are happy. By the way, does Missy know you are here?"

"Yes."

"Will she know what we have done?"

"Yes. She has known for some time that I have had urges for man-sex. She encouraged me to seek your companionship . . . to find out."

"Missy is a good woman to give you such freedom, and I am the beneficiary."

"Yes, she is a very good woman, and she knows you well, Adam, which in turn means she is not likely to feel threatened by our friendship."

"So, you expect this sex thing to continue?" I asked.

"I enjoyed it, Adam. I enjoyed it in my youth, and for too many years I denied who I am. You have freed me from that box."

John seemed to be on a high. He had done so much already. I could only think . . . what the hell, let's see where the boundaries are. "Would you like to fuck me?"

His expression flashed with a combination of shock, anxiety and what must be curiosity. "Really?" he asked.

"The great thing about anal sex . . . men and women both have assholes, and they all work the same."

"Really," he said, not as a question, but more as a statement of astonishment.

"Well? I would be privileged to have your cock plow my arse."

"I've never fucked a man before, and I've never been fucked before."

I smiled at him. "Have you done anal sex before?"

"Yes, with a woman."

"It is the same. The anus works the same for both men and women. Although, I will argue taking a cock in the ass feels better for a man, thanks to the prostate we men have."

"So you say." John held my eyes, while he considered his next words. "How would you like to proceed?"

"Well, let me see . . . we get that," I said, pointing at his cock, "hard again, and then we put it in here," I added, pointing to my butt. "Tab 'A' in slot 'B,' as the ladies say."

We both laughed hard, which had to relieve some of the tension, apprehension or anxiety John must have been feeling.

"Are you up for it?" I asked.

"Yes," John answered. His expression washed to away to a serious neutrality.

"Then, I shall act the part of fluffer, and we can get this party started."

"Fluffer?" asked John.

"Oh my, you are an innocent babe in the woods. It is a term from the porn industry that usually refers to a novice or apprentice who is responsible for getting cocks hard for the filming scenes, and sometimes getting the women wet for their ready participation."

"OK, so fluff away."

I jumped on his cock and balls with vigor. I could still taste the residual cum. He stiffened to my attention, and I had him to full erection within a few minutes. He was ready. I retrieved a small, squeeze bottle of Astroglide lubricant from the coffee table drawer, applied the slippery liquid to the target I wanted him to hit, and then applied more to his entire cock. I took up position on my knees, leaned over onto my elbows and presented my ass to him. John needed no more coaching from here. I could feel the smooth head of his rigid cock moving up and down my crack, homing in on the correct spot. He found it in short order and began to apply pressure. My heart beat faster in anticipation and bore down on my muscles to allow him entry. John kept this applied pressure, making it easier for me. In no time, I was rewarded with that glorious and unique sensation of penetration. He drove into me all the way to the hilt, taking my breath away, and then he withdrew completely, so he could repeat the entry pop several more times, opening me wider. John was not new to anal fucking. Someone had taught him well. Once he was satisfied with my grip on him, he began long, deep stroking into me. Damn, it felt good. He was brushing against my prostate, but not striking it quite hard enough.

"Try to increase your angle down into me," I said.

He responded perfectly, trying several modified positions until I got the sensation I needed.

I groaned deep and long.

"Are you OK?"

"Oh, yes, indeed . . . perfect. Now, pound that spot."

John performed his task with exceptional vigor, and his energy did the job. The hot waves of my orgasm washed ashore before him. I could feel my cum drip from my semi-hard cock. He knew something important had happened, so he picked up the pace of his stroking. I could feel him swelling inside me. He was rapidly approaching his climax. Yet, it was the sensations of his continued pounding that sent me back up the mountain of pleasure. The only question was, would he cum before I reached my second assent of the peak. The answer did not take long to arrive.

His loud, deep groans were convulsive and almost primal screams. The hot jets of his ejaculation inside me provided that last stimulation I needed. Another rush to the peak, gave me another few drips. I gripped him and pulled him with me to the floor. His weight and heavy breathing made my labored breathing all the more difficult, but the feeling of his closeness brought a most enjoyable warmth.

Neither one of us talked or moved for what seemed like the longest time. His deflation soon exceeded my libility to hold him and he popped out like a dog whose knot withdrew enough to decouple from his bitch. John rolled off of me and onto his back next to me. Several minutes passed before our breathing subsided to a more normal pace.

I turn my head to look at him. "I now pronounce you officially a gay man."

John produced a pleasant, satisfied laugh. "That was amazing. I had no idea."

"Oh, yes, you did. That was not your first time in an asshole and someone taught you very well."

He laughed again. "Well, thank you, Adam. Actually, no, I've done Missy more than a few times, and it was my older sister who taught me."

"Well, now, aren't you full of surprises."

We both laughed this time and enjoyed the afterglow of our mutual exertion. This had been a fine afternoon, and hopefully the beginning of a long and rewarding friendship. I liked this man. I simply had to thank Missy for sharing him with me. I also hoped I have helped him answer his question. Time shall tell the tale.

———

Simon

(This story is dedicated to Cindy M.)

—

The anticipation brought a shiver of expectancy as my imagination considered what might happen. Carla and I have been building up to this meeting for what seemed like years, but in reality, the time span was measured in months. We shared so many interests, and yet were quite different in our life experiences. Carla impressed me with her caring and compassion. I could feel her love of life in the words she chose to share with me during our near-nightly chats in Yahoo Messenger.

The challenge for me floated on the façade of confidence and calm. My first "Internet" meeting proved more daunting than I considered just 2 days earlier when we finalized the parameters of our meeting. I was about to spend the next 18 hours with a woman who existed only in words and images until this particular approaching moment. She drove three hours, and I drove four hours. How crazy is that for a person from cyberspace. I liked her words, but would I feel the same about her flesh?

Despite my longer drive, I intentionally arrived at our appointed hotel rendezvous ahead of our agreed to moment. I wanted to register, ensure the room was adequate and appropriate, and get myself settled before she arrived. I wanted this to be right.

Typical for modest Midwest towns, the Ramada was the best hotel in the city. The room had plenty of space and a large king-size bed. We would likely be sleeping in the same bed, whether we hit it off or not. The bed was soft, but not too soft. The shower had a large tub that could fit two, if we were so inclined. I even scanned the room service menu just in case we decided to eat in the room – decent but not fancy. The cold air of winter on the Great Plains meant we would probably spend our time in the room, which was just fine with me. I wanted as much time with Carla as possible without intrusion or interference from other guests and such.

The knock at the door startled me. My heart felt like it was going to jump out of my chest. I took a deep, cleansing breath and opened the door.

The cold blast of air did not dampen the hot flash I felt when I saw her eyes for the first time. Carla looked exactly like the images she sent me, except for the brightness of her smile and the spark in her eyes.

I reached for her bag and stood aside to let her in. As I closed the door and placed her bag on the table, I turned to her and stretched my arms to swallow her in my embrace. "I'm so glad you're here," I whispered and kissed her cheek.

"I'm glad to finally be here. The drive was a little more difficult than I expected . . . at least I made it."

I wanted to touch her, to finally feel the texture of her skin and the curves of her body, as I had dreamed for so many months. I yearned deeply to absorb all of her. But, I feared offending her more than my animal urges could overcome. Feeling a bit awkward and unsure, I moved her bag from the table to the bed. "Would you like to unpack and settle in . . . perhaps freshen-up after your journey."

Carla stood there, not moving, connected to my eyes. "First, I want a long hug and a real kiss."

My arms wrapped around her. Carla's warmth filled my soul. As our lips touched, I felt a surge. Her mouth opened, and I followed. Our tongues touched, and then danced among our pulsing lips. Her body pressed against me. She was swallowing me, as I wanted to be swallowed. As my excitement rose, Carla slowly withdrew. Perhaps, she was aware of my jumping heart rate or the swelling mound at the top of my legs.

"Wow, I never dreamed," I said.

"I hope you did not think I was too forward?"

"Of course not."

"It's just I have been waiting for this moment for what seems like a lifetime."

"I know."

We stared at each other for several breaths. Carla broke the moment when she moved her bag on the bed, closer to the chest of drawers and unpacked her things. Small talk about the cold weather, her kids, and our latest on-line chats filled the space, as she hung her clothes or put loose things in a drawer.

"Are you hungry?" I asked. I knew what I wanted, but I worried about jumping too quickly. I really wanted to see her naked before me, as I had dreamed through all those chat sessions. I wanted to be naked with her. But, I convinced myself I had to wait.

"I'm a little hungry. We could eat any time, but I would prefer to sit and talk a little more here. Do you think there is a soda machine close by?"

"Yes, I think I saw one at the end of this row."

"Would you mind, getting me a Diet Coke, and then we can talk?"

"Sure. I'll be right back." I grabbed the ice bucket and left.

The cold felt more intense, probably as a consequence of my excitement flush. The vending machine was indeed at the end of this row of rooms. There were actually three machines, two for drinks and one for snacks, as well as a good size ice machine. I spread the safety bag and filled the bucket with ice. Two Diet Cokes and a full ice bucket in hand, I returned to the room. She had moved the comfortable chair against the wall, beyond the small, round table and other matching chair. I washed two glasses, just to be safe, filled them with ice, and poured our drink, letting the fizz of carbonation dissipate, so they were full.

I handed a glass to her, stood in front of her, and extended my drink toward her. "Here is a toast to a weekend we both have waited for and I hope will be every bit as enjoyable as our fantasies."

She smiled, clinked our glasses and took a sip. She put her glass on the table, as I sat in the other chair. I took another sip before putting my glass down. She looked down at her knees.

I waited for her to begin.

After a few moments, Carla raised her head and looked me in the eyes. "The appropriate thing to do would be to get naked and enjoy several rounds of sex, but Simon, I have never done this before. To be honest, I am a little scared that I have done something dreadfully wrong, and that I have wasted your time and money."

I smiled at her. "Nonsense, Carla. There are no obligations. I do not want you to feel any pressure, to do anything you do not want to do. You are fully in control. The expectations of my fantasies and imagination are just that. You can leave at anytime you wish. Heck, you can ask me to leave and enjoy a little respite from the rigors of life. The most important objective is that you leave here whenever you choose and with a smile on your face in that you enjoyed a few minutes, hours or days. Your choices will not alter the enjoyment we have shared chatting over these last few months, or the enjoyment of future chats."

Carla smiled at me and searched my eyes. "My kids are with my mother, so I know they are safe and well cared for. Almost from the moment we agreed to this meeting, my apprehension and anxiety began to grow and corrode my confidence." She paused. I did not want to disturb her thoughts, so I simply held her eyes without expression. "You have been frank and forthright with me from our first chat. I believe you have been honest with me in every word. Yet, the long drive gave me plenty of quiet time for contemplation. I worry about your wife. I have never been with a married man. The more I think, the more I believe I cannot be 'the other woman.'" Her eyes told me she wanted my response.

"Believe me, I understand. This would have been much easier, if you had been able to at least chat with Joan to assure yourself. I am sorry I did not think of that."

"OK."

"We can call her now, so you can talk to her, so you can feel better, that nothing is being hidden and no one is being deceived."

"Would you mind?"

"No, of course not," I said, as I went to the telephone on the nightstand beside the bed. I raised the handset.

"No. Wait. That would probably be more awkward, since I am sitting in a hotel room, with her husband, within reach of the bed." I lowered the handset and returned to my chair. "You have repeatedly told me and explained to me that you are in a loving, open relationship, and this sort of thing is not uncommon for you, but it is sure new to me."

"Carla, the best I can say is, I hope our friendship endures this little hiccup. I do not want you to think less of me, or Joan, or yourself for that matter. If you left now, you could get home before bedtime. No worries. Or, we can go find a nice restaurant, have a nice dinner and talk some more, and then you could decide what you feel best doing. You could drive home, then, but it would be a pretty late arrival, or we could spend the night, get a good night's sleep, and leave in the morning, before or after a good breakfast. Again, your choice entirely."

Carla smiled, again. "You are so kind and generous." She considered her choices. "I am famished. I have not eaten since this morning."

"Fine . . . then, there we have our first decision. Let's go find something nice to eat, and then you can decide what you want to do with the rest of the night."

She nodded her head in consent. It was only at that moment that I realized she had not removed her winter coat. I retrieved and donned mine.

The restaurant recommendation of the hotel desk clerk had been a good one. We both enjoyed the Italian dishes we chose. Our conversation had been warm and expansive; some of it was a continuation of chat topics, with little hint of how Carla was leaning. Upon returning to our room this time, Carla removed her coat, which to me was a positive sign. She accepted my offer of another Diet Coke, as I sensed we had more direct discussions ahead. Carla was sitting in her chair, when I handed her glass to her.

"Does this mean you are staying?" I asked.

She smiled and said, "At least for tonight, I think."

"Excellent. That gives us more time to expand our knowledge of each other."

"I know this has to be frustrating for you, Simon. I'm sure like most men, you would prefer to jump right into sex."

"I'm not most men."

"Indeed, you are not. I will acknowledge your patience, as well as my desire. I cannot deny that I want to feel you inside me, but I suppose I am a bit of a traditionalist when it comes to marriage."

"No one is trying to convince you otherwise, Carla."

"I know . . . but still . . . ." I waited for her to continue her thought. "My conscience tells me I should not be having sex outside of marriage."

"Then, let's not enjoy sex."

"Not so fast," she said quickly and held up her right hand palm out.

"There is much more to friendship than sex."

"Yes, and I am grateful you think like that. I was taught and I suppose I believe that sex should be confined to marriage."

"OK, so let's take that tack. In the content of your belief and your statement, how do you define sex?"

"Intercourse," Carla answered. "Intercourse that can result in pregnancy."

"Vaginal intercourse, I presume. Then, anal or oral intercourse, or masturbation for that matter, is not sex?"

"Well, yes, I suppose they are sex, but my concern is pregnancy. That should be for marriage."

"Understandable. I thought you were on birth control."

"I am."

"I've had a vasectomy, tested and proven complete, so between us, I think it safe to say there is zero chance of pregnancy between us."

"Are you trying to talk me into sex . . . vaginal sex?"

"No, Carla. I am not. I am trying to learn and understand. But, I can see how my questions could be interpreted as pressure, and that I do not want between us."

Carla remained focused on my eyes, searching for meaning. I could see the struggle within her. Of all possible outcomes, I did not want her to feel pressure or have any regrets when she left.

She took a deep breath. "What if I said, I want you to take charge and do whatever you want with me."

I had to chuckle a little. "That is an offer many guys would jump at," I answered.

"Well?"

"Carla, I can't, I just can't do that. I have to know you are doing what you want to do, not for any other reason."

"I guess this is what they call a stalemate."

I laughed. She smiled. "Unfortunately, my dear, I am not a take-charge kinda guy in these conditions. I worry that my judgment may be pushing things too far. You have been very open with me . . . in your moral apprehension. I respect that."

"What would you suggest to break the ice?"

"Well, we can cuddle and watch a TV program or movie. I would gladly give you a nice massage . . . with or without clothes. We can play teenagers, make out, and see where it goes."

Carla studied my face, searched my eyes, and looked for clues, as she considered her feelings and choices. "A massage sounds like a nice start."

"OK. Massage it is."

"Since we've seen each other naked on cam, we might as well do this skin to skin."

"Fine by me."

Carla began removing her blouse and pants. She folded her clothes as she went, while I simply laid my clothes across the chair back. I was naked before her. I watched as she removed her bra and panties. We stood before each other, beyond an arm's length apart. Neither one of us showed any shame or reluctance. I held my arms out and embraced her as our bodies met. I hoped the skin contact felt as good to her as it did to me. We kissed passionately.

When we separated, I pulled the bedspread, blanket and sheet back, and arranged the pillows. Carla smiled, nodded her head, and then laid face down on the bed. I took the cue. I moved to the foot of the bed. Beginning with her toes and soles of her feet, my hands touched firmly but not too hard. I slowly moved up her legs. As I did, I straddled her and worked my way up her posterior.

"Ummm, that feels so good," she said, her voice somewhat muffled by the pillows. "You have magic hands."

"I'm glad you like it."

"Ummm."

My hands moved over her thighs and even inside her thighs, between her legs. She did not resist or show even a twitch of reluctance. As I reached the top of her legs, she allowed me to brush my hands across her pussy. While kneading her buttocks cheeks, my fingers stroked up and down the crevice and repeatedly touched her rosebud. To my surprise, she spread her legs slightly, to allow me better access. I responded to her movement. She liked what I was doing, but I did not want to rush events. I pressed on her spine, stroking outward across her back. My fingers traced the edge of her breasts. Soft groans of pleasure came from deep within her, as I worked her shoulders, her neck and even her scalp.

"Time to flip over," I said. I stood beside the bed to give her freedom of movement.

Carla did not hesitate, rolled onto her back, and watched me straddle her chest.

"Now, that is quite an image," she said softly and glanced down at my cock and balls resting on her chest between her breasts.

"Do you mind?"

"Not at all, other than I am tempted to touch."

"Your breasts?"

"No, silly, the goodies in my face," she laughed.

"No touchy. This is your massage, not mine."

"As you command, sir." She closed her eyes.

I reversed my sequence, starting at the top of her head. I copped a kiss as I descended. I also could not resist rolling her proud nipples after kneading her breasts as well as imparting a handful of sucks at each breast. I could feel her body twitch with pleasure.

"More," she whispered.

"Patience, my dear."

I continued on my journey over her body. On this segment of the trip, I purposely avoided the triangle at the top of her legs. I made sure I touched every inch of her thighs, her knees, and her lower legs, ankles, feet and toes. I kissed her big toes.

As I considered what might be appropriate to do next, Carla surprised me and drew her knees up and apart. By her action, she told me what she wanted. I could not disappoint her. My hands ranged slowly over her legs and her raised knees toward the neglected juncture. Her hips wiggled slightly when my fingers first reached her genitalia. My fingers gently explored each crease and crevice, appreciating the textures and curves. Carla's excitement was readily apparent. Her clit was swollen, proud and pronounced, tempting appreciative caresses, but not yet. Her intimate skin glistened and confessed her excitement. I probed the folds of her flesh, teasing entry to her love canal, but no insertion, and then returned to her clit. As I began to move over it and around it, she arched her back slightly and rotated her hips. She wanted more. I waited until I felt her twitch and moan softly before I took her in my mouth. I gently sucked on her and my tongue flicked over the head of her clit. Her reactive movements became more pronounced. The pressure of my sucking and frequency of my tongue licking, responded to her sounds and movements. I smiled to myself. We were working together for her pleasure. I felt the urge to insert a couple of fingers in her pussy, to work her G-spot, but I resisted, as I did not want to spoil the moment for her. As I kept up my efforts on her clit, I reached up to feel the soft flesh of her breast and found a hard nipple to roll between my fingertips; it seemed to add to her sensations. Her climax did not take much longer to attain. Her breathing became sharp and convulsive. Her soft moan turned into deeply, guttural, almost animalistic groans. Her legs shook in ecstasy. Carla's first peak seemed to last for a comparatively long time, and may well have been multiple peaks in rapid succession. She raised both her hands, as if to signal the intensity was reaching an unbearable level. Her breathing was heavy and labored.   I withdrew my attentions to the soft periphery, allowing peace for her recovery. I kept my eyes on hers until the heaving of her chest subsided.

Carla raised her head and opened her eyes to mine, peering across the length of her torso. "I have never experienced anything even remotely like that."

"I'm glad you enjoyed it."

"Oh my, yes, beyond words."

"Are you up for going again?"

"I can't ask you to do all that work, again."

"You don't have to. I am offering to render pleasure for you."

Carla answered by closing her eyes and lowering her head to the pillow. I slowly returned to my efforts for her pleasure . . . and mine. To my amazement, Carla's body responded quickly. This time, I took the risk to insert first one finger, and then another finger. She did not object or offer any sign of resistance. Quite the contrary, her body registered enhanced pleasure, which inspired me to renewed focus and vigor. The additional stimulation worked its delightful sensations through her body and mine. Her next climax arrived quickly and sharply.

The sensual sequence repeated a half dozen more times that night before she pronounced her satiation. She had enjoyed as much pleasure as she could tolerate. Carla pulled me up to her. We held each other and kissed.

"You taste of me."

I smiled broadly. "And proud of it, I must say."

"You naughty boy."

"And proud of that too."

"You are incorrigible."

I smiled and kissed her, again. Carla reached for me. I stopped her.

"You have worked so hard for my pleasure, Simon. The least I can do is return some pleasure to you."

"Thank you for allowing me the pleasure of access to your intimate parts."

Carla laughed – full and hearty. "Now, you have seen all of me."

"And tasted all of you."

"When will you allow me to taste you?" she asked with seriousness.

"Whenever you want."

"I want to now," Carala answered.

I chuckled a little, and then said, "I would suggest we have a good sleep and you allow the passions of stimulation to dissipate. I am keenly aware of your earlier expressed reluctance. I have no desire to offend your sensibilities. Take the night to think things through. If you still want to taste me or even a coupling, I will be honored to be of service."

"You are such a sweet man. Joan is a very fortunate woman to have you in her life, and I am blessed to have you in mine."

So ended our first night together.

———

Bob

(This story is dedicated to Arthur E.)

—

It had been an incredibly long day filled with lawyers, judges, clerks and paperwork. My daughter had passed away less than one week earlier, and her low-life, live-in boyfriend, Clarence, had bailed on her at the first sign of serious illness. Maggie's only child and my only grandchild, eight-year-old Jenny had been left with me, her only surviving blood relative. After today's legal obstacle course, I was now Jenny's official guardian and custodial parent.

Jenny was a beautiful girl, mature beyond her years, sharp as a tack, and rather tall for her age. She had gorgeous emerald eyes and shoulder length strawberry blond hair that she usually wore in a little ponytail at the back of her head. The legal day brought us together permanently two months prior to her ninth birthday.

"I'm going to go to bed, Grandpa," she announced a few hours after dinner.

"OK, sweetie. Give Grandpa a good hug." She wrapped her arms around my neck and kissed me on the lips, as she had done since she was a toddler. "Have a good night's sleep, sweetheart. I am so glad we have that necessary business behind us. It's just us, now."

"Me, too. I love you."

"I love you, Jenny girl."

Jenny skipped off down the hallway to the bathroom, and then her bedroom.

I switched off the television, took the last swallow of my almost warm beer, and switched off the living room and kitchen lights. Before I reached my bedroom, I made a left turn at my study / office. I figured I would check my email one more time. I answered a few well wishers, who knew the significance of the day, and caught up on my news sites for the day. Just as I was about to log off for the evening, a new message popped into my Inbox from my long-time friend Merv. It was a simple one-liner.

`hey bud, thinking of you.`

I smiled. Then, I noticed there were two images attached. The first image was clearly taken by Merv. A magnificent, black man with perfect skin was between Sally's porcelain legs and apparently pounding away into her. The image had the expected result. My shorts were painfully confining. I stripped off my shorts to release my rock-hard erection. I could not resist stroking my spear. As I continued my slow stroking, I opened the second attachment. There was the side of Merv's face between Sally's still spread legs with a bountiful cream pie oozing from her bald, pink pussy. He was licking up the man's cum from his wife's well-fucked vagina.

That last image did the trick. I began stroking with a more focused purpose in my mind and my eyes transfixed on the images of Sally and Merv enjoying themselves.

I sensed something odd. I glanced to the door. There was Jenny standing there naked as the day she was born. "Jesus!" I exclaimed and turned my swivel chair away from her. I searched for my shorts to have something to cover up with, and just then, I felt her hand on my shoulder.

"It's OK, Grandpa." I froze. *What did she mean by that?* "Can I help you?"

"What?" I said softly without looking at her.

"Can I help you?" she repeated.

"How much did you see?"

"Several minutes worth," Jenny answered with a slight giggle.

"I'm sorry. I should have shut the door. I did not mean for you to see that." My erection was not going down. "What's wrong? What do you need?"

"I couldn't sleep."

"Give me a second here," I said, renewing the search for my discarded shorts, "I'll get you a cup of warm milk."

Jenny kept her hand on my shoulder and applied just enough pressure to convince me to stop my vain search. "No, thanks. I would just like to help you?"

"You can't," I said in nearly a whisper. I still could not turn around and for some strange reason, my erection was still not going down. "It's not right."

"Why not? You are not going to hurt me, and I am certainly not going to hurt you."

"You are my granddaughter."

"And, you are my grandfather." She smiled. "We love each other, do we not?"

"Yes, we do, sweetie. Yes, we do."

"Then, what could possibly be wrong?" she said with a confident tone.

"It just is," I answered rather meekly.

I felt her push gently to turn my swivel chair toward her. I did not resist. My heart was pounding. I had no idea where this was going, but the urge to find out seemed rather overpowering. I could not sense the slightest hesitation or discomfort in her, standing so close to me completely naked and me with only a T-shirt on.

Jenny reached out and grasped my cock mid-shaft. Her touch was electrified and I shuddered upon feeling her soft hand on me. It felt like my heart was pounding so hard it might crack my chest. She began to gently stroke my cock. *This is not the first time she has stroked a cock.* With her free hand, she gently pushed my knees wider. I followed her lead. She knelt between my legs and did not miss a stroke in the process. She knew just how far to go with her stroking up and down. It felt so good. I closed my eyes and leaned my head back against the chair. *She is really good.* I opened my eyes briefly, as if to assure myself it was not a dream. She smiled back at me, when she noticed me watching her, and she remained singularly focused on her task at hand. Jenny switched hands expertly to keep from tiring. The feelings, sensations and sights made quick work of me.

"It's coming," I said, as I felt the rapid surge to the peak.

Just as I was about to climax, Jenny took me in her mouth and I exploded. My whole body shook. My knees rose. "Oh . . . damn . . . ah, ah . . . oh god," I gurgled as my climax shook my entire body.

Jenny used her mouth until the sensations were so intense they were approaching painful. I grabbed the sides of her head. Her tongue continued to dart all over my cock-head, as she licked and caressed. She grasped my balls firmly, but not hard, and pushed at the base to squeeze out every last drop of my cum. I looked down to see her eyes smiling even with her mouth still full. She drew back and licked up the few dribbles that had escaped her mouth. Jenny had swallowed my entire cum load. She pulled on my cock firmly a few times to squeeze out a few more drops. Each time her tongue touching my cock-head to lick up the pearls, more lightning bolts shook me.

When she was satisfied she had extracted everything she was going to get, she said, "Now, that was the milk I needed."

"Dear God, girl, where did you learn how to do that?"

"Clarence taught me."

"What!" I exclaimed. "Did he . . . ," I stopped when she raise her hand.

"He never forced me to do anything, Grandpa. He may not have been good for Momma, but he was always good, kind and gentle with me."

"When?" I could not finish the question.

"Well, I guess the answer depends upon how you define the starting point."

"At the beginning . . . ," I said rather lamely. I patted my lap. She sat across my legs and placed her right arm behind my neck and across my shoulders. "I'm listening."

"As far back as I can remember, Mom and Clarence allowed me to watch their sex. We used to take showers together. One day, I saw Clarence jacking off when Mom was at work. I asked him if he would show me how to do it."

"How old were you? Do what?"

"To jack his cock. I guess I was about six, or maybe five."

"That's pretty young for sex."

"Why?"

"You are still a young child, Jenny. You have a lot of growing to do. Sex is an adult thing."

"Why, Grandpa? Momma always told me sex was a normal, important part of life. She wanted me to learn from her, rather than some stranger."

Where the hell did Maggie learn that and arrive at that position? "Well, you learned well, my dear."

"Thank you, Grandpa. Do you want another one?"

I chuckled nervously at the thought. "No, that is enough for one evening. Thank you for asking." So many questions. I do not want to overwhelm her or make her feel like she is being interrogated. But . . . so many questions. "When did you develop your taste for cum?"

This time Jenny giggled. "I had seen Mom lick up Clarence's milk many times. She clearly liked it. I asked more than a few times what it tasted like and why she liked it? One time, she gave me some. They called it snowballing. I've loved the stuff ever since."

The image of Maggie feeding her baby chick Clarence's cum had the usual effect.

Jenny felt the change against her leg. She smiled, looked down and grasped my now hard cock. "Well, look at that. By the way, Grandpa, you have a magnificent cock," she said, as she gently squeezed and stroked my erection.

"Thank you, Jenny, but you've only seen one other one, so hardly a large sampling."

"Oh no, I've seen others."

"Have you, now? Where?"

"Mom and Clarence used to have friends over to play."

"Really?" *Now, that is news to me. Where on earth did Maggie learn all that?*

"Yeah. It was great fun watching them when I could. Most of the time, they did not want me watching."

"Did you ever participate?"

"No way! Mom said it could cause big problems."

"Did your Mom teach you about the law also?"

"Yes, Grandpa, she did. I understand that other people think it is wrong for a girl my age to be enjoying sex."

"Correct, and you should never forget that. You must be careful. Now, it's getting late. You need to get to bed, young lady. You have school tomorrow."

"Can I sleep with you, Grandpa?"

Now, there is a thought. "No, sweetie. That is a little too far . . . I have many more questions, and a lot to wrap my mind around. Is there something wrong with your bedroom?"

"No. It is just fine."

"OK. Please get a good night's sleep. Perhaps we can talk more tomorrow. I have so much to learn."

"Sure." She hopped up, and turned to give me a hug and kiss on the lips.

I patted her bare bottom before she left the room. I logged off my email and put the computer in Sleep mode. I switched off the remaining lights and went to bed. Too many thoughts rumbling through my brain made it difficult to reach sleep.

The next few days proved uneventful. Neither Jenny nor I raised the sex issue until the following weekend.

At mid-afternoon on Saturday, out of the clear blue, Jenny asked, "Can I milk you, again, Grandpa?"

Her question caught me rather flat-footed and unprepared. "I just don't know, Jenny. The law says what we did the other night was wrong."

"But, it's not wrong. The law is wrong."

"That may be, but it is still the law."

"Then, the law does not deserve to know. I need a good dose of man-milk and yours is really tasty. Besides, would you rather have me go get it from a stranger?"

"No," I answered rather meekly.

"Then, can I have yours?"

"I guess so. If you insist."

Jenny gripped both sides of my shorts. "May I?" I nodded my acceptance. She pulled my shorts down, allowing my already hard cock to spring out. "Nice," was all she said, as I stepped out of my shorts on the floor. She did not hesitate, took me in her mouth, and began working my eager cock. There is no way she learned this skill on her own. She stroked with one hand on my shaft her tongue and lips caressed my cock-head, and her other hand fondling my balls. Jenny had been focused on my cock-head, and then all of a sudden she sent lips-balls-deep into her throat. *Wow! She has learned a lot and learned well.* The next time she took all of me I felt a finger wiggle its way back to my rosebud. I instinctively squatted slightly to give her better access. Just the pressure of her finger was sufficient to send me over the edge. My legs shook and nearly collapsed as the climax shot bolts of electricity through my entire body. She lightened up to reduce the intensity, so she could milk out every last drop of the juice she sought from me.

Jenny finished, withdrew, looked up at me, and said, "Now, isn't that better?"

I could not help smiling down at her. "Yes, my little darling, it most certainly is. What about you?"

"What do you mean?"

"Have you had an orgasm, yet?"

Jenny laughed. "Yes, I have them all the time, now. Momma showed me how to twiddle my clit."

"Amazing. Can I give you one?"

"Sure. I won't complain. How do you want to do it?"

"Have you been licked off before?"

"Yeah. That's my favorite way."

"Fine. Then, let's get you comfortable and let me give you an orgasm."

Jenny needed no further encouragement. She stripped off her shorts and panties, went to the living room couch, and sat down with her butt on the edge of the couch. She leaned back, and raised and spread her legs. Jenny was way ahead of me, but I tried to catch up. I knelt in from of her. I had never seen such a young pussy, and rarest among the rare, one spread wide before me. Her clit was already swollen with excitement, as I descended to my pleasure and hers.

I sucked on her clit like a small cock and flicked the tip of my tongue over her clit-head. She squirmed and groaned with pleasure. I gently pressed my finger between the folds of her flesh, expecting resistance. There was none. I continued to work her clit, as I pressed my finger slowly into her. Apparently, I was too slow. She thrust her hips at me. Even more amazing, she was wet with her own lubricant and wanting more. *She has had stuff in here before.* I began to massage her G-spot with clear results. *She really likes this.* Her breathing became more rapid and convulsive. She arched her back and rolled her head back against the couch cushion. *Is she really going to climax?* I did not have to wait long for the answer. Jenny's knees pulled back farther, her toes curled under, and tremors emanated from her pelvis, shaking her legs and torso, as she expelled a very deep, guttural groan of pleasure. I kept going on her to sustain her peak until she grasped my head tightly. I lightened gradually as her tremors subsided. I looked down at her pussy with my index finger still inside her. I could feel and see her pussy twitch after she descended from the peak. The tension in her entire body slowly relaxed and she lowered her feet to the floor, although she kept her knees spread.

"Wow, Grandpa!" she exclaimed with still heavy breaths. "That was the best I have ever had. Where did you learn to eat pussy like that?"

I laughed robustly. "Years of enthusiastic practice, my dear." She joined me in laughter. Her pussy was still twitching, as I finally and slowly withdrew my finger from her. She kept her knees spread without the slightest hint of modesty. "Perhaps would be a good time to continue our talk."

"Yeah, sure," she answered and patted the couch cushion beside her.

I took my cue and sat next to her. She placed her hand on my chest and cuddled up against me.

"What do you want to know?" she asked softly.

I have so many questions; where to begin? "You said earlier that your momma taught you to masturbate. How long ago was that?"

"Maybe a couple of years ago. I watched her masturbate. I tried to do like she was doing, but I was not doing it right. She saw me trying to imitate her and asked me if I wanted her to teach me how."

"Do you remember how she taught you?"

"She told me first to put my hand on her hand as she did herself, and then she did me." She giggled. "We used to do it together all the time before she got sick."

"Who taught you to deep throat a cock?"

"She did. We used one of her dildos at first, and then we used Clarence." Jenny giggled again. "He was always willing to be the teacher's aid."

"I'll bet."

Without realizing it, I was erect again. She looked down, saw it, smiled and grasped my pole. "All this penis talk gets you excited huh?"

I laughed. "Yeah, I guess it does. I am learning a side of my daughter and granddaughter I never knew, and it is just amazing to me."

"You want to see something even more amazing?"

"Sure . . . I guess."

Jenny stood up on the couch, stepped her far leg over me, so that her pussy was in my face. I looked up at her. She held my eyes with hers as she lowered herself. Jenny grasped my erection, again, and guided it to the spot she wanted. She slowly lowered herself onto me. Her hot flesh felt like it was burning me. I slid in easily, as she remained dripping wet. She got about half of me inside her before I bottomed out. Jenny began to do squats on me. *Here is another one that is not her first time.* She was tight, but she clearly felt no pain. Jenny kept her hands on my shoulders and never looked away from my eyes. *Damn, I cannot believe this. My eight-year-old granddaughter is actually fucking me.* Jenny kept bouncing on me, seemingly taking a little more of me each time. She smiled.

"Can you take me from behind?" she asked.

"Sure."

"So, I can play with your balls and ass?"

"Of course."

Jenny dismounted, got on the floor and onto all fours on the rug. She lowered her shoulders to the rug and reach between her legs with her hips held high and ready. As I positioned myself behind her, I placed my left hand on her hip and started to reach for my cock, but she grasped me before I got there and guided me to her ready and waiting lips. I slowly pressed into her. Her groan of pleasure spoke volumes. I began stroking into her, trying very hard not to go too far. I certainly did not want to hurt her. Jenny began rhythmically stroking and applying pressure to the rear base of my balls. Another finger found my rosebud and this time pressed into me. I tried to relax, to let her in. *Does she really know what's in there?* We kept going like that for several minutes. Sure enough, she found the spot she was feeling for. Jenny began like a windshield wiper motion with her inserted index finger. *Damn, how does she know about the prostate at such a young age?* Her efforts made short work on me, and I shot my load into her . . . well at least what I had felt after already shooting once in the day. We remained coupled for several minutes as the sensations subsided and we extricated ourself.

She rolled over and knelt in front of me. "Do you want my cream pie?" she asked with a twinkle in her eyes and broad smile of her face.

"You are just a fountain of surprises," I answered. "Of course I do."

Jenny gently pushed me back, signaling that she wanted me on my back. I lay flat on the floor. She quickly straddled my face and allowed our mixed juices to drip out of her pussy and into my mouth. Several times, I raised my head to lick her and probe her love-tunnel for more juice. I was not embarrassed in the slightest that I enjoyed the taste of my cum and especially the mixture.

"That feels so good," she said. When there was no more to give, she lay down beside me, cradled in my right arm and her right arm and leg across me. "We are going to have so much fun," she added softly.

"Yes, we are."

"I know you will teach me so much more."

"You already know a lot, Jenny."

"But, I know you can teach me more."

"I will try to raise you right."

"I miss Mom."

"Me too, honey. Me too. It is just a shame I did not know what I know now back when she was still healthy."

"Perhaps I can make up for that."

"I'm sure you will."

"That was not your first time with a cock inside you, was it?"

"No."

"Clarence, as well?"

"Yes, but always with Mom there, and a few other friends of Mom and Clarence."

"Other men?"

"Yes . . . well, and one boy."

"How old was he?"

"Thirteen or fourteen at the time. He was the son of one of their couple friends."

We must have drifted off to sleep. I was the first to wake and the house was dark. I did not budge, wanting to let her doze as long as she wanted. My brain tried to process everything that had happened in the last few days. No one will believe this, even if I could tell anyone. My logical mind told me it was wrong, but my practical mind knew this was natural and good for her . . . and for me. I had no idea where our relationship would go, but I knew in my heart it was going to be an unworldly experience.

———

Gary

(This story is dedicated to Gerard L.)

—

The 'Sunshine State' lived up to its full potential on an afternoon during what the Northern Hemisphere called winter – crystal clear, blue skies with nary a cloud in sight and a light trade wind breeze to cool off the mid-80's temperature. This was perfect naked weather, which is precisely why so many of us moved to and lived in the Sunshine State.

David and Cassi often hosted weekend, pool parties at their orange orchard ranch, which offered the perfect setting for their parties. The single-story, modest size house sat nestled smack-dab in the middle of a section and a half orchard of mature, bountiful, orange trees. The distinct, sweet scent of orange blossoms added a nice touch to the lovely winter day. The large, full-length patio was covered in cool-decking to make it easy on bare feet at the peak of summer heat and also incorporated an absolutely perfect, hardwood, lattice awning over two-thirds of the patio length with healthy, multi-colored, wisteria vines filling in the gaps of the overhead lattice-work. Their large saltwater pool incorporated a nice, low, diving board at the deep end; a rock formation, multi-level waterfall for the soothing sounds of water and water slide the children absolutely loved; and, mushroom fountain at the shallow end for the smaller children. Everyone had something to help them keep cool on a hot summer's day. The partially sunken, large, at least ten-person hot tub offered the adults a delightful site in the open end of the patio. At night, with the house and pool lights out, the Milky Way painted the sky above them for a glorious backdrop and playtime.

They had a large, built-in, barbecue at the far end of the patio, opposite the hot tub. As was often the arrangement, they also had a long table for the accumulation of potluck dishes. Several of David's ranch hands served as the grill-cook and waiters. Everyone attending contributed to the selection of picnic dishes and drinks of all forms. David and Cassi usually provided the hot-dogs and hamburgers.

These parties were most often family affairs – couples, single parents and their children, ranging from infants to teenagers, all well known families. While there was never any requirement or pressure, everyone who did not need a diaper was naked . . . completely, although some chose to wear water-tolerant footwear. Even David's ranch hand helpers were naked, and one of them answered the door.

"Good afternoon, Mister Gary and Miss Debbie. Welcome."

"Thank you, Carlos. I see the party is well underway," I said.

"And, someone must be glad to see me," added Debbie, while she admired Carlos's erection and lack of any inhibition.

Carlos glanced down at his stiff cock. "Yes, well, Miss Debbie, it is product of this job."

"Do you need someone to take care of it for you?"

"Thank you for offering, but no, I am here to support Mister David's party."

"If you change your mind, let me know," she said, as we entered. As Debbie passed Carlos, she grasped his cock and gave him a few strokes while she held Oren, her 18-month-old daughter on her opposite hip – my third grandchild. I carried our cooler of beer and soft drinks and the large bowl of pasta salad made as our contribution.

"Thank you, Miss Debbie," Carlos said behind us, and then closed the front door. "Everyone is on the patio," he added, as we walked through the elegant kitchen and breakfast room.

What a magnificent sight as we walked out onto the patio. Naked boys and girls played in the pool, the slide and under the fountain. The adult women and men stood around talking under the wisteria awning. No one was eating just yet, but the food array on the buffet table was quite varied and appealing. I added our contributions to the table, and then noticed that Debbie and Oren were not behind me. After situating things, saying hello for a few folks, I went back into the house to get undressed. Before I got to the kitchen door, Debbie came out naked, well except for the rubber flip-flops on her feet. Her modest breasts swayed beautifully as she held Oren's hand and walked her nearly naked, toddler daughter to the shallow end of the pool.

I deposited my folded clothes next to Debbie's and Oren's stack, and decided I would barefoot it on this day. By the time I returned to the patio, a few adults were eating, but to my surprise the action had already started.

Debbie was bent over with her arms and head resting on the back of a cushioned patio chair, being plowed by some young buck I did not recognize. Even better, Kimmie – 12-year-old daughter of Cassi and David, also sans clothes – had positioned herself under Debbie suckling at a breast like a calf at her mother's udder and rubbing Debbie's clit as well as her own. The scene worked its magic on me. I moved a lounge chair in the shade, so I could watch Debbie's fun time. I was soon surprised to feel a hand grasp my rigid cock. It was Carol – Kimmie's friend and constant companion – young, blond hair, blue eyes, a nice bronze, all-over tan, and budding, conical breasts.

"May I?" Carol asked.

"If you wish, by all means, please do. It's all yours."

Carol began gently stroking my hard-on. The tension built quickly. The combination of Carol's exquisite touch and the scene of Debbie's pleasure proved very stimulating. I felt Carol's warm, wet lips descend over my shaft, but I kept my eyes on Debbie. I briefly wondered, who is going to cum first? The answer did not take long to arrive. Debbie's young buck threw his head back, arched his back and groaned deeply, almost growled, as his hips pounded into her convulsively and his legs started to wobble. When he was finished, he bent over her resting his forehead on her back. His chest heaved from the exertion. Kimmie abandoned Debbie's breasts and deftly positioned herself underneath Debbie, between her legs, and waited for the treasure soon to come. While I waited for the next phase, Carol was working my throbbing cock with unusual expertise, sucking and thrusting on my cock-head with her tongue feverishly licking the soft, sensitive skin inside her mouth, as she stroked my shaft, and fondled and pulled on my balls. She had clearly done this quite a few times before now, and she had been taught very well. The young buck eventually deflated and slipped out of Debbie. Like a hungry chick, Kimmie gobbled up the drippings as they came to her, and then began lapping up the residual directly from the source. Debbie wiggled her butt as the new sensations washed over her. When Kimmie was satisfied she consumed everything she was going to get, the two females hugged and kissed. Carol continued to work my cock, and I was getting closer to delivering what she sought. Debbie pulled up a lounge chair next to mine, and opposite from Carol.

"I see you're enjoying yourself," Debbie said, glancing her eyes at Carol's head still working my cock.

"Oh yeah . . . quite the scene . . . she took the opportunity," my climax was now approaching rapidly. I held up my right index finger, signaling her to wait. The hot waves of orgasm surged through my body, and the pulses of my cum shot into Carol's hungry mouth. She took every drop – not even one pearl appeared.

"You want some," Carol mumbled.

I shook my head.

"Sure," answered Debbie.

Carol moved around to Debbie's side, stood over her, and fed some of my man-milk into Debbie's up-turned, open mouth. "Ummm," both girls voiced simultaneously. When they were finished trading my juice, Carol moved on and Debbie lay back on her lounge chair.

"Who was the young buck plugging you?" I asked.

"I don't know. I've never seen him before. When I came back out to the patio, I had just put Oren down when he appeared with a raging hard-on. I asked him if I could help. He said, sure, and glanced at my pussy, so I bent over the chair, and he fucked me."

"Quite well, from my perspective."

"Oh my, yes. Definitely a cock I'd do again. I'll find out who he is and where he fits in, from Cassi later."

"Sure."

We both watched little naked Oren playing in the shallow end of the pool with several other naked children. There was something special about watching generations of females and males frolicking in the warm, Saturday afternoon sunshine. More sex was beginning around the yard, without signs of shame, inhibition or modesty.

Without taking my eyes off the evolving activities, I said to Debbie, "And, you got a treat from Kimmie."

"Quite so. She has an experienced tongue and mouth."

"She certainly appeared to be enjoying your cream pie."

"She offered great sensations after a good hard poke, and I didn't have to drip everywhere."

Just then, Oren walked up – naked as the day she was born – waved her hand and smiled at me, and then attached her mouth to Debbie's right nipple. Debbie closed her eyes, lay her had back against the chair back, and wrapped her arm around her daughter. She was still producing for her daughter, and she was quite content for others to enjoy her breast milk. Then, to my surprise, Kimmie appeared and without encouragement lay down on Debbie's left side and took her left nipple in her mouth to suckle as well.

"Looks like you need someplace to put that monster," a familiar voice observed from behind us.

I turned to see my good friend and near neighbor Mark, who had apparently just arrived. He was nude along with all the rest of us.

"Welcome to the party, my friend. It should be no surprise with scenes like this," I nodded to Debbie and her two peaceful, suckling children, "that I have a throbbing hard-on."

"Well, let's do something about it, shall we?"

Mark bent over a nearby chair. I knew what he wanted and I needed. I rose from my lounge chair, and positioned him and his support chair so that I could see Debbie and her girls while I did Mark. I spread his cheeks to see my mark, applied ample saliva lubricant, and directly pressed my cock-head against his rosebud. He must have been ready. The entry pop occurred quickly and comparatively easily. His groan of pleasure announced our coupling. I began stroking into him. By the time I look back to Debbie, her eyes were on me. She smiled broadly and winked at me. I had already shot one load this afternoon; as such, the second one so soon was probably not going to be as easy. I had been stroking into Mark for several minutes when I noticed that Oren was apparently asleep in her mother's arms and Kimmie had had enough. The next thing I became aware of was Kimmie kneeling down behind me and gently fondling my swaying balls as I continued to plow Mark's ass. Her soft, caring touch amplified my sensations. She never ceased to amaze me how comfortable and confident she was around sex of all kinds at such a young age. Her parents had raised her and taught her well. I continued stroking into Mark, aiming my attention at his magic spot. Kimmie moved her attention to Mark, grasping his semi-hard cock, and squeezing and pulling on it like a cow's teat. Mark wiggled his hips and groaned as the sensations mounted with intensity. The combination of our efforts must have done the trick on Mark. I could not see and only imagine he had started to produce. Kimmie was under him like a calf on its mother-cow, and also returned her fondling, caressing touch to my balls. It was her middle finger pressing on my rosebud that was enough for me. The rapid ascent to the peak sprang on me. I grabbed his hips, pulling them toward me as I thrust into him, pounding him hard.

"Oooohhhh gggaawwdd," I heard from inside me, as the hot waves washed over me, again and again. When I felt the repeated pinnacles pass, I held his hips tightly against me, feeling the last vestiges of my convulsing cock were pumping my man-milk into Mark. I waited patiently for Kimmie to finish her work on Mark. When his groans of pleasure subsided and Kimmie smacked her lips with contentment, I backed off just enough to allow my cock to be squeezed out.

"Much better," Mark said with a broad smile on his bearded face.

"I'm so glad to be of service."

"As you always are, my friend . . . always willing to accommodate a hungry cum-slut." Mark turned to Kimmie standing beside him and patted her head. "Kimmie, you are just the greatest."

"Thank you, Mister Mark, and thank you, again, for letting me play with you."

"Our pleasure."

"Indeed," I added.

Kimmie walked away quickly and dove into the cooling waters of the pool.

"Well done, boys," Debbie added, with Oren still asleep, nestled in the crook of her arm and her head on Debbie's chest.

"Thanks, my dear. Would you like me to get you something to eat or drink, since Oren has you tied up?"

"A Diet Coke would be nice. Thanks, Dad."

Mark and I went to the buffet table. Mark made a plate of delicious food, while I poured a soda over ice in a large plastic cup and delivered it to Debbie. By the time I returned to the table, Mark had his selections and was munching from his plate, while chatting with Cassi. Her body always impressed me. She was in her early 30's, birthed one child, enjoyed a very active and bountiful sex life, yet it was her appearance that commanded the most attention – long, thick, blond hair; trim, exquisite curves with no excess flesh; full, mature, pendulous breasts with small, tight areolas and prominent, erect nipples; and hairless pussy with a distinctly protruding clit . . . so incredibly tempting . . . clearly excited.

"Great party," I said.

"Thanks, Gary. We try. And, Debbie hit it first thing with my cousin."

"Is that who that young, buck cock was?"

"Quite so. Petey is all of 16 years . . . my aunt's son."

"He seems to be quite the player."

Cassi laughed a strong, hearty laugh. "Yes. He has grown up around sex and with sex. He has a most handsome dick, doesn't he?"

"What did I miss?" asked Mark.

I laughed. "Cassi's Cousin Petey had a poke at Debbie in fine fashion as soon as she hit the deck."

"And, Daughter Kimmie joined in," said Cassi.

"Oh my, sounds like quite the pile," Mark added. "Sorry I missed it."

"There will be more, I'm sure," Cassi whispered. "The party has only just begun."

"You always throw the best parties, Cassi," said Mark.

"Thanks. Well, time to mingle. Perhaps one or both of you boys could have a go at this," she said, lowering her head and pulling her pussy lips back, exposing all of her swollen pink clit.

I immediately dropped to my knees in front of her. She put a hand on my forehead.

"Not just yet, my eager little beaver."

"Oh shucks," I answered.

"Later boys," she said, turned and walked away.

Did I say, she had the most exquisite, round, flawless bum? She wiggled in a delightful, seductive manner. She was fun to watch, moving like a mature leopard.

Mark and I returned to Debbie, who still had Oren asleep on her chest. I lay on my lounge chair. Mark retrieved another lounge chair and pulled it next to mine. When we looked around, the sights had become all the more stimulating – just about all combinations and forms of carnal delights scattered around the backyard, patio and pool.

"Well, now, ain't that a sight to behold," Mark observed, watching Kimmie and Carol stroking and sucking on Petey.

"They know what they are doing."

"They've been around sex all their lives. They are quite comfortable around cock and pussy."

Oren woke up. "Momma. Potty."

"OK, baby."

Debbie helped Oren to her feet, got up, took her daughters hand, and led Oren into the house. A few minutes later, my naked daughter and granddaughter came back out.

"Hi, Grandpa," Oren said, waved, as she ran past me to the pool.

Debbie sat back down. "Your granddaughter loves being naked."

"As her Momma and Grandpa do as well."

"I'm gettin' hungry for some of your man-juice, Dad."

"You're welcome to a good dose anytime you wish, my dear. By the way, Cassi told me your young buck is her cousin . . . all of 16 years old, I must say. Name's Petey."

"You beat me to it."

Looking across the pool, young Petey was currently engaged. "And, it looks like your young buck is balls deep in another girl."

Debbie turned her head to catch the scene and smiled. "Good for him. No one else is wagging their cock at me, so it's up to you, Dad."

"Help yourself, sweetie."

Debbie turned to sit on the edge of the chair toward me. I was nearly hard when she grasped my cock and descended upon it.

"I'll help," Mark added, as he turned toward me, and began gently fondling and pulling on my balls.

Debbie worked my shaft like the expert she was, and with Mark's exceptional assistance they made quick work of me. To my surprise, the distinct rise toward my climax did not take long to arrive. Debbie recognized the changes.

"I'm going to take this one in the puss, so Mark can have a nice cream pie," she announced and did not wait for approval.

Mark backed off with eager anticipation. Debbie stood, swung her right leg across me, positioned my manhood as she wished, and descended smoothly and effortless onto me. I could feel her love-hole muscles working me as she pumped me for my juice. Her reward did not take long to arrive. This one was unusually high and strong, probably the distinct gripping of her muscle with each upward motion of her cyclic effort. I was always impressed by my daughter's expertise. As soon as she was satisfied she had received all she was going to extract from me, she slowly dismounted and nimbly stepped across me to straddle Mark's yearning face. She worked her lower abdominal muscles to squeeze out and drip my deposited man-milk into his waiting mouth. When the flow diminished, Mark attached his mouth to her pussy. Debbie groaned with pleasure, as Mark worked his skills on her. Her climax arrived quickly and sharply. Her legs quivered and her chest heaved, as she struggled to maintain her position over Mark's face. After a minute or so of afterglow, Debbie gingerly stepped over Mark's chair.

"Sorry for the squirt," she said.

"No need. You know I love it."

Debbie leaned over and kissed Mark, and then licked his lips. "Oh my, I gave you a really good squirt, too."

"Yes, you did, my dear, and you know I love it."

"You are such a perv."

"And, don't forget a true cum-slut, man-whore."

"You nasty old man."

"And, proud of it, darlin'."

"OK," I interjected, "you two love birds can knock off the gushy chatter."

"Oh, Dad, you are such a spoil-sport."

As Debbie returned her fatigued body to the lounge chair next to me, David arrived with a lawn chair sat down in front of the three of us. "Y'all have been having your own little party over here in the shade."

"Just keepin' an eye on Oren," I said.

"Among other carnal pursuits . . . as I observed and enjoyed."

"Glad to be of service, my friend. Great party, as usual."

"Thanks. We try."

"I know you've told me part of the story, but how did you raise your daughter to be so comfortable and skilled with sex?"

David smiled and captured Debbie's eyes, "Your daughter is quite the nymph, I do believe."

"Yes, she is, and I am very proud of her; but, she is 26. Kimmie is only 12."

"Well, actually, the truth is quite simple. She has been around sex all of her life. In short, with Cassi and me, she grew up with sex. What she has learned, she has picked up from watching us. Her curiosity and desire paced her learning."

"The natural process has worked quite well," Debbie added.

"We think so."

"Oren is learning the same way."

"Yes. Y'all have been most generous with her. If Kimmie is any measure, you will be absolutely amazed how much she has absorbed when she blossoms."

"How old was Kimmie when that point arrived?" I asked.

"I think Cassi would know for sure, but as I recall she was around four or five."

"How did it happen?"

"Cassi and I were doing the old in-out one evening . . . pretty vanilla, as I recall. Kimmie was watching, as was often the case. I had just barely pulled out when she was there to grab my wet cock. She asked if it was OK to taste it. I told her sure, if you wish. She began licking our combined juices off my cock-head and shaft. It just seemed so natural. Much to my surprise, her little tongue and caressing hand had me hard again in short order, and then she guided me back into her Momma. Very heady stuff, for us, back then."

"I can understand that."

Cassi arrived with another lawn chair and sat next to David, in front of Debbie. "This looks like a serious conversation," she observed.

"They were asking about Kimmie's blooming moment," said David.

"A beautiful moment it was, I must say."

"We worry about the law . . . other kids talking," I said with some solemnity and concern.

"Yes, well, there is always that," Cassi answered. "We have struggled with that as well." David nodded his head in agreement. "At the end of the day, we decided to be frank and direct with Kimmie. The reality is, we live in a socially conservative society . . ."

David interjected and picked up the thought, ". . . that has passed so many damnable morality laws to enforce Puritan and Victorian attitudes about sex. We wanted Kimmie to be responsible, to understand the society in which we live and in which she will grow up, and most importantly, to have a healthy respect for and enjoyment of her sexuality, whatever that happens to be for her. Cassi grew up much the same way."

"Did you, now?" asked Mark.

"Yep, sure did. My parents were very open and free spirited. I am immensely grateful they were as generous they are."

"Are they still with us?" asked Mark.

"Yes . . . in their 60's now."

"Do they know about Kimmie's sexuality?" I asked.

Both David and Cassi laughed. Cassi answered, "Yes, Gary, they do. Kimmie has played with both of them when they come to visit, or we visit them. Shoot, they still play with us," she said, motioning to David, "when we see them."

"Amazing," added Debbie. "That is so cool."

Kimmie arrived dripping wet from the pool and plopped down in Mom's lap.

"Damn, Kimmie, you're cold."

"That's the point of the pool, Mom." She kissed Cassi on the cheek. "Whatcha y'all talkin' about?"

"You," I answered.

"What about me?"

"How you became so comfortable with sex."

Kimmie tweaked Cassi's right nipple and stroked David's limp cock a few times. "Easy with the best-est parents like mine."

Everyone laughed. Oren arrived and sat on Debbie's lap. "Momma . . . sleepy," she announced.

"We'd better get her home," Debbie announced. "Plus, I have a client tonight."

"Busy, busy," David said.

"Thanks for havin' us, y'all. Great party, as always. We look forward to the next one."

Everyone stood, hugged and kissed. We said our good-byes to every-one. Mark decided to leave with us. Another great afternoon goes down in the record books.

———

Gus

—

I had been working in Italy alone for over a year. My wife Julie had remained in Prescott to retain her university teaching job that she had waited so long to obtain. We used email and texting for daily communications. Fortunately, technology enabled us to see each other on the weekends. We Facetime'd virtually every Saturday, and sometimes on Sunday as well. Actually, with the nine-hour time zone difference, it was Saturday evening for her and early Sunday morning for me. This particular day was no different.

"Good evening to you, sweetheart," I announced, as I saw her beautiful face appear on my propped up iPad.

"Good morning to you, honey. How are you?"

"Pretty good. I had a good week and a good night's sleep. How are you?"

"I'm really great. I have a surprise for you."

"OK."

Julie took her iPad, turned it around, and pointed it down. A man's head was between her legs and appeared to be munching away on her kitty. "Say hi to Gus, Henry."

The young man looked up from her pussy, smiled, withdrew his fingers from her and offered a quick wave. "Hi, Gus."

"Hello, Henry. Do a good job and give her lots of pleasure."

"I'm trying," he said and returned to his task.

I had cammed with Henry a few times in mutual masturbation. He was one of Julie's students, who had shown particular interest in her and no reluctance to cam and chat with me. I had encouraged Julie to go for it . . . discretely so as not to jeopardize her employment.

Julie turned the iPad back around to her face. "Today is his lucky day."

"Apparently. Good for you. I hope he is up to the task of pleasuring you."

"So far so good, honey. He took me to dinner at The Barn Door, and we just got home. Ooooo, yes, that's good," she said and closed her eyes. "Ummm," she purred. When she opened her eyes, she said, "He's good, honey. He's still going to town," she said and flashed a view of the top of Henry's head still between her legs, "while I chat with you."

"I'm so glad you're finally enjoying some pleasure." I flashed a quick view of my right hand jacking my rigid cock. "You got me excited."

"Good. You can't see much with his face buried in my pussy. Do you want to watch him fuck me?"

"Oh my, yes. I'd love that."

"OK, Henry," Julie said. "Time to get serious. Mount up." Views flashed around as they shifted positions. She settled on his cock. "A fine specimen, I must say, honey."

"Yes, he does have a great cock, doesn't he. Too bad he's not into cock, as well."

Julie ignored my comment. "Here, let me see if I can give you a close-up as he enters." She moved the iPad closer, so that his cock and her pussy filled the screen. "OK," I heard her say off screen. His cock-head slowly disappeared into her. She groaned deeply, as he buried himself to the hilt into her. Julie kept the iPad on their engagement for several seconds as he began stroking into her. The scene was so exciting. I had to stop, feeling the throbbing of my cock, to delay the peak that was so close. I wanted this sensation to last.

Julie moved the iPad around, giving me different perspectives of their union, and then turned the device back on her face. She spoke silently with her lips I love you. I returned her thought with heartfelt joy. Her carnal pleasure took hold. Julie's eyes rolled back, and then closed. Her head arched back, and then she must have released the iPad, since I had a rather odd partial view of them in their moment of pleasure with the ceiling as background.

I could hear Julie coaching Henry regarding what felt good for her. Her left knees came back, nearly blocking the camera's field of view. The slopping, gushing sounds of their union and the slapping of flesh became more discernible and prevalent. Even his moans of pleasure were added to hers. The rhythm was increasing. I could barely contain myself. I wanted to erupt, but I fought to hold off.

Julie was the first climax. I heard her characteristic guttural grunts and groans, and saw her thigh convulsing in her climax. "Yes, yes, give it to me," she clearly encouraged him. The pace of his stroking became a blur.

"Oh, god . . . here it comes," he groaned.

"Yes, that's it. Give it to me." He nearly roared with pleasure. "Oh, yes." Julie's legs moved to grip him and help him pump into her. "That's it." Her legs began twitching, again. She was probably enjoying a mini-climax in all that fervor.

After 20 seconds or so, Julie lowered her leg, so I could see the side of them. He appeared to be still joined with her, but they were both nearly motionless, except for the heaving of their chests. Both their skin glistened from their exertion. Henry eventually began to slowly withdraw from her. My cock was so hard and throbbing. I was ready to explode, but I waited.

"Would you get me that towel over there, please," Julie said, pointing to her left. She picked up the iPad and her face filled the screen. She was smiling broadly. "Whew," she said. "I doubt that was as good for you as it was for me."

"Oh, I don't know," I answered, and gave her a view of my cock and stroking hand.

"Oh my," she said. "Here, place it under my butt, please." She turned the camera to her groin. I could see his hands pushing the towel under her butt cheeks. "Here is your favorite," she said, as she moved the device for a close-up frontal view of her swollen and engorged pussy lips. I could see her tightening her abdominal muscles. Soon, the creamy, white juice began oozing from her pussy. "Do you want some?" she asked off screen.

I heard him answer, "No thanks," as I said, "Abso-fuckin-lutely."

Julie turned the camera back to her face. "Apparently, our young Henry does not like cream pies like you do, honey." She turned the camera to him. He smiled and shook his head.

"You don't know what you are missing, Henry," I exclaimed. "Give me another view of your cream pie, sweetheart." She did as I asked. "Hold it there. Now, it's my turn," I announced. I switched to the back camera and turn my camera, so my cock was pointed directly at the protected screen. I used the back camera, so I could see her pussy and my cock in the insert image. I had been dancing on the edge a long time, and it only took a few feverish pumps to shoot my cum load toward the camera. My third or fourth squirt hit the camera aperture directly, blurring the image.

I licked off my hand and switched the camera back to the front one. I licked my hand a few more times, so they got the idea.

"Well done, honey." Julie pulled her camera up. Henry was sitting right next to her and fondling her right breast.

"Yeah, well done, Gus," Henry added.

"I'm sorry you don't enjoy cream pies, Henry. Julie's are the best."

"I'm good," he answered.

"Well, that was quite a surprise, indeed. Thank you so much, sweetheart, and thank you Henry for servicing my wife."

"My pleasure, Gus. Anytime I may be of service." He stood. Julie took a quick flash of his flaccid cock. "I'll go now, and leave you to for some private time."

"Thanks, again," I said.

Julie again put the iPad down. She stood, hugged him and kissed him passionately. "Thank you, Henry." She grasped his cock. "I want some more of this." Julie kissed him again, and then released him. She returned to the couch, folded the towel over, and sat back down on it. She picked up her iPad and pointed it back to her face. I could hear the muffled sounds of his dressing.

"Good night," he said in the distance.

"Good night," Julie answered and waved. "See you later." She turned back to the camera. "What did you think of the surprise, Gus?"

"I loved it, sweetheart. Well done."

"Thank you for encouraging me. I doubt I would have been able to do that without your support and encouragement."

"You are most welcome. We both benefited."

Julie pointed her camera back down to her pussy. She was still oozing. She inserted a finger and scooped out more of Henry's cum. Julie held up her finger in front of her pussy and let the cum drip from her finger.

"Yummy," I said.

She turned the camera back to her face. She looked away, probably drying her finger on the towel, and then back to me. "I thought you would enjoy that. He is a big cummer. I know you would enjoy it, if only he would let you."

"Indeed. I've watched him jack and cum on cam a few times. Yeah, I'd love to have some of that, and who knows what tomorrow holds."

"You got that right," Julie said. "He was such a good sport about that. He was quite apprehensive when I told him at dinner what we were going to do for you. It took me more than a little effort to warm him up to the idea. I told him repeatedly it was no different from jacking with you on cam."

"I'm glad you did."

"Me, too. He's good with that thing, Gus. I know you would love it, too."

"I'm sure I would. Are you going to do him again . . . some more?"

"If it's OK with you, yes, I would like to do him some more, to see what he is capable of performing."

"Sure thing, sweetheart."

"Are you sure you are OK with this . . . with watching me fuck him?"

"As long as you are enjoying yourself and happy, yes, I am good with this. We are so far apart these days. I feel like what we just did brings us closer together."

"What if something happens and you are not available, or we can't connect on Facetime?"

"That's alright. Shit happens. I would like to watch, to be a part of your pleasure, but I recognize it can't happen all the time."

Julie flashed the camera to her breasts. She cupped her right breast and held it like she was presenting it to me. "Nice, huh."

"You got that right . . . the best; and, I get to play with 'em all the time when I'm home."

"Yes, you do." She turned the camera back to her face and she pursed her lips in a gestured kiss. "Would you like to do a threesome with Henry?"

"Sure, I would. Maybe on one of your future times, you can have him ass-fuck you. If he likes it, maybe we can convince him an ass is an ass, and we can get him to top me."

"Good idea."

"Or, you can peg him . . . to see if he likes it."

"Ah, yes, another good idea, although I suspect that might be a little much for him. He's only 20. He has made it quite clear he is not into cock and cum like you are."

"That's OK. Just a thought. But, who knows, perhaps he has just not discovered his inner-self just yet."

"Possible, I suppose. I'm getting tired. Will you excuse me? I need to rinse off all this sweat and clean my pussy. After all, I do not have you here to clean it up for me."

"You are so sweet. I miss you very much, Julie. Again, thank you for sharing your little adventure with me. It was very special. By the way, I meant to ask you, is Henry in one of your classes?"

"Yes. He's a good student."

I laughed. "Yeah, we saw that demonstrated just a while ago."

We laughed together. "Have a good day, Gus. Thank you for being such a good sport with the sex shit."

"My pleasure, sweetie. Have a good night's sleep. Hopefully, we can chat tomorrow. Ciao, ciao."

The screen went blank. She was gone. I sat there at my kitchen table and thought about what I had just witnessed. The possibilities were endless.

———

Steffie

(This story is dedicated to Sharon L.)

—

The week and especially the last day of the week had been an intense, extended struggle. I did not look forward to spending the weekend alone. Allen was out of the country on an extended business trip to Japan, Hong Kong and Singapore.

Max was always waiting at the door with his tail wagging feverishly. I dropped my business bag, gave him some good lovin', and then let him out to the backyard. Even the reclusive Mr. B, my Orange Tabby cat, came out of hiding to get some lovin' as well.

I retrieved my bag, put it on the desk in my study, went to the bedroom and stripped out of my clothes, hanging up my suit and depositing my underwear in the hamper. I preferred naked at home. Allen and I were usually naked when we were home. Our backyard was surrounded by an eight-foot high, stone wall that matched the accent masonry of the house. The lush trees, scrubs and a wide variety of flowering bushes, all expertly maintained by a professional gardener, gave us a rather attractive, peaceful and private environment. I felt safe, even by myself . . . well, without Allen, as I did have Max, and he was a protective, 100-pound, Black Labrador Retriever.

Max was eagerly waiting at the sliding glass door when I returned to the family room with its adjoining kitchen. I made sure to feed Max and Mr. B, and then decided on a simple bowl of Thai noodles for myself. With everyone fed, I went to the family couch and called up the nightly news on the DVR. It did not take long for Max to nuzzle me for attention . . . and access, since I knew what he wanted. To be truthful, I wanted it too . . . actually, I needed it.

I opened my legs wide and rocked my hips forward. His tongue went to work. For reasons I know not, he loved it. The anticipation and sensations of his tongue yielded the desired effect for me . . . and for Max. His red rocket was by now quite rigid and exposed, and his hindquarters were beginning to gyrate.

"Yeah, Max, me too," I said to him.

He stopped his licking and looked up at me with clear eagerness in his eyes. I often caressed his cock and growing knot, but this time, I did not. I wanted him to last as long as he could.

I took a large throw-pillow from the couch, put it on the tile floor, and knelt on it. I bent over, presenting my posterior to Max. He did not hesitate and mounted me like he would any other bitch of his. He stabbed his red rocket at me several times, and before I could reach to guide him in, he found his target. I felt his hot organ enter me. I gasped, as I always did. True to form, Max began his pumping. He did not fill me up like Allen did, but he got credit for vigor and enthusiasm. I could feel him pressing his knot against me with each full in-stroke. As is so often the case, the duration of his stroking did not last long. He ejaculated before he could complete the engagement by burying his knot inside me.

Max remained motionless for several seconds. I could only hear his panting and feel his chest heaving against my back. I felt his red rocket slip out of me, and then he dismounted, but did not move away. I turned my head to look at Max. He looked at me with an expression of 'thanks mom' in his eyes.

"Good, boy," I told him. "But, tonight momma needs more. Hope you're up for it."

While Max stood still, I sat up next to him and gently touched his wet and slippery cock. His knot was not quite deflated, so it kept his organ exposed beyond the furry, skin sheath that usually covered it. I imagined it would be sensitive, but I just loved touching it, feeling the curves of it. I captured a few, residual drops of his cum, or perhaps it was my juices, and put my finger to my lips. I recognized that salty, rich taste.

"You deserve some, too, my boy," I said, as if he could understand me.

Max still did not move other than his panting. I reached between my crossed legs and inserted two fingers to collect up his deposited spunk, mixed with my wetness. There was plenty. I withdrew my fingers and touched them to my tongue.

"Yummy."

I held my fingers near his nose. The reaction had become quite predictable – like ammonium carbonate – smelling salts – to a nearly unconscious man. Max recognized the smell and what he was implicitly being asked to do. His tail wagged furiously and his nose went directly to my pussy. He immediately started lapping up what had oozed out. The process did not take long to work its magic. As his hindquarters began to quiver again, I returned my knees to the pillow on the floor and lowered my torso to rest on my elbows, giving Max a perfect target. He wasted no time mounting me again. This time he struck home on the first stab, pushing all the way in, as far as he could go. Max's stroking had slightly less urgency than the first episode, which suggested he would last longer. This time, the index and middle finger of my right hand went to and bracketed my clit. As Max stroked deep, my fingers worked my clit. My mind drifted in images and fantasies . . . a big, thick cock filling me up, ravaging my pussy. I surprised myself at the rapidity of my approaching peak. Max rose to the occasion in this session. The convulsions of my orgasm shook my entire body. I heard my deep groans of pleasure as some distant echo, as the rushing, hot waves crashed against my consciousness. Then, I felt Max's knot literally pop into me. The sensation pushed me to another sharp peak. The pulsing of my muscles gripping his knot did the trick for him. I could feel Max shooting his latest load into me – what a sensation! I truly loved it. Contrary to the first coupling, Max did not escape. I held his knot. He dismounted and turned so that we were butt-to-butt, both of us panting now. Our bodies struggled to recover from the exertion. I purposely did not move, waiting for Max's inflated knot to subside. Several minutes passed. I felt the pressure of his impending withdraw and Kegel-ed to hold him joined with me. More minutes passed before the withdrawal exceeded my ability to hold him. I thought I could hear the pop when we separated, finally.

Both of us rolled over onto our backs on the floor, allowing our bodies maximum potential for recovery. I had no idea how long we lay there. I was the first to move. My legs wobbled more than I expected. The exertion took more out of my body than I realized. I staggered to the refrigerator and took a long swig from a bottle of *Pellegrino acqua frizzante*. The cool fizziness felt good to my throat.

I slowly waddled back to the couch and collapsed. Max's tongue hung out of his mouth onto the tile, as his panting continued. I stroked his heaving chest a few times. "Good boy." My mind wandered from thought to thought – some reality, some imagination. I had no idea how much time passed. Eventually, I felt that peculiar urge blooming in my groin. I needed more from Max. He was the only cock available to me.

I left Max on the floor, went to the bedroom nightstand, and retrieved my bottle of KY lubricant. Returning to the family room, I noticed that Max's sheath had re-covered most of his red rocket. I decided to wait for Max to return to his usual quiescent state. Some unrecognizable program on television did not distract me from the variety of thoughts rumbling through my consciousness. Again, time suspended. Darkness had descended outside – some abstract measure of time passage. I waited for Max's tongue to retract and his panting to cease. The time had arrived, and now, I eagerly anticipated our last coupling for the night.

Since Max generally had less staying power than me, I took the KY and generously lubed my rosebud. For months now, I have wanted to see if Max could do it. As the moment of challenge approached, the twitching in and around my genitals told me I needed this effort by Max. I reached for his cock and gently began to jack him. He hardened to my caress and protruded from his sheath. Just like a man, Max laid on his back and spread his legs to allow full access. I grabbed the KY and lubed him up as well – liberally. I added some more to my ass. Now was the time.

"Show time, Max, buddy."

I took my position, and Max knew his duty. This time, I reached between my legs to grasp his beckoning red rocket. I guided him, as he mounted me one more time. I felt him pressing at precisely the correct spot. Again, Max rose to the task before him. Success took several seconds to achieve, but he actually did it. His stroking was just as purposeful as earlier this evening. I added more lubricant without missing a stroke, so Max did not get sore. His efforts felt so good – a unique sensation. Fortunately, Max was a strong male dog who responded with consistency to his instincts. Max remarkably kept his relentless pace to the conclusion he sought . . . and I wanted. I added lube to him and me several times. I loved feeling his slippery pole moving into me like the piston of a fantastic machine. His stroking changed to quivering convulsions immediately preceding that delicious feeling of his hot cum squirting deep inside me. He did it. We had a new trick in our repertoire of pleasure.

I pushed and dragged myself onto the couch. I did not much care what leaked out of me. I would clean it up later. Once again, Max lay on the cool, tile floor for his latest recovery. I had no idea how much time passed. My eyes remained closed. The distant sound of whatever television program occupied the time slot did not register on my awareness. Max eventually decided to do his own clean up. I could hear him licking. In time, he cleaned up my oozing holes. He was a good dog. When he was satisfied, Max weakly jumped on the couch, laid down next to me, and placed his head in my lap. I stroked the soft fur on his head and ears. We both drifted off into deep sleep. Neither of us cared that the lights were still on and the television broadcasting. We remained together in our embrace until the following morning. It was not until the soft light of dawn woke me that I wondered what some imaginary neighbor would have thought, watching Max and I through the open windows doing our thing last night?

Mary

(This story is dedicated to Mickey B.)

—

Gordon and I had been talking about this meeting for over a year. The road to this point had been rocky and difficult, with what appeared at the time to be insurmountable lows. We married 20 years ago, produced two, beautiful, healthy children, and lived generally routine suburban lives. Like all families, we had our share of problems – accidents, periods of unemployment, money strain, and family tensions. On the whole, we were doing pretty good . . . that is until Gordon informed me that he liked cock, other than his own. I was shocked! I truly had not even the slightest inkling of his predilection. I did not have a cock, so the problem became clear and obvious. What were we to do with his revelation? Well, more accurately stated, actually, what was I supposed to do with it, since he had already taken it upon himself to confirm his urges? His confession had gushed from him in unstoppable, overwhelming waves. I nearly drown in the heavy surf of his confession. My mind had numbed from the onslaught and constricted down to one gnawing thought – why had he told me all of it at that moment? Had he contracted some venereal disease? Was he indirectly telling me he had fallen in love with another man and leaving me for the other man? What did this tell me about my body, my sexuality? Why?

The process of unraveling the massive tangle around that question took several weeks . . . no, many months. We sought individual and couple counseling. Just sitting down at the dinner table with the kids and pretending everything was hunky-dory became a daily Herculean chore. It took me more than a few days before I found the courage even to talk to him. I was hurt, embarrassed, gravely disappointed, flabbergasted and deeply confused. As my withdrawal deepened, the kids began to voice their concern. While I did not confide in or disclose to them Gordon's secret, the children pushed me to break out of my turtle syndrome.

We eventually confronted the elephant in the room. The reconciliation sequence had been long, tortuous and fraught with fits and starts. The professional counseling, both for me and for us, helped me see and feel beyond my sense of betrayal. As I gingerly stuck my head out from under my shell, I came to recognize and realize that Gordon genuinely loved me, and wanted to preserve the family and our relationship. Gordon had worked tirelessly to regain my confidence and trust, while he grappled with his own conflict, guilt and isolation.

The medical tests eliminated the apprehension swirling around unprotected sex with another man . . . with other men. Gordon's patience and persistence slowly convinced me he was not going anywhere, with anyone else. There was no pregnancy, and I could only laugh at that thought. The evolution of our relationship progressed through various stages and brought us to a new sense of stability.

Today, I was about to meet Rodney – Gordon's friend with benefits, his fuck-buddy. The drive to Rod's apartment took 45 minutes, and clearly Gordon knew the route well. I had talked to Rod a handful of times on the telephone. He sounded nice enough, and he had conveyed his understanding and support for the marriage of Gordon and me, and our family unit. I think he had been honest with me, but time would tell the tale on that aspect.

Rodney's apartment complex was definitely upscale with lots of well-maintained greenery from colorful flowerbeds to full, healthy trees. Even guest parking had nice, covered, protected spaces. I followed Gordon on the meandering, brick walkway to Rodney's ground floor apartment.

Rodney answered the door. He was taller than I expected, and just as handsome as his photographs depicted. Gordon and Rodney hugged and kissed . . . not a passionate kiss, but definitely a familiar kiss.

"You are Gordon's lovely wife, Mary."

"Yes, I am, and you must be Rodney, whom I've heard so much about."

"I hope not all bad."

Gordon chuckled a nervous acknowledgment. This was the awkward stage for all of us.

"No, quite the contrary, which is why I consented to this meeting."

"Won't you come into my humble abode?"

We entered and waited in the foyer for Rodney to close and lock the door, and then lead us into what appeared to be his living room, or rather more accurately could be his combined living room, family room, if he had a family, breakfast nook and kitchen.

"What would you like a drink?" Rodney asked.

The early afternoon hour preceded the cocktail hour, but a glass of wine seemed appropriate given the circumstances of this meeting. All three of us chose a glass of a delightful, California, Pinot Noir.

Oddly, Gordon and Rodney sat on the couch, not exactly touching, but within arms reach of each other, while I elected to take the single chair, like I was some kind of therapist for this gay couple.

After a few nervous sips of wine, Rodney spoke. "I have no idea what to say, other than thank you very much for coming, Mary. Gordon has told me of your struggles with all of this, and I hope I, we," he nodded to Gordon, "can assure you I am no threat to your marriage. I also truly and genuinely hope that we," he nodded to me, "can become friends, as well."

"Yes, well, we shall see," was all I could say.

"I have never done this before, so I have no idea how it is supposed to work, so please forgive me and allow me to jump right in."

Gordon looked at me with apprehension in his eyes. I nodded my head in consent.

"I think Gordon will agree, the relationship between him and me did not start out on the most honest of terms. I did not know he was married until well after our relationship formed. I am truly sorry, and I think he is as well, that we have hurt you."

"You didn't. He did."

"And, I am truly sorry, Mary," interjected Gordon.

"Yes, well, what is done is done," I added.

"Nonetheless, here we are. The fact that you are both here, in my apartment, is a tribute to the strength of your marriage. To be direct and perhaps blunt, I love Gordon. He is a rare and uncommonly good man. I asked Gordon if I could meet you and hopefully win you over."

"To what?" I asked.

"To allow me to become part of your relationship, your marriage."

"Oh, wait, I've heard of this. Are you suggesting we enter into polygamy?"

"Polygamy is illegal in this country. Until that law changes, I am suggesting a polyamorous relationship."

"Really?"

"Yes."

"So, you are bisexual?"

"Yes, just as Gordon is. He has continued to please you physically."

"Once I let him back in."

Rodney laughed softly. "Yes, after an understandable period of abstinence or self-pleasure, I suspect you can feel his love for you."

"OK. I'll give you that. He has been a good lover, a good father, and . . . and . . . a good husband, other than his betrayal and cheating."

"Gordon and I have discussed that, and we both agree that our relationship cannot continue without your consent, and preferably participation."

My mind began racing through random flash-thoughts. *What was he suggesting? Was he really saying what I think he is saying? I could tap that. What am I supposed to do with that? Why isn't ol' Gordo talking? He is an attractive man?* Then, my mind filtered down to one presiding thought and I acted without premeditation.

I stood and quickly stripped off all my clothes and stood there in all my glory, before two shocked men.

"Mary!" protested Gordon.

"Yes, well," I said, looking directly into Rodney's appreciative eyes, "what will you do with this?"

"Mary!" Gordon protested, again.

Rodney smiled, stood, unzipped his shorts, and allowed an impressive erection to spring forth from its confines. "Does this answer your question?" he said, glancing down at his proud, rigid cock.

"Nice, but no, not yet."

"OK, then, please allow me to show you."

Rodney gently switched places with me and pressed on my shoulders for me to sit next to Gordon. Once I was seated, Rodney slid his warm hands between my knees and slowly slid them up the inside of my thighs, spreading my legs before him. Fortunately, I had shaved smooth in anticipation of what might happen at this meeting. As Rodney's fingers began exploring my lady-parts, Gordon turned and took my right nipple in his mouth; he knew quite well what felt good to my nipples and breasts; he took to his part in this with enthusiasm. Rodney probed my interior with his fingers and tongue, and used my ample wetness to lubricate my clit. I lay my head on the back cushion of the couch, closed my eyes to focus on the physical sensations, and instinctively spread my legs wider. Rodney was good. He handled pussy probably as well as he handled cock . . . well, at least Gordon was impressed with how Rodney handled cock. His tongue licked my swelling clit, as one hand sent fingers inside me and the fingers of his other hand spread my labia majora aand pulled back my labia minora. His lips latched on me like he was sucking a small cock, while the tip of his tongue flicked rapidly across my clit. Yes, Rodney was real good. While Rodney tended to my pussy, Gordon added soft, nipple bites to his suckling and reached across my chest to squeeze my other breast and now hard nipple, just as I liked it. I wanted his handsome cock inside me, but he was so intent on his oral pleasure I let him continue until he wanted something different. Rodney expertly worked my G-spot, while Gordon shifted his position and add passionate kissing to my treatment. This was heaven. Both men clearly enjoyed what they were doing, and I was the beneficiary of their attention. The characteristic electricity signaling my ascent of the orgasmic mountain did not take long to arrive. I was not sure how they recognized the signs of my ascent. I just know they did. Gordon squeezed my nipples hard and twisted them slightly – one with his fingers and the other with his teeth. Rodney picked up the pace of his efforts. The tremulous convulsions consumed my body. The intensity surprised me.

From somewhere deep within me came a deep, growling sound. "Ooohhhh gaawwdd." The peak was actually a series of sharp peaks that lasted longer than any orgasm I had ever experienced. I must have squirted some woman-cum. When I finally opened my eyes, Gordon hovered over me, grinning from ear-to-ear, with a strange sparkle in his eyes. Rodney remained between my legs, licking his chops like a sated wolf, as he enjoyed my vaginal contractions and gently spread my excretions around the smooth, soft flesh of my pussy. *Damn, now that was an orgasm.* I lay my head back and closed my eyes to allow the heaving of my chest to subside and mostly to enjoy the afterglow of that impressive event.

With more control returning, I opened my eyes again and immediately noticed both men were naked and both displayed fine, proud erections. I grinned at Rodney. "Tab 'A' in Slot 'B,'" I said softly and smiled broadly.

Rodney needed no further clues. He moved smoothly and gracefully to his task. I watched him as he took his cock in his right hand and used it as a delicate instrument, rubbing my lips and clit, and barely probing my hole. I wanted him to push in . . . to the hilt, but he teased me, dancing and darting about my scabbard for his sword. Rodney sensed the tension of my anticipation approaching my threshold of tolerance. He inserted his cock-head, and then withdrew. He pushed in a little farther, and then withdrew, again. The process was repeated a half dozen more times until I felt him balls-deep and filling me with his manhood. Rodney took to his task with purpose and vigor. Then, just as I was beginning to enjoy his stroking, he stopped, withdrew, turned me around, and gently bent me over. Gordon moved to me. I took him in my mouth. Rodney re-inserted and positioned himself so that each thrust pressed his cock-head against my G-spot, and each stroke, in and out, rubbed against it. He reached around my hips and skillfully rubbed my clit, as he stroked into me. The delightful sensations between my legs enabled me to take pleasure in Gordon's cock, as I had never enjoyed it before. Their collective efforts worked their magic. That electric buzz grew within me. My rise was not as fast as Rodney's acceleration. I could feel him swell within me. His pace quickened. He grasped my hips, slapping our flesh and pounding into me. He was moving quickly toward the peak. To my surprise, Gordon shot his man-milk in my mouth. I loved that sensation, the taste. I sucked and milked him dry. Just as I finished draining Gordon, Rodney pumped his load as deeply as he could into me. I did not notice, but Gordon and Rodney must have silently gestured to each other, as they switched places. Gordon flipped me over, again, and buried his face between my legs like a ravenous animal gobbling up and devouring my cream pie. Rodney fed me his cock. I tasted my juices mixed with his, as I licked it all up and sucked out the last few drops. Gordon had enough. I considered whether I should just rub myself off, but I let that thought go as both the guys sat down on the couch, on either side of me.

"Well, that was quite the session," I said, to start the conversation.

"I hope you enjoyed it," Rodney commented.

"I love you, sweetheart," added Gordon.

"I can certainly feel the love, and I now have a better understanding of why my husband likes you so much." Silence filled the space of several minutes. "So, what are we supposed to do now?" Gordon and I had discussed the options, but I wanted to hear what Rodney thought or wanted. I moved back to my seat across from the two men.

"We've discussed . . . ," Gordon started, but stopped when I held up my left hand.

"Yes, we have talked about this, but I want to hear what Rodney has to say."

Rodney cleared his throat to buy a few extra moments to choose his words. "Mary, you and Gordon have talked, and Gordon and I have talked . . ."

I held my hand up, again. "Rodney, I am here to talk to you. How about let's get to the point."

"I am very nervous, Mary. Please forgive me."

"You are forgiven," I answered and gestured for him to get on with it.

"I would like the three of us to have a warm, open and loving relationship."

"Those relationships don't happen in one fucking."

Rodney cleared his throat, again. "Yes, I certainly understand that, but good relationships have to start somewhere."

"Yes, they do, Rodney. I do not want to be Debbie Downer here, but let's review. I have been married to Gordon for nearly 20 years. We produced two beautiful, teenage children together. While there have been bumps in the road, I always thought we loved each other and loved our children. Then, I learned a year ago, that he has been sucking cock behind my back without a word or the slightest indication, and on top of that, he tells me he has been carrying on with you for several years, again, behind my back. I say this, because I need to say it to you." I held Rodney's eyes. He did not blink or look away. "Gordon has heard all this before. He hurt me . . . terribly. I thought I was safe from my father, only to learn that sense of safety had worn extremely thin." I paused to look at both men on either side of me. Again, Rodney did not blink and remained expressionless. Gordon smiled meekly and nodded his head. I turned back to Rodney. "And, what made his betrayal even worse and cutting, he was denying me the sex I sought and needed, the intimacy I required, all the while getting sex from you and strangers, bareback no less, exposing himself, and those few times we did fuck . . . me . . . to unspeakable risks and diseases. So, how the fuck am I supposed to feel?"

"I understand."

"Do you!" I snapped. "Really? Have you ever been betrayed by someone you love?"

"Yes, actually, I have," he answered, softly, almost inaudibly.

"Then, why would you ever do that to me?"

"Since we are being direct, I will say, because I did not know Gordon was married, until a year ago, which is exactly what started this process. I felt strongly enough about Gordon that I convinced him he had to come clean and give you a chance, if our relationship was to survive. I did want our relationship to survive. I told him I would wait. I have waited over a year to get to this point. Once he confessed his marriage to me and told me about you, I just knew I could love you, too. He does love you deeply, Mary, which is why he headed down the path of laying everything on the table."

"OK. I understand all that. Gordon lied to you as well, and he has taken his punishment, at least from me. So, if I may be so bold, are you suggesting you move in with us and we become a triad?"

Rodney smiled. "I do not think you are ready for that."

"Our children are not ready for that."

"Yes, that too. But, yes, someday, that is precisely what I would like, but only if that is a mutual decision by the three of us."

"By the five of us. We cannot do something like this without the concurrence of our children. Our oldest child, our daughter, will be off to college in another year, but she is still part of our family."

"I would like to meet them."

"In time. Just not yet."

"Then, what can I do to assure you of my sincerity?"

"Give me time," I said. My mind went to another thought. *I want to see for my own eyes the cock crazies that have been occupying Gordon for the last few years.* I smiled at Rodney, and then I winked at Gordon. "I would like to watch the two of you fuck."

"Well, that was rather blunt," Gordon observed.

"Really?" asked Rodney.

"Yes. I've never seen two guys doing it . . . well, other than in pornos."
I stood and moved back to the single chair.

They scooted closer and grabbed the other's flaccid cock.

"Shall we go to the bedroom?" Rodney asked.

"If you wish," I said. "Whatever works."

Rodney led Gordon and me into his ample, well-appointed, master bedroom. The bedspread and sheets on his large, super-king size bed had already been pulled back. Rodney had anticipated what was about to happen.

They did not waste time, especially since all of us were still quite naked. They focused on each other. Rodney lay on the bed, and Gordon straddled Rodney's head and inserted his cock in Rodney's mouth, and then descended on Rodney's cock. I was left to find my place. I moved a small chair in front of a dresser, beside the bed, so I had a good view of their activity. They were both clearly enjoying their connection. Their rigid cocks glistened as they appeared, and then disappeared. Without words, they changed positions.

Gordon got on all four of his extremities, while Rodney retrieved a plastic bottle of lubricant from the adjacent nightstand. Gordon looked at me, winked and smiled. Rodney applied plentiful lube to Gordon's butt crack, as he worked his now open ass. Satisfied all was in readiness, Rodney moved behind Gordon, placed his left hand on Gordon's left hip and his right hand grasped his hard-on, and guided himself to the proper spot. When Gordon felt the pressure on his man-cunt, he closed his eyes and lowered his head and shoulders to the bed. Rodney slowly pressed into Gordon, who pushed back against Rodney. When Rodney's cock popped into him, Gordon audibly groaned and smiled, although his eyes remained closed. Rodney repeated the entry process several more times before he started stroking into Gordon in earnest. I could feel the distinctive effects in my body. The urge to rub my magic spot grew rapidly. My eyes did not break from the scene on the bed. Before I knew it, my knees had drifted apart and my right hand was active between my legs. My awareness brought me back to the present.

I stood and went to the bed. Their bodies swayed together with their joined pleasure. Gordon jolted when I touched his dangling cock. The shock passed quickly, as I began squeezing and stroking his cock like a cow's teat. I had never been so close to fucking and especially two men fucking. The smell of sex filled the air around us. Our combined attentions made quick work of Gordon. Several generous streams of man-milk shot from his cock onto the sheet below. His contractions of climax did the trick for Rodney as well. He emptied himself into Gordon. The energy of the two men subsided. They lay on their backs; Gordon closest to me. I bent over and took Gordon's deflating cock in my mouth to taste his last few drops. I stood beside the bed with my hands on my hips.

"Most impressive, guys," I pronounced. "I think we can all understand the cock crazies, now."

"Glad to be of service, sweetheart," Gordon said. "Any other requests."

Was there anymore in there? What else do I need? "No, my sweet, I think we have what we need." I looked to Rodney's eyes. "Thank you for your patience and indulgence. Gordon and I need time to discuss how this is going to work. You are a good man, Rodney. I understand why Gordon loves you." Rodney nodded his head in acknowledgment.

Gordon stood and hugged me, and then kissed me passionately. Rodney rose to embrace us both. I kissed Rodney, and then Gordon kissed Rodney. After what seemed like minutes, we parted.

Rodney clasped both my hands. "Thank you for meeting with me, Mary. I know this has not been easy, given the circumstances that brought us here. Hopefully, this afternoon has moved us forward to mend the fences. I await your verdict. I love Gordon, perhaps not as you love him, but I pray you will learn to love me as well."

"You have been most generous, patient and tolerant, Rodney. Thank you."

We dressed. More hugs and kisses. We had much to discuss, but it was a good afternoon.

———

Betsy
(This story is dedicated to Stuart P.)

—

Saturday night parties remained entertaining events after the intensity of the week's classroom and homework. The professors always kept us overloaded and off balance. The weekends were pressure relief. This particular weekend, our sorority party coincided with the Saturday afternoon, men's swimming meet between the Cornell men's team and the midshipmen of the Naval Academy. Several of my Tri-Delta sisters had attended the meet with me. Some of us appreciated the swimming skills on display, but most of the ladies just went to ogle the nearly naked, hard body men. The Navy men prevailed in the day's competition, but it was close and came down to the last freestyle relay.

Several Cornell men attended our party along with a half dozen midshipmen. The good thing for everyone stood on the willingness and generosity of our guests in contributing to the food and drink . . . all of which flowed freely.

As was our practice and house rules, we gathered in the large, house, living room after all our guests had departed, in part to check to make sure our sisterhood was safe and in good spirits. We also took the time to at least clean up most, if not all, of whatever mess may have been left by the party-goers and freshen up the house, so we did not have to face that in the morning. Several of my sisters were still a bit tipsy, but everyone was ambulatory and coherent. I had a few beers, and I was in pretty good shape compared to my sisterhood in general.

"So, everyone is OK?" asked our chapter president Anna.

"Yep, good party," answered Susan.

"You got that right," added Helen.

"So, who got laid?" I asked. From the sharp verbal or gestured responses, about a quarter of our two dozen members affirmed their participation in some form of sexual relations, since many of our membership were switch-hitters, which broadened the definition of the term. "OK, then, of that lot, how many enjoyed their pleasures of the flesh?" Nearly all of that group responded in the affirmative. Yes, it had been a good party, and a good night.

Anna commanded the obvious. "Let's get this place cleaned up, so we can all get to bed."

"We have a slight problem," Megan said.

"What's that?" Anna asked.

"One of the Navy guys I was playing with is passed out on the floor in the basement."

Without a word, a majority of the sisterhood made their way downstairs. There before them in the middle of the group-room floor was a naked man with his arms and legs spread like the Da Vinci sketch, and surprisingly a magnificent erection standing proudly at the juncture of his legs. His penis appeared to have been well used. He had a cock-ring at the base of his scrotum and penis that was undoubtedly the source of his erection maintenance in his state of inebriation.

"What did you do to his dick?" Susan asked.

"Judy and I drained him," answered Megan.

"Yep, we did," added Judy. "Bone dry."

"We tag-teamed him. He passed out about halfway through it . . . maybe an hour or two ago. We just kept going on him. I mean really . . . look at that dick. Believe it or not, he can still climax like that," she said, pointing to the naked body on the floor. "Well, at least it looks like he is climaxing. But, he hasn't produced any cum we can detect in the three or four orgasms. Anyone want to have a go, while we have him here?"

Melissa did not hesitate. She reached under her skirt and pulled off her panties.

"Before you jump on that live dildo there," said Anna, "how long has he had that erection?"

"What time is it?"

Anna was apparently the only one of us wearing a watch. "One-thirty."

"Well," Megan said, "I guess about three, maybe four hours."

As the only medical student in the house, I had to jump in. "Come on, now, you've all heard those ED drug advertisements. We need to get that cock-ring off of him and get an ice pack on that man's package. We could injure him."

"It looks like they already have," Anna observed. His penis had pinkish welts, probably from over use. Beyond the obvious, it was a fine specimen of male genitalia and larger than average for a white guy in both length and girth.

"Oh, come on ladies," Melissa said. "I haven't had a cock in weeks. Let me ride that thing a little." She reached between her legs, probably inserting her fingers, and held up her hand, displaying her clearly wet fingers. "I'm already wet." Everyone laughed.

"OK," I said. "But, we need to get that cock-ring off of him before we cause damage."

Melissa straddled the man and lowered herself onto him. "Oh my," she gushed, "he is quite the specimen." She took him in to the hilt and ground around on him before she began stroking on his pole. While Melissa was satisfying herself with the live dildo, Helen and Susan stripped completely naked, leaving not even their socks. They apparently wanted their turn on the live dildo. Meanwhile, Melissa continued her effort. Then, to our amazement, the man's legs began to shake and his arms twitched. Megan was correct. It actually looked like he was climaxing without the slightest sound. Melissa continued several more minutes before she too climaxed. Helen was on her knees with her face beside Melissa's left hip, apparently waiting for her to dismount. Melissa got the hint, but took a moment to catch her breath before she uncoupled. As she withdrew from him, the man's cock remained just as rigid as it was before their union.

Helen did not wait for Melissa to step away from him. She began licking the shaft, as if she was enjoying a large phallic lollipop. She wanted Melissa's juice. Helen swallowed the man. We always marveled at her deep-throat ability. It only took Helen a few minutes to get everything she was going to get. "OK. I've had enough." Helen left him.

Susan moved toward the motionless, recumbent man, but stopped short. She stared at the erect male member in front of her and apparently lost her appetite for her carnal pleasure using that member. "I'll pass on this one." Susan stood naked, staring at it. "I think he has had enough of our attention. I'm going to go masturbate," she declared and departed.

No one else moved. "OK," I said, "it's time to save this man's . . . abused cock." I examined his dick. It was worse off than I imagined. The large, thick, rubber band that served as his cock-ring was very tight. I tried several ways to remove it without success. I was concerned I might tear his sensitive flesh. "Does anyone have some good cosmetic scissors?"

Megan went to the basement bathroom and retrieved a nice pair of scissors. I opened and closed them several times to get the feel of them. I was only able to get enough space to insert them near the base of his scrotum. I carefully cut the band off of him. A better color began to return to his penis, but the welts grew, making his cock all the more disfigured.

"Would someone get me an ice pack from the refrigerator?" I asked. "We need to get his cock to go down, or get him to the hospital for medical treatment." Anna went upstairs to retrieve the ice pack. I went to the basement bathroom, found a fresh washcloth, soaked it and wrung it out. I returned to the unconscious man and very gently washed his package. The more I was able to examine it, the nastier it looked. I could not imagine what my sisters did to leave him in such shape.

Anna returned and handed me the ice pack. I anticipated such cold on a sensitive part of his body might rouse him . . . and perhaps convulsively.

"Stand back," I said. The ladies all stepped back several paces. I knelt beside him, took a quick look to make sure everyone else was clear, and wrapped the ice pack around his swollen cock. Surprisingly, he did not even twitch. I kept the ice pack in place with my right hand and felt for a pulse at his right side, carotid artery. He had a strong, regular pulse. He would be OK, as long as I could get this erection down. The ice pack slowly worked and his penis began to deflate. The process must have taken 10-15 minutes. When I was satisfied he was sufficiently deflated, I removed the ice pack for the last time and put it on a nearby end table. The remaining ladies moved closer.

"Wow!" exclaimed Melissa. "That is one ugly dick." She was correct. It was like a gnarly, puffy, partially deflated balloon.

"Is he going to be OK?" asked Judy.

"Yeah, I think so. He's going to be pretty sore for a few days, but he'll recover. He may not ever forget what happened on the night he does not remember. But, when he sobers up, he will not forget what happened to his dick."

Several girls laughed.

"What were you doing?" I asked, again.

"We fucked him, sucked him and jacked him. He was good with it, while he was conscious. We told him we wanted to see how fast we could drain him. He thought it was cool. Unfortunately, he passed out before he stopped producing. We kept going until nothing came out. Even after we were done, several sisters wanted their turn, just like Melissa did."

"Well," I said, "this gives an all new meaning to our motto."

The ladies laughed and cheered, and then shouted almost in unison, "Let us steadfastly love one another."

"Yeah, baby," added Megan, loudly.

"OK, ladies," pronounced Anna, "enough fun for one night. We need to get him dressed and outta here, so we can go to bed." Several of the women began to move to the stairway. "Whoa, whoa, whoa! You enjoyed the show, you can help clean up the mess."

"Where do we take him?" asked Judy.

"Does anyone know where his team is staying?" Melissa asked as well.

"Nope," Megan responded. "Not me."

"Trying to dress him, in his uniform, like that," Judy said, pointing to his motionless body, "will not be easy. Perhaps we should just let him sleep. When he wakes up, he can tell us where he needs to be. Then, we can help him."

Anna scanned the group. "You know the house rules," she reminded the others.

"But, Anna, please," protested Megan. "It will only be a few hours."

Anna again scanned the basement group. "OK . . . just this once. We cannot make this normal."

"Thanks, Anna," Megan responded.

"Cover him up with a blanket. Someone will have to stay down here with him. When he wakes, we need to get him out of here as soon as he awakes."

"I'll stay with him," Judy volunteered.

"I'll stay with her," added Megan.

"OK. So be it. Cover him up. This," she gestured to the man, "is indecent. Let's finish cleaning up and get some sleep."

The Tri-Delta house progressively returned to some semblance of normal. Yes, it has been one helluva party, but it was finally over . . . at least for the sisterhood. The party would last several more days for our only remaining guest.

———

I slept in . . . at least by my standards. I was certainly not the last to awaken from last night's party. After a quick freshen up, I made my way downstairs to the kitchen. I poured myself a tall glass of orange juice, and got a small bowl of granola and yogurt. Megan, Judy and Anna were the only sisters at the table, and apparently the only other sisters awake at mid-morning.

"How is our guest?" I asked.

"He left a couple of hours ago," answered Megan.

"How was his tallywacker?"

"Looked worse this morning . . . but hey, at least it had color."

We laughed. "Small blessings."

"Indeed."

"How did he do? Was he in pain?" I asked.

"He was pretty woozy and more worried about missing the team bus departure at 10."

I looked at the wall clock in the kitchen. "About now?"

"Yeah," Megan responded. "If he was in pain, he did not let on to us. Judy and I helped him get dressed, gave him an apple, and got him a cab to this hotel. He was a gentleman about it all."

"Nice guy," added Judy. "And, oh my, really nice cock."

"Did he know what happened?"

Megan giggled. "He thanked Judy and me for a fun night, but that was all he could remember."

"Did he see his dick?"

"Yes. He looked at it and touched it. He went to the bathroom before he dressed, so I guess he had to aim that thing. I did not check on the bathroom to see how he did."

"Well, I guess the booze had not worn off. That abused dick has got to hurt . . . or eventually it will."

"Probably so," commented Judy. "I know I'm a little sore this morning."

"Me, too," Megan added.

"But, the good kinda sore," Judy chuckled.

"I'm just glad it's over," interjected Anna, "and didn't go sideways when he woke up."

"Yeah," Megan said, "I guess we worked him over pretty well last night." Everyone laughed. "I don't know what got into us . . . helluva night."
The other women began to join in the group. *Yeah, it could have been much worse for all of us. I wonder if we will ever see him again. I'd really like to give that cock a ride.* Today was another day. It was back to the grind of the university's work.

—

Diana

(This story is dedicated to Rebecca C.)

—

My light, nearly transparent, floral print wrap offered a little extra cooling in the warm, summer day's walk across the street to my bestie's home for an afternoon of chit-chat by her pool.   The breeze was just enough to make the leaves speak with the only sound other than my soft footfalls on the pavement and walkways.

The knock on her strong, natural, oak door brought an oh-so-faint 'come in' from beyond the door. The solid door moved easily, despite the 'heavy' feel it offered. Joanne always kept a neat, clean house, especially notable given the presence of her two young children.

"I'm out by the pool," she said, instinctively knowing it was me.

Joanne reclined naked in her full glory in the shade of their patio awning. I always admired her ample breasts as well as her confidence in her body. Joanne was a very attractive woman.

Joanne and Pete had an absolutely awesome backyard . . . delimited by natural terrain, high, stone walls and lush vegetation of many varieties that made the yard colorful and delightfully fragrant. The large, curvaceous, salt water pool had been custom built to blend into the surrounding rock of the hill behind their property as well as the quarried stone of the yard walls. They built in an ingenious slide for the kids as well as a cove under one of the two waterfalls to add sound to the ambiance. The patio deck used thermal resistive coating to keep it cool in the full sun and a sturdy awning that covered half the deck next to the house. Magnificently creative and functional, their backyard was always a pleasant and pleasurable place to spend a few hours.

"There is tea and lemonade in the frig, and an open bottle of Chardonnay in the chiller on the counter."

"I'm OK for now."

Their two-year-old daughter Jessica was playing contently in the pool. They raised their children as water-babies to be safe and comfortable in the water. Jessie was as naked as her mother and equally as free as her mother. Their six-year-old son, Ryan, was at school down the street and would not be home for another hour or so.

I wanted a little sun, so I pulled the adjacent deck chair into the sun. Joanne and I had been friends for many years, so I knew well I did not have to ask if I could be nude as well in front of her children. I doffed by wrap and bikini. The sun felt good laying on the deck chair. We listened to Jessica entertaining herself for several minutes.

"So, what have you been up to, Diana?"

I kept my eyes closed and answered, "I completed my wifely chores and thought I'd catch a little sun with my bestie before Pete gets home for dinner."

"How are things with you two?"

"Better, I should think."

Joanne pulled her chair into the sun next to me. "Did y'all try that club you mentioned last weekend?"

"Oh my, I haven't told you? Yes, we most certainly did. A swinger's club called The Eros House. Everyone was naked and doing just about everything you can think of, in one room or another."

"Pete and I have talked about it, but just never done it."

"You really should. Hey, we could take you."

"That would be fun. Let's do it.

"Mommy, I'm tired," announced Jessica.

"OK, sweetie. Why don't you come here, and we'll get you ready for naptime." Joanne raised the back of her chair to sit not quite upright.

Jessica sat on the edge of Joanne's chair, still wet, leaned over and took Joanne's right nipple in her mouth.

"Oh my, you are cool on my hot body," said Joanne, but neither of them moved.

I watched them together for several minutes. Jessica had her eyes closed, sucking quite regularly, while Joanne embraced her and stroked her wet hair. I reached over and stroked Jessica's shoulder, as she continued to suckle at her mother's breast. Joanne closed her eyes and laid her head back against the chair to enjoy the moment. There was no way I could disturb the moment between mother and child.

Eventually, I heard the slight groan, almost like a whimper, as Joanne arched her head back. Her left leg began to quiver and her toes curled under. Jessica's pace of sucking had slowed. I felt that unique itch in my groin. I wanted to reach down and take care of it, but I worried I might interfere with the mother-daughter moment beside me. After a few moments, Joanne looked into my eye and smiled.

I mouthed but did not speak, "Really?"

She mouthed back without disturbing Jessica, "Yeah. I love it." Joanne winked at me, and then turned her head back and closed her eyes again.

By the time Jessica sated herself, and her mother, she detached, sound asleep. Joanne maneuvered herself as she held Jessica, rocked a few times and stood. She cradled her daughter in her arms, to carry her inside and to bed.

I turned over to give my backside some sun. I was nearly asleep myself, when I heard Joanne lower the back on her chair and lay down face up. "I didn't know you got off breastfeeding," I said, without opening my eyes or turning toward her.

"Well, it's not something that ever came up in conversation. It just started a few months ago."

"Does Pete know . . . out of curiosity?"

"Yes. Actually, he has helped me a few times, when the kids are with our parents."

"Well, I'll be damned." A minute or two passed, as we enjoyed the warmth of the sun. "Has anyone else helped you?" We both looked at each other simultaneously.

"No. Are you offering?"

I laughed and closed my eyes. "Now, there is a thought."

"You are welcome to a breast, if the urge strikes you."

"Thank you, my dear. I must confess, I felt a very strong urge to diddle, as I watched you get off."

"You can, you know. Won't bother me a bit. In fact, I would gladly assist, if you would like me to."

"Another good sugg . . ." We both heard the front door close hard. "Is that Pete?"

"No, probably, Ryan."

"Is this OK?" I asked, looking at each other again and moving my eyes up and down our bodies.

"Yeah, sure. He is quite comfortable with nudity. He sees us naked all the time."

Ryan came out on the back porch. "Hi, Mom."

"Welcome home, sweetie."

Ryan shucked his backpack and began to undress himself, placing his clothes on the picnic table.

"How was school today."

"I don't want to talk about it. Good afternoon, Missus Jamison."

"Good afternoon to you, Ryan," I answered.

Once he was naked, he dove into the pool and swam a couple of laps. Without another word, he got out of the pool and walked directly to Joanne's chair. He sat down on her chair just as Jessica had done, and leaned toward Joanne's right breast.

"You'd better take the left one," Joanne said, matter of factly. "Jessica just had the right one."

Ryan reached across his mother and grasped Joanne's left breast in his hands. He gently kneaded her flesh, as if preparing a meal. Joanne's nipple rose in anticipation. Ryan took her nipple and began rhythmically sucking on her. He continued to use both hands to gently squeeze her breast. Joanne held her son and stroked his hair, as she had done with Jessica. Joanne kept her eyes on me. Within just a couple of minutes, I watched her eyes lose focus, stare off into the distance, and then roll back in their sockets, as once again, she arched her head back and closed her eyes. Her climax did not take long to overwhelm her. Her legs shook in more pronounced tremors than with Jessica, and this time, her groans of pleasure were quite audible. Ryan did not skip a beat, apparently unaware or oblivious to the pleasure his mother was enjoying by his mouth. The boy continued his efforts without a care in the world or the slightest self-consciousness beyond the sensations he felt consuming his mother's milk. I was fascinated watching Ryan pawing his mother's breast, almost like a content, big cat, making biscuits on his master's lap. The process continued and within minutes, Joanne displayed all the signs of another powerful orgasm. Again, Ryan did not skip a beat. Then, as if by some imperceptible cue, Ryan detached, sat up and released his mother's breast.

"Thanks, Mom. I needed that."

"You are most welcome, Son."

Ryan stood, went back to the pool and dove in.

"That can't be real," I said.

"Sure it is," she said, as she spread her legs and inserted a finger. "Here, feel it."

"Are you serious?"

I looked at Ryan, who was just turning at the far end of the pool. "No, I can't do that."

"Why not? It's just a body like yours, and you can feel the proof while it lasts."

"Can I feel it, Mom?" asked Ryan, with both arms folded on our side of the pool.

Joanne nodded her consent.

Ryan left the pool again. Joanne removed her finger and allowed her son to insert a finger into her vagina.

"Do you feel that?" asked Joanne.

"Like you are squeezing me," he answered.

"Yes. That is how a woman's body reacts to an orgasm."

"Wow, that is so cool." Ryan looked at my eyes. "Can I feel yours, Missus Jamison?"

My eyes darted to Joanne's eyes, apparently with an impression of stark terror, as if I was about to be accused of being a pedophile. Joanne smiled and nodded her head, giving me permission. Ryan looked at me without expression, waiting for my answer with his finger still inside his mother.

"I did not have an orgasm," I answered and turned over. Amazing myself, I sat on the edge of my chair, facing Joanne and spread my legs.

Ryan moved between us, and innocently and gently inserted his finger into my vagina. "You are warm and very slippery." He moved his finger in and out a few times, and wiggled it a little to feel the interior.

I laughed. "I'm sure I am. This has been a very exciting afternoon."

"But, you are not twitching."

"No, I am not."

Ryan withdrew his finger and stood. "Thank you, Missus Jamison."

"You are welcome," I answered.

"Are you OK, Son?"

Ryan turned to face us with such innocence and absolutely no discernible shyness or shame. This time, his penis was quite erect, standing straight out. He acted as though nothing had just happened or was different with his body. "Yeah, I guess," he said.

"What happened at school or before you got home?"

"Nothing really . . . just a rough day."

"I hope you feel better now."

"I do."

"Perhaps we can talk about it later."

"Sure. I'm going to go play a video game."

"Alright, sweetie."

Ryan kissed Joanne on the lips and headed for the house.

"Your sister is taking a nap, so please be quiet and let her sleep."

"Yes Mom," he answered without looking back. Ryan gathered up his clothes and backpack, and went inside.

Once Ryan was inside and the door closed, I raised the deck chair back and to the usual seated position. I looked over to Joanne, whose eyes were now closed. "Ryan had a erection," I whispered.

"Yes, he did," she answered without moving.

"Aren't you concern your openness with the children might go too far? Hell, some folks would say what just happened was way too far."

Joanne sat up, turned toward me, placing her feet on the deck. "Do you think anything that happened this afternoon is wrong?"

I looked into her eyes, searched her expression, and then I sat up to face her, more to allow subdued conversation. "Joanne, you have been my best friend for many years. Neither one of us has colored within the lines. Frankly, I think the love, intimacy, bonding and closeness you clearly have with your children is simply magnificent."

"Then why did you say what you did . . . as if there is something wrong, disgusting or nasty?"

"Joanne, please, I'm not making that judgment. I am only reflecting our society around us."

"I am quite aware of society's attitude about anatomy, nudity, sexuality, and especially childhood sexuality. We can talk about the morality of the religious and social conservative attitude toward sex and the consequences of teenage pregnancy, venereal disease and such. I was lucky in my sex education. You probably were as well. I know Pete had similar childhood experiences, and I suspect your Brian would have a comparable story. Pete and I talked a lot about how we wanted to raise our children before Ryan was conceived. We want them to be comfortable, knowledgeable and confident about their bodies and with male and female bodies, and genitalia are just body parts."

"I must say I've not thought about that, and Brian and I have certainly not talked about it; but, clearly we should."

"I am not saying what is right or wrong, just that we want our children to know their bodies, including their sexuality. We most definitely do not want their sexual experience to be a matter of chance or happenstance."

"Quite understandable."

"The key for us is their curiosity. We do not want to hide anything from them. We think they will decide. If we think events outside the home are exceeding what they know inside our family, then we will take appropriate steps to ensure they have the correct information to be responsible sexually, to appreciate their place and conduct within a restrictively conservative society, and to be respectful of other who will not agree with them, with us."

"It's just a lot to take in," I said, as my thoughts ground through so much information, imagery and curiosity. "Would you mind if I asked some questions?"

"Of course not. I hope we can be open with each other."

"Pete is naked around the children as well?"

"Yes, of course. We both are. Our whole family is generally naked at home and when no one will be offended."

"Have they touched Pete?"

"You mean his cock?" I nodded. "Yes. Jessica hasn't shown much interest, yet, but she is going on two, not quite three. Ryan has actually felt and watched Pete go from flaccid to full erection."

"Wow! I'm amazed."

"Only because you have not thought these things through. If you think of body parts as just body parts and sexual reaction as just a normal, natural, physiological process, you see these things in an entirely different light."

"Have the children watched you fucking?"

"Yes . . . again . . . when they are curious. We see no reason to hide our pleasure from them."

"Have they seen you masturbate?"

"Yes, both of us and each other."

"Wow!"

"What if Ryan wants to fuck you or Jessica?"

"Well, that is getting close to the line, isn't it?"

"There must be a line out there somewhere, even for you and Pete."

Joanne withdrew into distant contemplation. I left her alone for several minutes for my thoughts to absorb the topic of conversation and the words spoken. I eventually reached to her and placed my right hand on her left shoulder.

"Are you OK?"

She did not move or react. Her eyes focused upon some distant, unseen place. Another minute passed. Her eyes returned to mine with an unusual softness in her expression.

"Yes, yes . . . quite alright. I was just thinking how far I want to go with this topic."

"We can stop here or anytime. I do not want to make you uncomfortable or anxious. What you do is your business, in my mind, and none of mine . . . as no one is injured or abused."

Joanne's expression turned in an instant to a hard, defiant gaze. "Do my children seem abused?"

"Oh God, NO! Joanne, please, your children are deeply loved and cherished. Even a casual observer will see that. I was just saying . . . well . . . I think I was trying to say, I am impressed with how enlightened you and Pete are, regarding the sex education of your children. Most folks ignore it, pretend it does not exist, and leave their children to learning about sex to the uncertainty of strangers. If we ever have children, I hope Brian and I can be so enlightened."

"Thanks, Diane. It is a very sensitive topic. Both Pete and I are keenly aware of society and especially the law. I know there are moralistic, over-zealous prosecutors out there who would deem the innocence of how we are raising our children as sexual abuse and readily condemn us forever as pedophilic, sexual predators. One of my absolute biggest regrets with our kids is exactly that – we must teach them that according to society their parents are wrong. We must teach them about the inhumanity of the law."

Joanne searched my eyes for several seconds, perhaps to ascertain my sincerity, or my receptiveness. "To answer your prior question, there is a hard line at pregnancy," she answered and smiled warmly.

"So, you would?"

"I think, if that point ever comes, I would allow it."

I stared deeply into Joanne's eyes. She was serious . . . and amazingly confident in her response. "No shit! Double wow!"

"If I carry my argument to its natural limit, I think it would be the natural approach, to talk to him about his feelings, the sensations, the options, so that he understands and appreciates what is happening, as part of his education. I refuse to think of it that way."

"Wouldn't you be worried about an emotional attachment?"

Joanne laughed hard and loud. As her laughter subsided, she chuckled, "I think we already have that emotional attachment."

I laughed. "Well, now that you mention it, I see your point. But, what about Pete?"

"He thinks he could help . . . with love . . . like sharing other life experiences. We want the kids to be able to separate the pleasures of sex from commitments of relationship, so that they can put life experiences in the proper bin and treat them accordingly."

"I am staggered by all this, to be blunt, Joanne. I think you were raised like we all were. Sexual contact between adults and children is sexual abuse, wrong, nasty, and actually according to the law statutory rape; and, sex between parents and their children is incest. How did you overcome those societal prohibitions?"

"In short . . . critical thinking." I waited for her longer response. Joanne understood my patient non-reaction and added, "As we began talking through this issue and the ancillary aspects, we also questioned the basis for those societal prohibitions. We saw the multitudinous imprints of religion and the extension of that control via common law. The one aspect that is a real, *bona fide* constraint is pregnancy. Combinations within closely matched genetic material often produce serious DNA defects – the consequences of inbreeding. Beyond the genetic problem, there is the obvious specter of abuse of power, taking advantage of power position of an adult-child or parent-child relationship. Birth control dealt with the primary threat. We struggled with this last element. How do we determine when a child feels an implied or associated threat? Our only solution, available only to us, was to let the children control whatever sexual experience their curiosity urge them to learn. We can guide their learning, but they must control the pace. So, when or if the day comes that Ryan wants a poke with me, I will make sure . . . we will make sure he knows what he is asking and what it means to have vaginal intercourse, or even anal intercourse for that matter."

"Well, I asked." We both laughed again. The laughter turned into convulsions of levity. We both recognized the seriousness of our conversation and the need to relieve the tension. Control and recovery took several minutes, as each of us took turns cross-infecting the other with waves of laughter. In time, we settled down. "Joanne, you are an amazing woman. You clearly have this under control. I must admit I eagerly await the progress of your journey."

Joanne smiled and nodded her head to acknowledge my words. "We want to see how this turns out, too. We have no guide and we are in uncharted territory. Whatever mistakes we make, we believe our love for our children, and their love for us, will overcome the mistakes we make. Our greatest concern remains our fear of the law and misinterpretation by ignorant people, who have not thought these things through."

"I will do my best, Brian and I will do our best to help you, to protect you."

"Thank you, Diana."

"Thank you for sharing such intimate stuff with me, Joanne. All this sex talk has made me horny."

Joanne again searched my eyes. She smiled, stood and lowered the back of my deck chair.

"Why don't you lay back, close your eyes, relax and let me do you. After all, I've had three, and you've had none so far."

"Are you serious?"

"Yes, my dear. I want to do this."

I could see the seriousness of her offer and what I took for love in her eyes. Briefs thoughts of discovery evaporated quickly with the excitement of her implications. I hoped I was not jumping to unreasonable expectations. I smiled back to her, turned, raised my legs to the chair, and laid back.

"Relax. Close you eyes and just enjoy the sensations."

I followed her instructions. I heard her chair move as she stood. One hand touched each of my feet. She lightly ran her hands over each leg, feeling the skin and curves, up my calves, over my knees, and over my thighs. At my hips, her warm, smooth hands moved together across my lower abdomen. Her touch moved down, barely brushing my genital 'V,' and then continued down the crevice between my thighs to my knees. She applied gentle pressure to the inside of my knees. I followed the guidance of her hands, as she spread my knees wide and above my hips. Once she was satisfied with my position, her hands moved slowly toward my puss. Her fingers probed and traced the creases of my flesh. My clit throbbed, swelling with excitement and anticipation.

"Oh my," she whispered her appreciation, as a finger moved over the curves of my enlarged organ.

Joanne's finger began to move back and forth across my clit, increasing that special ache emanating from the spot. I wanted more. I needed more. Joanne soon traded her finger for her tongue, flicking her tongue rapidly across the exposed tip of my clit. Her tongue caressed my clit and occasionally probed my love socket. She had to be getting a good taste of me.

"Uhhhh," I groaned when Joanne's lips enveloped my clit and she began rhythmically sucking on it like a small cock. Her tongue continued to flick over the head of my clit as she sucked.

One finger entered me easily. I had to be very wet. Soon, she had two fingers inside me, stroking them to the hilt and tickling that magic spot deep in my Va-jay-jay. Joanne was good at working a pussy. She clearly had done this before, more than a few times, and had a very good teacher.

The peak approached quickly, faster than I ever experienced. She could sense it. Joanne could feel my body reacting and the tension building within me. Deep, guttural groans burst out of me as the volcano of my climax erupted. Those hot, electric waves shook my whole body and my groans of pleasure became almost super-natural. Several additional peaks kept my convulsions pulsing through my body. Eventually, I began to descend from the mount. Joanne backed off.

"No, please, don't stop," I begged. I met her eyes with her face still buried between my widely spread legs. She winked at me, and then renewed the vigor of her efforts. I closed my eyes, lowered my head to the chair, and let Joanne work her magic. "Yes, yes, oh God, you are good."

Joanne returned to her effort. This time, she added a finger pressing on my rosebud. She got partway in, which sent me over the top in short order.

The peaks were sharper and more electric, as she stimulated my anus as well as my vagina. I enjoyed it all.

I exhaled heavily and looked up, again. This time, Joanne had raised her head. I reached for her. She knew what I wanted. We embraced, held each other and kissed. I could taste myself on her lips. It was an incredible moment of intimacy. I noticed movement and turned my head to see Ryan standing two arms lengths away from us. Joanne pulled back, saw Ryan, and we separated.

Ryan smiled. "Can I feel now?" he asked.

I looked at Joanne, who nodded her consent. I leaned back on my elbows and spread my legs again. Ryan came over and inserted a finger, again.

"You are twitching this time," he announced.

I smiled and chuckled. "I'm sure I am. Your mother is very good."

"Thanks, Diana," she said.

"No, thank you very much, Joanne. That was mind-blowing."

Ryan explored my genitals for a few minutes with his finger. "What is this?" he asked, with his finger lightly grasping my engorged clitoris.

"That is her clitoris, Ryan," answered Joanne.

"Wow. It is like a small penis," he said innocently.

Ryan finished his exploration. I closed my legs, turned, sat up on the edge of the chair, and tried to stand. My legs were weak and rubbery. I laughed. "That must've been more powerful than I thought," I gushed. I eventually stood, wobbled and braced myself.

At that instant, Peter appears from inside the house. "Well, it looks like everyone has had a good afternoon." Ryan ran into his father's arms and was immediately lifted into his full embrace. They kissed and hugged, and then Peter lowered his naked son. "Great to see you, Diana." I had decided to be as unashamed as Joanne, who went to her husband and kissed him.

"Always a pleasure to see you, Peter." I looked into Joanne's eyes. "I'd better be going. Brian will be home soon as well. Thank you for a most delightful afternoon, Joanne."

"Thank you, Missus Jamison," Ryan said. He looked up to his father. "I got to feel Mom's and Missus Jamison's vagina twitching," he added proudly and unabashedly.

"Did you now," Peter answered. He looked to Joanne, and then to me. "It must have been a very good afternoon."

I felt a twinge of embarrassment. I could only smile at Peter. "Well, I suppose I should put something on." Everyone laughed. I put my bikini back on as well as my wrap. I kissed Joanne on the lips, more than just a peck. I kissed Ryan on the forehead and whispered to him, "Thank you." He smiled back. I rose on my tiptoes to kiss Peter on the cheek. "And, thank you, Peter." I departed their house, walked the short distance to our house, and so ended a most extraordinary afternoon. I had so much to think about and consider.

———

Luke

(This story is dedicated to Lewis B.)

——

Nick and I always looked forward with eager anticipation to our monthly parties with the guys at Robert's elegant home in Kansas City. His spacious home occupied the center of a five-acre lot that was more like a private forest than a residential neighborhood. He had designed the house himself and taken extra care with its construction. As an accomplished, single, gay man, he had done an exceptionally good job with his furnishings and accoutrements. Showing considerable foresight and selection, most of the furniture was quite utilitarian and best of all, washable, so no one had to worry about missed drippings of any kind. The large, saltwater pool filled roughly half of the backyard, which was surrounded by comparatively tall, manicured, juniper trees and a wide variety of flowering bushes, offering a full spectrum of color in the spring and summer. The pool was an elaborate custom construction that had a large rock formation in the far corner, incorporating a delightful, multi-stream waterfall and rock slide with pockets of plants and vegetation to add color. Underneath the rocks was a hidden grotto that was accessed by a nearly submerged entrance. A large, ten plus person, hot tub had been built into one edge of the pool, making transition from the hot to the cool water just a slip & slide over a simple smooth, water level barrier. All in all, this was a perfect party home for a bunch of gay men.

Robert was a prominent, highly successful, approaching elderly, corporate lawyer, who demonstrated a long history of pride in his sexuality, although he did not broadcast his preferences. We met him nearly a decade ago at a regional conference of school administrators, at which he had given an exceptional talk on nurturing the corporate – public school relationship for the advancement of our children – using the possessive, second-person plural pronoun in the collective community sense. He had never been married, to our knowledge, and no children of his own, although nieces and nephews visited him, from time to time. Robert had become a good and faithful friend.

Nick and I tried to attend every month, but we did not make them all. We managed to attend eight to ten times a year over the last handful of years. Attendance varied from one to two dozen men, depending upon the season, timing, local events and such. There were nearly 20 men present when we arrived. Robert actually answered the door naked, as was often the case.

"Welcome back to my humble abode, Luke and Nick."

"Thank you, Robert," I said. "It is always an honor to be included. We brought a couple bottles of wine."

"Thank you, dear fellows. You know where they go."

Most folks made a contribution of some food dish, in addition to the catered dishes Robert provided. Our three and a half hour drive made perishable foods impractical, so we usually brought wine, which went to his collection of bottles on the large kitchen counter.

We greeted those we knew and introduced ourselves to those who were new to us. We were the only two still dressed, so we worked our way toward the designated guest room that served as the dressing and storage room to shuck our clothes, and join the group. We folded our clothes in order of removal and set up stacks among the other stacks on the large king-size bed.

We collected a plate of food and a drink. Most folks were sitting out on chairs, benches and such, around the pool. The warm, late spring day and noontime sun coaxed more than half the guys into the shade of the sturdy, redwood awning over most of the cobblestone patio. Nick and I chose the large picnic table on the patio, out of the sun. Mostly casual chitchat about the weather, pending legislation, current entertainment events and the like occupied the space between bites and sips. There were always delightful men with interesting lives that spread across a very broad spectrum from a truck driver and a construction worker, with a most impressive body I must say, to a couple of doctors and other lawyers like Robert.

When most of the guys finished with their early feeding, some had already begun their sex play, just oral or masturbation, so far. Robert came out to the patio with two, also naked, men – an older gentlemen and a younger man, who bore a striking resemblance to the older man. "Everyone, if I may have your attention," Robert said, and waited for the talking to stop and all eyes on him. "I would like to introduce Jerry and his son Jim." Greetings came from everyone, including us.

"Hiya," Jerry said. Son Jim just raised his right hand.

"Why don't you eat first," Robert said to the newcomers. "This is a friendly bunch. They will introduce themselves as you go."

Jerry and Jim sat at the picnic table across from Nick and me.

"Welcome to our august group," I said. "I'm Luke, and this is my partner Nick."

"Nice to meet you," Jerry answered.

"It is so nice that you are comfortable being naked together," Nick said.

"Yes, Jim has been raised with nudity all his life."

"And, with sex," Jim added, with a broad smile.

"Well, now, do tell. What do you mean by that?"

Jerry nodded his head as approval or sanction.

"My parents have always been very open sexually, even with other partners, from time to time. To my knowledge, they hid nothing from each other, or from me."

"Impressive," I said. "If I may be so bold, how did father and son wind up at a naked, gay men's group?"

Both Jerry and Jim laughed. They apparently understood the joke, even though no one else did. Jerry looked around, and then Jim did the same. They must have been thinking the same or similar thoughts.

"We could show you," Jerry said, "but, the sex hasn't really started, yet."

"Oh my. I can't wait."

"We have always been a rather open and uninhibited family. My wife, Jim's mother, passed away when he was 12. We had done mutual masturbation by then, and he had handled all our body parts, including fingering the missus during one demonstration."

Our expression must have given away our inner surprise, or perhaps shock.

"I was a very lucky boy," Jim offered.

"What did you think?" I asked. "That seems like a lot for a boy to absorb."

"Not really. It was all very natural to me, like it was supposed to be that way. I have always felt nothing but love from and for my parents."

"How far have you gone?" Nick piped in.

Jim smiled. "As far as two men can, I suppose."

"Really?"

"Yes."

"A few years after Margaret's passing, Jim asked what it felt like to fuck someone," Jerry began. "We talked. I tried to answer his questions directly. I told him the anus for both women and men responded the same. He would have to find a woman to feel a vagina. I told him, if he wanted, he was welcome to feel it with me."

"And, he did," interjected Nick.

"Yes, I did," responded Jim. "I fucked my father all the way to the end that night. A few months later, I wanted to feel what he was feeling. He has been a very good teacher. We have been doing it ever since."

"Wow!" I exclaimed.

"Not to be disrespectful and meaning no offense," Nick said, "would you have fucked your mother?"

Jerry and Jim both smiled, as if they expected the question. "Margaret had a very open mind and free spirit. I think she would be proud of what has grown between Jim and me."

"Yes," interjected Jim. "That is my opinion. I never got to talk to her about it, so I do not know. However, I can recall my feelings from the first time I saw my mom and dad fucking. I knew it had to feel good, because they both were so obviously enjoying the process. I certainly wanted to know how it felt. My mom loved me. She loved Dad. I think she would have let me, if I asked and she had confidence Dad was OK with it."

"And, I would have been OK with it. She was a very good woman – big heart, bigger soul, and a very giving and caring person."

Robert came up to the picnic table. "Luke, Nick, you two have tied up our newest guests long enough. How about you let them meet the others?" Robert's cock was not far from Jim's shoulder.

"By all means," I answered for both of us.

"May I?" Jim asked Robert, glancing at his cock.

"Well, sure, if you wish," Robert answered.

Jim took Robert's cock in hand with one hand and his balls with the other. Robert's cock responded promptly to the stimulation. Jim licked, sucked, stroked and virtually worshiped Robert's cock, and even took Robert's cock down his throat to the hilt, which was an impressive feat, given Robert's exceptional manhood. I had watched more than a few cocks being sucked close by, but this episode was one of the more special ones. I felt Nick's hand grasp my handsomely erect pole. I reached for and gripped Nick's equally erect cock. We began stroking each other, as we watched Jim perform on Robert's cock. Jim was clearly making quick work of Robert's pleasure. The combination of the discussion, the scene and Nick's expert hand produced those readily recognizable sensations within me. It must have been the same for Nick. My partner was the first to go. I felt him quiver and his warm man-milk on my hand. I groaned as my peak arrived and shot my load on my belly and Nick's hand.

"Oh dear god," Robert growled, as his knees buckled, and he grabbed the table for support. He seemed to have several more, smaller peaks, as Jim swallowed his cock and would not detach. "You are good, Jim."

Jim had not missed one drop. He took it all, swallowed it with pleasure and savored the taste. "My pleasure, Robert," he said.

Jim stood, followed by Jerry. "Thanks for the invigorating conversation," Jim said to us.

"You are most welcome," I responded. They walked away. Nick and I both licked up the cooled man-milk deposited on our hands.

"What do we do, now?" Nick asked. We were not accustomed to shooting our loads so soon after arrival, and we were not as young and bountiful as we once were.

I grinned broadly and kissed him passionately. "You know perfectly well," I chuckled. "We may have to give 'em a rest, but there is plenty of cock to play with."

By the time, we rose from the table and dealt with our dinnerware, two of the other men were on their knees servicing Jerry and Jim near the pool. Two guys were fucking like dogs on the grass, and another set were doing it in the pool. Nick dove in the pool. I went to the hot tub. David and Stephen were the only ones in the hot, bubbling pool, as I slowly entered.

"Looks like you and Nick were impressed with our newest members," Dave said.

"I would say that is an accurate statement," I answered.

"Father and Son, we don't get to see that every day," added Steve.

"Nope. Wife and Mother passed a decade ago."

"What happened?"

"I didn't get to ask. Father and Son have been intimate ever since. The boy must be in his mid-20's, and clearly he knows how to suck cock."

"My kinda man," Dave said, adding a modest laugh.

"Did we see it correctly . . . you and Nick jacked each other, while you watched the boy perform on Robert?"

"You saw correctly, my friend."

"You want to suck mine?" Dave asked, so matter-of-factly.

"Gladly."

David pushed himself up to sit on the edge of the hot tub and spread his legs to allow me access. He was already quite rigid. He had no taste as I took him in my mouth, wrapped my lips around his shaft, and began licking the head of his cock and probing its slit with my tongue. David leaned back, supported by his arms. His cock and balls were as smooth as a newborn. The soft, delicate skin moved freely over the rigidity of his shaft. I gently fondled and pulled on his balls. Stephen began to fondle me, while he stroked himself. He had a very nice touch. I continued to suck and stroke David, and moved the middle finger of my other hand to his rosebud. The unique texture told me I had the spot. I rhythmically added pressure to the spot. As I worked David's cock, balls and his man-cunt, Stephen began to press his rigid cock between my butt-cheeks on the proper spot. He gradually applied pressure, allowing me to bear down on him. I tried very hard to maintain my attention on David, while Stephen pressed his entry. I must have groaned with David's cock keep in mouth, when Stephen popped in. David raised his head to see what was going on, smiled, and then returned to the images of his fantasies. I just loved that sensation of entry. Stephen knew what he was doing. He withdrew and repeated the entry process several more times to heighten my pleasure and anticipation. Each of us performed our parts in our delicious dance of sensual enjoyment. David was the first to go. His pinnacle sent Stephen into a frenzy. He pounded into me at precisely the correct angle, pace and force. I continued to coax the last few drops from David's cock, as Stephen attained his peak and pushed me to my own climax. It felt good to release, again, even if there were but a few drops.

"Now that was a most impressive coupling, Luke. Well done . . . for all of us," David proclaimed.

"Yes, that was indeed a good one," I responded.

The three of us sat on the edge of the bubbling hot pool to cool off a bit from our joint exertion. Our lower legs dangled in the warm water. The comparatively cool air felt good.

"I wonder if the father and son did anything before his wife's passing?" David said, apparently casting his thoughts aloud.

"Jerry said they had done mutual masturbation before her passing, along with some touchy-feely stuff between the three of them," I answered in a rather subdued tone.

"Kinda nice to have a father who loves you as a first," David added.

"My first was a neighbor boy, two years older than me," said Stephen.

"Mine was an uncle. My family never knew . . . well, at least that I know of," David offered. "A few years later, I figured out that the family knew Bobbie was gay, but it never seemed to bother anyone or raise any questions . . . at least that I was aware. Uncle Bobbie and I played a few more times, and then it stopped when he move to San Francisco. He is now married to another man his age – Thomas – really nice guy."

"Does Uncle Bobbie know you're gay?" I asked.

"Well, to tell the truth, I don't know. I've never talked to him about it."

"Who was your first?" asked Stephen of me.

"My best friend before puberty, actually."

"Did you enjoy it?"

"Absolutely . . . from the get-go."

Jim came up beside us. "May I join you?"

"By all means. Please do," David responded.

Jim immersed himself in the hot tub. David followed him into the water, and Stephen and I joined them.

David started the conversation with Son Jim. He was always the bolder one among the group. "Luke was telling us a little of your story." Jim just smiled and nodded his head. "If I may ask, how do you feel about doing your father?"

I felt a twinge of shock at David's rather direct, personal question, but that did not seem to bother Jim in the slightest.

"I love him, and he loves me. What is not to like?"

"Good point," David said. "We," he added, nodding his head to Stephen and me, "were talking about our first times. Mine was an uncle. Stephen's was an older neighbor boy. Luke's was his BFF in his youth. I can't imagine doing my father."

"I am quite the lucky one."

"Apparently. You seem to have a very good relationship."

"We do, indeed."

"Does it affect your other relationships? I mean, does it decrease your desire for other relationships?"

"Well, actually, no, quite the contrary. I have a girlfriend. I would call her my fiancée, but I have not asked her, yet."

"Interesting. So, you think of yourself as bisexual?"

"Yes."

"Does she know?"

Jim smiled broadly. "Most certainly. I told her straight away. I did not want anything hidden from her, as I was raised. And, to be as frank and direct as you have been, she has done Dad a few times, as well. She has even watched Dad and me playing."

"Now, that is quite impressive," interjected Stephen.

"We do not advertise any of this, but as Robert said at our introduction, this is an open-minded group."

"Yes, it is," I contributed.

"I imagine he was a very good teacher," David continued his inquiries.

"The best, I would say. He has always been very gentle. My parents were both very open with me – honest and direct. They really hid nothing from me. I had considerable direct knowledge of things sexual by the time I reached puberty."

"How long have you been with your girlfriend?"

"We met during our junior year at KU. I'm 26, now, so that would be six years."

"A long courtship," Stephen commented.

"Yes, I suppose so, but we are in no hurry."

"Do you live with her?"

"She lives with us."

"Really? Where is she tonight?"

"Home, watching the dogs."

"Does she know you and Dad are here . . . with a bunch of naked, gay men?"

"Yes, she most certainly does. As I said, nothing hidden. She would be here as well, if women were invited."

"Wow, that is most impressive," David said. "Do you think you will ever get married?"

"Yes, absolutely, but as I said, we are in no hurry. I am a civil engineer for the city, and she is a corporate lawyer."

"Oh wow, so is Robert."

"Yep, that is how we found out about this group," Jim said.

"Will wonders ever cease?" pronounced David.

"I sure hope not," Jim responded.

All of us laughed hard. The conversation was enthralling. Not long after this moment, I felt Jim's hand working my cock, which was soon fully erect, again.

"May I?" asked Jim, looking into my eyes.

"If you wish," I responded and pushed myself out of the water. "I don't think I have any man-milk left in me tonight. I've been well milked already."

"No worries," he answered before taking me in his mouth. After a few pumps, he stopped to look directly into my eyes and said, "I've admired your cock from the moment we arrived."

"I certainly do not have a specimen like Robert, or David for that matter."

"You have a magnificent cock-head . . . very shapely," Jim added, and then descended on my shaft, again.

"I have never heard that before," I mumbled.

Apparently, Jim's efforts were inspiring. Stephen and David picked up their own action. The scene around me, on top of truly expert oral work, provided heady sensations. Jim was good . . . really good. My mind drifted among the physical stimulation and images bursting from the earlier words. The combination made for quick progress from Jim's efforts, as the distinct waves of pleasure mounted swiftly toward the crash of my climax. I could feel the groan of released energy shaking my body. Jim knew to let up, caressing my balls and shaft, allowing me to come down softly.

"Did you get any?" I asked him.

"Enough to know I love the taste of you."

"Well, thank you kindly. Glad to serve."

"Looks like we have inspired others," Jim said, glancing to David and Stephen, who were now feverishly coupled.

"So, y'all have had some fun," Nick said from behind me.

I looked over my shoulder to connect with his eyes. "Perhaps an understatement, I must say."

"I'm tired, Luke. I'm afraid it's time to go."

"Yes, dear. These guys have worn me out," I said and stood. I grasped Nick's hand, bowed to the small group and added, "We bid you adieu, gentlemen. Thank you for a most enjoyable evening of fun and frolic. Until the next time . . ."

Nick and I made our friendlies and offered our gratitude to Robert for hosting the party. We rinsed off in the guest shower, as was the party practice, dressed and said our good-byes. We would have plenty to talk about and compare notes on before we made it home. What a night!

———

Dawn
(This story is dedicated to Dena L.)

———

I knew I was going to be the center of attention this evening – the object of pleasure. I prepared every hole my body possessed. I was certain they would be well used tonight and I had to be ready.

Johnny picked me up a little after seven. The drive to The Lounge took the usual 45 minutes . . . more than enough time to give Johnny a complete blow-job. He had a good off, and I got a good dose of his man-milk that I thoroughly enjoyed.

Once we checked in at the front desk, we went to our respective locker rooms. I never really understood why there were separate locker rooms, since everyone got naked, or at least partially naked – some women chose to keep panties on. Less than a handful of members on any given night remained dressed – very few . . . some nights there were none. I knew I had to be completely naked – no socks, no panties, nothing – for what was about to happen to me

I stepped out into the dimly lit great room. Only the round, raised, center stage was lit, as usual, with spotlights, so the audience had a clear view of the main event.

"Here she is," announced Johnny. "Our main attraction for the evening."

Several unseen people clapped. Johnny took me by the hand and led me to the stage. A few copped a feel of my breasts or buttocks as we walked. An elderly woman, short silver hair, with nice light green eyes, stood on the stage dressed in her minimalist dominatrix outfit – a small bustier that left her nice mature breasts exposed and suspender straps to hold her print stocking up and her pelvis exposed as well. I had not seen this woman before, but she just looked like she knew what she was going to be doing to me. Her pussy was smooth and completely bare, leaving her prominent clitoris as the feature of her groin. A mobile equipment rack had been moved behind at the edge of the stage.

"She's all yours," Johnny told the dominatrix lady.

"Thank you, Johnny." She took my hand as I ascended the two steps to the stage. She positioned me before her equipment rack. "Let's get you ready, my dear." I nodded my head in agreement. "From this moment until you are finished delivering pleasure, I do not want to hear another word or sound from you, except for your safe word, which will be three grunts in rapid succession. Do you understand?"

"Yes, ma'am."

"What did I just say!" she said sharply.

I nodded my head in affirmation rather than reply.

My mistress had me keep my arms at my side to remain fully exposed to the audience. She first fitted me with a small but effective cloth blindfold. A special fitted hood was positioned with a nasal apparatus that she inserted in both my nostrils, and then smoothed the hood back over my entire head. The smell of cum was very prevalent until the nasal inserts were plugged in.

"Make sure you can breathe easily through your nose," she commanded.

I could and nodded my affirmation, again. I assumed and expected she, or someone, would be administering vaporous amyl nitrite, otherwise known as Rush or popper, to enhance my receptiveness for penetration. She tied off the hood tightly at the back of my head. The domme lady checked the position of the mouth opening, and then installed an oral brace to ensure my mouth remained constantly open.

Hands began to touch me, as the domme lady worked. I felt at least three pairs of male hands with degrees of roughness and at least one set of female hands. They squeezed and caressed the curves of my breasts and buttocks. They also probed the folds of my pussy as well as my vagina. I could readily feel my wetness. This was already exciting and the real games were yet to begin. While the hands were roaming over my body like hungry vultures circling their next meal, the oral brace was adjusted for the desired opening.

Once soft set of hands seemed to shoo away the others, moved a few forward and gestured gently signaled for me to lay down. I could feel wide, fur-lined cuffs being buckled to my wrists and ankles. I could hear the metallic clinking of hardware being attached to each of the cuffs and to my surprise another fitting at the top of my hood. I could also hear other metallic clips and connections being made that did not immediately affect me.

I heard some distant male voice exclaim, "Oh yeah. This is going to be good."

Another said, "Fresh meat."

I imagined hungry, horny men practically drooling at the edge of the stage, waiting not so patiently for my body to be fully prepared for their pleasure. The ratcheting of what had to be a hoist announced what was about to happen. The ropes or chains attached to my extremities lifted my legs and arms. Once they were taut, I realized my arms were spread slightly wider than my shoulders, but my legs were spread much wider in what amounted to a shallow 'V.' As my body rose off the floor, my head dangled. The domme lady stopped my raising and adjusted the strap attached to my hood, lifting my head until it was level and supported. She lifted my entire body a little higher. I felt fingers dancing over the folds of my pussy, until I heard the smack of flesh that had to be her swatting those hands away. She was apparently not finished preparing me for the night's entertainment. I felt what had to be her exposed and rigid nipples brushing against the skin of my inner thighs; the sensation sent shivers through my entire body.

Her hands were on my belly, caressing my skin, softly and gently. She fondled my breasts, feeling the curves and squeezing my nipples. She knew just the right pressure to apply. Small electric jolts twitched my muscles as I hung there.

I smelled the distinct odor of amyl nitrite. Something was about the happen. First, my right nipple and then the left nipple were clamped tightly. A sharp stab pierced one nipple and then the other. I tried very hard not to twitch or groan as the pain rushed through me and disappeared. More attachments were made to what were apparently steel pins through my nipples. The clamps were released and my nipples were pulled up, stretching my breasts. The strings or ropes were tied off, so my distorted breasts were part of the show.

Clapping must have been a reaction to the domme lady's gesture to the audience that I was ready for their pleasure.

More amyl nitrite flowed before the first cock slammed into my pussy. While the first cock was feverishly pounding into me, myriad hands of all grades began touching me, stroking and fondling me. To my surprise, one of the men deposited his cum load in my gaping mouth. With my hose block and amyl nitrite flowing, I could not fully appreciate the taste, but it was clearly man-milk. It did not take long for the man in my pussy to climax. The sight of me hanging there with all the stiff cocks around me had to be very stimulating. When the first one finished, another man quickly replaced him. This one was thicker and bigger. I so desperately wanted to groan in pleasure, but I could not forget the domme lady's admonition. The big guy took a little longer to shoot his load into me, but I soon felt those distinctive convulsions and hot spurt.

The feeling of a tongue probing my pussy somewhat startled me, causing me to jerk slightly. As a consequence, I got a sharp smack on my buttocks with a riding crop. The domme lady was reminding me not to react. The tongue kept probing my pussy, and then even my ass. It was a soft, pointed tongue, longer than usual, since I could not feel a face to have some hint whether the tongue belonged to a man or a woman. Satisfied there was no more juice to be had at the moment, the tongue withdrew.

Fingers began to stroke my brown-eye flower. It felt slippery . . . applying lubricant. More amyl nitrite flowed. Sure enough, I then felt a cock head pressing against my sphincter. I instinctively tightened my abdominal muscles, bearing down to let him pop in. I received another smack on my ass. She did not want me to help get him in. Hands grabbed my hips through my legs to hold me tighter as he pressed harder into me. I could almost hear the sound of him popping into me as my sphincter let go. He withdrew and re-entered several more times, as if to make sure my rosebud was opened. He began stroking into me. I felt cool liquid at the junction. That had to be generous applications of more lubricant. Several more deposits in my mouth came before my ass-fucker reached his climax. As soon as he was finished shooting his load in me, he withdrew.

A hand slapped my clit a half dozen times. On the sixth smack, a mild electric current was applied through my nipple suspenders, causing my body to involuntarily twitch from the electric shock. Again, I was smacked on my ass with the riding crop; this time harder than the previous times. I fought within myself to resist the current.

The tongue returned for a short time, rimming my gaping anus. The tongue did not last long this time. Another cock, thicker than the last one, entered my ready ass. He did not waste time with preparatory subtleties and immediately began pounding into me. After a dozen or so long, deep thrusts, balls deep, I felt a genuine electric shock through his cock into my core and out my stretched breasts. He had to have an electrode attached to him somewhere. He continued to pound into me. The current was increased. My body began uncontrollably twitching, shaking and shuddering as the onslaught continued. The smacks of the riding crop on my buttocks had not effect. I could not stop my body's reaction to the anal pounding and electric current shooting through me. The slapping of his flesh against mine joined the slapping of the riding crop. The convulsion of my shockingly rapid and sharp climax shook my entire body violently. I had no idea whether my response was all me, or a combination with the current flowing through my body. I had no control whatsoever and felt my urine shooting forcefully out of me, which must have been too much for my current ass-fucker, as he nearly roared in his climax. He body shook spasmodically as my orgasmic convulsion subsided, and then he just fell away, hitting the floor with a distinct thud.

Everything stopped suddenly. I could feel naked people brushing against me, but I was not the focus of their touching. I was incidental. I could only guess that my last fucker had collapsed and people were tending to him. There were muffled words that I could not discern.

The domme lady was close to my right ear and whispered, "It seems your very capable body was too much for one of your customers, my dear."

I did not respond or react in any manner. "While they take care of him, I'm going to put you in a different position. Don't forget my instructions at the beginning of this session." Again, I did not respond, but I immediately thought, *what the hell is she going to do to me now?*

She lowered me smoothly and gently to the floor. Either the collapsed man recovered and moved, or they moved him. My arms and legs went to the floor in the same position they started. I was detached from everything and the cuffs were removed. She left the spikes in my nipples and took my mouth brace out.

I was given no rest. A hand lifted my knee and pushed my foot back to my buttocks. Coarse, rather itchy rope was wound around my leg to restrain it in that position. The process was repeated on my other leg. Two sets of strong hands lifted me onto my knees. Another coarse, itchy rope was wrapped around my shoulders like some form of harness. Once the leg bindings were complete, the domme lady pushed my torso forward, squishing my breasts against my knees and she applied more rope to hold me in that position. My hands were moved my shoulders, bound in that position, and then tied tightly to my sides. Somehow, she must have fashioned lifting lines. I was lifted off the floor in that position. The topknot hood ring tied off above also supported my head. I was not yet in position when the first cock thrust into my pussy and began feverishly stroking into me. He soon deposited his load. Another cock immediately took his place. I took cock after cock for what seemed like many minutes. I lost track and count of how many dicks squirted into me.

Eventually, I became aware of someone underneath me. Whomever it was, male or female, began diddling my clit and must have been laying beneath me, presumably with his or her mouth precisely position to catch the drippings from my pussy, of which there had to be ample overflow. Occasionally, one of the men preferred my ass for his pleasure, presumably because my ass was tighter than my pussy. It made no never mind to me. While the endless stream of cocks penetrating me continued without interruption, a vibrator expertly applied, replaced the manual stimulation of my clit. Another climax peak shook my body and resulted in more smacks with the riding crop, but this time on the upper part of my buttocks, so as not to interfere with the man having at me at the moment. Every so often, one of the men fucking me would smack my buttocks sharply with his hand.

While the seemingly never-ending string of cocks pressed on, other ropes pulled my knees apart. A broad strap was positioned across my upper abdomen and lifted to support my mid-section, since my torso weight was no longer resting my thighs. The vibrator continued on my clit. Hands began to fondle, squeeze and tug at my breasts. My nipple spikes were twisted and released. Several more orgasms gushed through my body and brought the now expected result. My clit was becoming sore from all the stimulation. In fact, the various pain sites on my body began to blur and mysteriously transform into what felt like a blanket of warmth wrapped around me. Mercifully, the vibrator stopped.

Then, the strangest thing . . . I felt a cool round object touch my chest at several places. *Someone is actually checking my heart health to make sure I'm still alive. Wow! I've never had anyone do that before. I must be doing pretty good at remaining inanimate, if they felt the need to check me.* It felt oddly reassuring.

One drop of cold water startled me as soon as it touched my hot skin, mid-spine. My body had to be glistening with sweat. The contrast in temperature felt like a small jolt of electricity. Then, another drop produced the same result closer to butt crack. When a glass of ice cold water hit my back, it took my breath away. My chest convulsed in rapid, sharp, shallow breaths, while some man continued to pound his cock into me. My whole body swayed with his rhythm, and then transitioned to rapid jerks as he jackhammered me to his moaning climax.

The stream of hard cocks just kept coming at me, and cumming in me. Most preferred my pussy, but some, perhaps one in five or a dozen, I had no idea how many, chose my ass.

Just as I began thinking this evening's event would not give me a throat fuck, my head was raised from horizontal and a rather thick, hard cock slowly went into my mouth. It tasted of cum and pussy, so it may have been one of the cocks that already fucked me once, or more, and now renewed to erection wanted another hole. Another good dose of amyl nitrite loosened my throat and enabled me to quickly overcome my immediate gag-reflex. I had to work hard to keep my teeth off his shaft while he continued to stroke into my mouth, since my head was being held at an odd, uncomfortable angle. The two men, one at each end, must have thought it rather humorous when I heard soft laughter and tried different joint rhythms in unison, opposed, different frequency, or any combination they could think of. Several times they thrust together, as if they were trying to get their cock-heads to touch inside me. Amazingly, they both shot their loads within what seemed like a minute of each. I swallowed a rather small load, and only a brief taste of his fresh cum when he withdrew his cock from my mouth and lowered my hooded head back down to its supported horizontal position.

I had no idea how long I had been hanging above the stage or how many cocks I had taken. The domme lady's confidence, calm voice queried,

"Our main attraction tonight appears to have exhausted our audience. Are there anymore interested fuckers before I release her?" I heard her step several times on stage, as she was probably turning to scan the whole as best she could since the only light was on the stage and of course the illuminated exit signs required by law. "OK. Hearing none, we are done with this event for the evening." Applause and cheers, both male and female, punctuated the conclusion. I could hear people shuffling around, moving chairs, along with muffled conversation.

"Well done," the domme lady whispered in my ear.

I was slowly lowered to the stage floor. The ropes were removed in reverse order from how they were applied. Several hands gently moved my arms and legs, to flex my joints. Two sets of strong hands lifted me off the floor and sat me in a chair. A cold, wet cloth was placed on my pussy, partially to sooth my well-used flesh but also to soften caked on cum and any other deposits in the area. *Oh damn, that feels good.* Several cool, soft washcloths began to wash my legs right up to my covered pussy. My abdomen was gently washed. Some kind of ointment was applied evenly to my nipples. The tingling sensation suggested it some kind of anesthetic and/or disinfectant. The spikes were slowly removed from my nipples, and my breasts were gently washed. *Probably to clean up the blood from the piercings*, I told myself. Fresh, wet, soft cloths again washed my body from the bottoms of feet to my shoulders. Soft hands spread my knees. The towel was removed from my pussy. Fresh, cool, wet, soft cloths carefully washed my pussy and ass, going over the same flesh several times to make sure I was clean.

My hood and blindfold were the last to be removed. Blessedly, the stage lights had been switched off and the room lights turned on and dimmed. The domme lady knelt in front of me and gently washed my face and neck in a very caring, motherly manner. As my eyes adjusted to the light, I noticed she had two rather ripped young men dressed in slave outfits with their genitals exposed standing behind her. Johnny sat in a chair at the edge of the stage watching the process.

"You did very well, my dear," the domme lady said, as she finished her cleaning of my body. She remained kneeling between my spread legs. "You were very popular. You will have a place here whenever you wish the attention. By the way, my name is Betty."

"I'm Dawn," I coughed out, trying to get my speech to work, again.

"May I?" she asked and glanced at my crotch. I nodded my head. She leaned forward, kissed my clit, took one swipe with her tongue, and kissed it, again. She looked up at me without moving and spoke as if my pussy was a microphone. "I would like to get to know you better, if you are OK with that."

I chuckled. "I don't know if I can take that everyday." We both laughed. "But, yeah, I would like to know you better, as well." I looked over at Johnny, who just sat there smiling, and then back to Betty. I whispered, "Do you do cock or just pussy?"

This time Betty laughed. "I prefer pussy, but I do cock, as well, especially if it is a nice looking, cut hunk of manhood."

I look backed to Johnny. "Stand up," I said to him. He did so. He was not hard, but not flaccid either. "Betty, meet my friend Johnny. He brought me here tonight."

When I look back to her, she was smiling. "That one qualifies."

"Excellent. Let's trade numbers before we leave."

Betty stood and extended her hand. I did not feel confident enough in my legs to stand, so I took her hand and shook it. Deal! Betty gestured for her two helpers to assist me in standing. They each placed a forearm under my shoulder and lifted me to a standing position. I flexed each leg several times, as they steadied me. My legs were still stiff, but they were good enough. I nodded my head, and they let me stand by myself.

I walked out, dressed and met again in the lobby. As agreed, we traded numbers and tentatively agreed to meet next Friday night for dinner and whatever might happen afterward.

On the drive home, Johnny recounted his observations of the night. He filled in some blanks beyond my senses at the time. He had also joined the line of fuckers, confessing to depositing two more loads in me during the night's festivities. Johnny was clearly still excited by what had happened, but frankly, I just did not feel up to more. I just wanted to sleep and let my body recover. It had been one helluva night.

Allen

(This story is dedicated to Jeanne P.)

—

I had wanted Jennifer to experience San Francisco for a long time. She had never been to the city before. The city by the bay remained one of my favorite cities in the whole world, and I was rightly proud of the city where I had grown up. The fine, early summer day complete with a light on-shore breeze made the day's excursion and tour all the more enjoyable. The usual fog had receded to the ocean, leaving a bright sunny day. Yet, like clockwork, I knew the fog would roll back in during the evening hours and blanket the city.

We drove through Haight-Ashbury – a very colorful part of the city. We also visited Coit Tower, had a delightful early lunch at Fisherman's Wharf, and an exquisite, shared, chocolate sundae at the Ghirardelli Chocolate and Ice Cream Shop in Ghirardelli Square. We even took a short cable car ride to the top of Russian Hill and looked down the many twists of Lombard Street, before hopping back on another cable car to return to Ghirardelli Square and our car.

I really wanted Jennifer to experience Golden Gate Park – one of the best city parks in the world, in my humble opinion. We found a parking spot, vacated just as we approached, along John F. Kennedy Drive, not far from the De Young Museum. We took most of the afternoon to walk around the central part of the park. We took in the exceptional sights of the Japanese Tea Garden, the magnificent floral display of the San Francisco Botanical Garden, and walked around Stow Lake.

The interesting part of the day's excursion began when Jennifer flashed her breast. She made sure she was beyond arm's length from me. She knew I would want to touch her. It did not last long, but it was a clear view. I looked around. Other people could have seen her flash. Yet, I could detect no evidence anyone noticed except me. I went to her, embraced her and kissed her passionately.

"So, you are not wearing a bra today," I observed the obvious.

"Nope."

"What else aren't you wearing?"

"Wouldn't you like to know?"

"Yep."

"Patience, my eager one."

"Easy for you to say," I said and glanced down.

"Oh my," she said and moved close beside me. She reached out and gently squeezed my swollen and restrained manhood. "You are a nasty little boy, getting so excited so easily."

"Yes . . . well . . . it is what it is." I looked around. There were not many people in the park on this particular weekday, but we were not alone. "I can't walk around like this. It's too obvious."

"It's perfectly natural, Allen. There is nothing to be ashamed of in a fine erection."

"So you say." She continued rubbing and squeezing me. "You are not making it better."

Jennifer giggled mischievously. "No, I'm probably not, but it sure is fun." This time she looked around, and then took my hand and led me through a small opening in the hedgerow. We adjusted our position a couple more times before she was apparently satisfied there was minimal risk of discovery. She knelt in front of me on the leaves and pine straw. Jennifer expertly removed my distended woodie. She stroked it a few times, which felt so good, and then she took me into her mouth. She bobbed on my pole and stroked it for several minutes. I felt the telltale sensations of the impending volcanic peak, only to have things stop abruptly when we heard the muffled conversation of an approaching couple, who would pass just a few yards away from us. Jennifer froze, holding my johnson, but looking toward the walking path. A young couple walked passed our spot, continuing their conversation about the birds they were spotting and apparently oblivious to our proximity.

When their voices faded, Jennifer looked up at me. "Do you think you can make it to the car?"

The thought of a little more protection, or at least familiar space, convinced me to make the trek for the promise of a more rewarding climax. "Sure," I simply responded.

"You'd better put it back," she said. "I don't want to risk pinching you with the zipper."

I did as she requested.

We exited the hedges and walked more purposefully toward where our car was parked. Cars were parked in front of and behind us. I had not noticed before, but a solid hedge was close to the passenger side of the car.

"Do you think you can get in the passenger side?"

"I think so. Front or back?"

"Front. There is more leg room."

I unlocked the car first, and then made my way, shuffling along the narrow curb space between the hedge and the car. I opened the door and squeezed in.

Jennifer closed the door behind me. She moved to the driver's door, quickly got in, closed the door and crawled across the console. She straddled me and sat on my knees. "I'm ready," she said, lifting her skirt and revealing her smooth mound and slit. "Feel," she commanded.

Sure enough, she was dripping wet. I managed to rub her clit with my slippery fingers.

Jennifer closed her eyes and purred with pleasure. Then, abruptly, she said, "No." She dropped her skirt and grabbed my wrist. "I want you inside me."

I knew what she meant, but I easily inserted two fingers and reached for her g-spot.

"No. Not like that," Jennifer said, not resisting in the slightest. "I want the real deal." She opened my zipper. I was still quite hard when she extracted my stiff dick. "This," she added, almost growling softly. She stroked me a few times, wet her fingers with her own lubricant, and rubbed my cock-head and slit, as if she was admiring the curves. She grabbed the seat recline lever and leaned me back, to make it easier for her to mount me. She scooted up on me, spread her skirt, held my shaft and guided it to her wet spot. Jennifer rubbed my cock-head across her lips, getting the tip nice and wet, and rubbed her clit, before she positioned and easily, effortlessly and smoothly descended onto me. We both groaned with pleasure. We remained motionless for several seconds, just enjoying our renewed union. Jennifer kissed me deeply and began to thrust her hips. I could not resist and added my hip thrusts in opposition to hers.

Just then, a couple walked passed our car to the vehicle in front of us. We stopped. Jennifer giggled nervously. We did not move, trying not to attract attention. The man opened the driver's door for the woman, and then walked around the rear of their car and in front of our car. I watched him closely to see if there was any sign that he noticed us. I felt Jennifer squeeze me several times with her vaginal muscles. The man never looked at us or even toward us. He shuffled along the curb, got in the passenger door, and they soon departed.

"There we go," I said.

We renewed our hip motion. Jennifer cocked her hips forward to gain clitoral stimulation. We were making good progress, when motion on the left side of the car caught my attention. Another car slowed. I held Jennifer's hips to freeze our activity. The windows of the other car were heavily tinted. I could not see if anyone noticed us or saw us. We watched and did not twitch, as the driver parallel parked his car in the open space in front of us. Still, no sign of detection. Any outside observer would not have to see bare flesh to recognize what we were doing. After all, we were facing each other, torso to torso in the front passenger seat. Jennifer kept Kegel'ing on me, as a motionless reminder she was not finished. I smiled involuntarily. I could not avoid admiring her resourcefulness and persistence.

A middle-aged, nice looking man got out, shut his door, and opened the rear, driver-side, passenger door. He helped an elderly lady slowly get out. The front passenger door opened. An attractive, well-endowed, brunette woman, probably his wife, got out, shuffled back to close her door, and then opened the rear, passenger-side door. A boy, perhaps 10 years old got out and worked his way around the back of their car. He did not see us or show any sign of detection. Then, an eight-year-old girl was the last to exit the car. She paused at the right rear fender, waiting for her mother to close the door and follow her. By this time, the man had most likely told his mother or mother-in-law to lean against our left front fender. We felt the car shudder slightly, at least enough to be felt by us. All this going on and Jennifer continued to rhythmically grip me.

The girl led her mother back to make her way and join the rest of the family. The cute little girl, whose chin barely cleared the hood of our car, stopped between the two cars, turned directly toward us, and pointed. "Look Mommy," she said loudly enough for us to hear her inside the closed car.

The woman quickly glanced directly at us and undoubtedly recognized exactly why we were oriented in such a fashion. She flushed noticeably with some embarrassment. The mother quickly turned her head toward the street and nearly pushed her forward. When she reached the elderly woman, the girl again turned directly to us. "What are they doing, Mommy?" she asked, again loudly enough to be heard in our closed car.

What on earth is she going to tell her daughter and son about what the little girl saw that afternoon?

Now, the entire family was looking at us. To my utter amazement, Jennifer looked away, perhaps to hide her face, and continued to kegel on me. *This woman is determined not to let go of what she is gripping.* The mother leaned over and whispered something to the girl.

"Really," the girl said with spirit.

The boy just stood there staring at us.

The elderly woman actually smiled, and then wagged her right index finger at us, as if to say, "naughty, naughty." She reached for and pulled the girl in front of her.

"Grandma, I can't see," she clearly announced. Her eyes appeared just beyond Grandma's left hip. She was then pulled back.

Apparently, frustrated, Mom took the hands of her children and walked them forward out of our sight.

Jennifer's continuing efforts worked their motionless wonders, despite all these distractions.

The father looked down, as he moved to the trunk of his car. As he did, grandma turned partially around, looked directly at us, made a circle with her left hand and inserted two fingers, thrusting them in and out of the circle. She pushed her cheek out with her tongue.

"I'll be damn," I said, watching grandma give us the very sexual gesture. "Grandma's a player."

Jennifer looked around to witness grandma's gesture. "Well, look at that." Jennifer thrust her hips a couple of times for grandma.

Grandma winked at us, and then instantly turned away, as the father retrieved and donned a full backpack from the trunk and closed the trunk. He did not look back at us, again. He offered his left arm, which grandma took. They walked forward to join Mom and the kids, and never looked back to us.

Jennifer gave me a hard squeeze. I was still there. We looked around to see if there would be any more distractions. I could not see another human being, or critter for that matter.

"We're clear," I whispered.

Our coupling renewed in earnest. The interruption had set me back slightly on our journey to ecstasy, and yet I instinctively knew Jennifer had not regressed as far as I had. However, I was always quicker on the ascent than Jennifer. This time had to be different. She was doing most of the work and deserved the appropriate reward for her efforts. I diverted my mind, as she pumped me. *Maybe grandma and her family were coming back soon. Maybe someone would walk by looking in cars.* To my amazement, I sensed the signs of Jennifer's ascent – her quickening pace, the forward rotation of her pelvis, and most prominently the staccato choppiness of her moans and groans. Yes, she was close. I tried my best to help her attain the peak she deserved. Hips bobbed up and down on me. She picked up the pace. *She must be close.* Or, she sensed my rapidly approaching climax. *Damn, she is good.* I did not so much as twitch, fearing I might disturb her rhythm and concentration.

"Oh yes," she mumbled in an almost guttural manner. "Oh yes," she repeated, this time more distinct. She was now pounding on my hips. *Look at the trees, the leaves moving, such a beautiful day.* I tried anything to stay behind her. *No, no, no . . . don't think . . . no . . .* I lost control in an instant.

The hot waves of orgasmic surge enveloped my entire body, while bolts of electric current convulsed every muscle. I heard myself groaning loudly. I could no longer see. This one lasted for the longest time, as Jennifer thrust down on me. Then, I heard her rather loud groan, "Oooohhhh gaaawww . . ." She stopped thrusting and transitioned to grinding her groin on me. Her head settled into the crook of my neck. Jennifer's chest was heaving and her groans became sporadic muffled moans that mixed with her labored breathing. Her hips stopped. We lay motionless, joined together.

That's clapping. I strained to look beyond her head on my left shoulder. A small crowd of perhaps a dozen people, mostly young adults, stood by the left front fender. "We have an audience," I said softly.

"Oh, damn," she said, when she raised her head and looked to her right.

There were all clapping and apparently enjoyed our union. We had not intended to provide a show, only to consummate our passion. We did not do this for anyone else.

"What do we do?" asked Jennifer.

"Let's wave. Maybe they will go away."

We looked at the people outside the car, smiled and waved to them. They did not move and continued clapping and cheering. Several additional people joined them, undoubtedly wondering what all the commotion was about. To my utter surprise, Jennifer flashed her right breast, which brought even more cheers, even from the women in the audience.

"Should we uncouple?" Jennifer asked.

"I think not. We haven't exposed any pussy or cock, yet."

"Maybe that is what they are waiting for."

"Perhaps. I'd suggest we remain still until they disperse." I felt her kegel on me, again. I laughed, "No. I mean completely still. You don't need to be raising me from my sated limpness."

We both laughed.

"You were incredible, Jennifer. You never cease to amaze me."

Jennifer smiled. "I'm glad you enjoyed it. I sure did."

"You did all the work."

"Easy to do, when you're in love."

"I love you so much."

We kissed deeply. The clapping resumed. The slightly diminished crowd probably thought we were renewing our copulation. "We'd better remain completely still. We don't need to be encouraging them. We need them to go."

Jennifer lowered her head, placing her forehead on my left shoulder. We tried to stay very still. We talked about the plan for the remainder of this day and the following day – the last day of this trip.

Sure enough. Our audience eventually moved along, although the process took longer than I expected. *I'm not sure what they expect to see.* Once we were satisfied we were alone again, Jennifer dismounted and shifted her butt back on my legs. She grabbed several tissues from the console and wiped up the residue of our mixed juices from between her legs and around my now limp dick. She lifted her skirt several times to make sure she was getting everything from herself and me. *I wish I had my camera. What a freakin' hot pic this is.*

We shuffled around awkwardly, mostly to reassemble me, since she chose to remain panty-less. I scooted across the console to the driver's side. "We probably should be getting along. We have a reservation for an early dinner at La Folie on Polk Street at five-thirty."

"Sure."

I checked around the car. Clear. I started the car, checked one more time and slowly pulled out. As we it made around the family's car ahead of us, they returned. We waved. The wife did not look pleased. The husband and grandmother returned our waves.

"Well, that was a nice adventure," I said. "Thank you so much for loving me."

"That is the easy part, my darling."

What a day!

Angie

—

I knew this year's birthday present would be different and perhaps even a little risky. Yet, when the idea came to me several months ago, it just felt correct . . . worth the risk . . . well, not that much of a risk. Greg and I both turned 46 years of age this year. His birthday was two months before mine. Later this year, we would attain the 21st anniversary of our marriage. We had been swinging for six of those years, and we considered ourselves polyamorous. So, perhaps my novel birthday present idea was not so far out there for us.

By prior arrangement, I picked up Johnny on the way home from work. Johnny was one of our regular playmates at club parties. He was a self-declared pansexual man married to Gloria, who had consented to my idea and her husband's participation in the scheme. The plan was for me to arrive home with Johnny before Greg arrived. He had a much farther commute than me, so that was a fairly safe bet. All he knew or expected was a nice dinner out, as we usually did for each other's birthdays. What he did not know for this particular birthday was my surprise between arrival home and dinner. It would probably be a late night for all of us. Also part of my plan, Johnny and I would shower together in our "party shower," so that we were both fresh and squeaky clean. I intended to be waiting for Greg stark naked at the entryway from the garage when he arrived.

"Are you sure this is OK?" Johnny said immediately when he answered the door.

"As sure as I can be. After all, this is a surprise for Greg. We've never done this before."

Just then, Gloria joined Johnny at the door. We hugged and kissed. Gloria and I had been intimate more than a few times over the years. "I hope this goes well," Gloria said.

"Me too. Thank you so much G. for lending me your hubby for this."

"My pleasure, darling. I look forward to hearing about your adventure. I hope Greg appreciates all your effort on this."

"Time shall tell."

"I'd invite you in, Angie, but I do not want to spoil your plan. Y'all better be on your way." Gloria kissed Johnny passionately. "I will not expect you home tonight, honey. Play nice. Do your part well, my valiant stud."

"Thanks, sweetie. I'll try," Johnny answered.

With that, we were off. Gloria remained at the doorway until we were gone. I drove several miles in silence, until Johnny asked, "Do you really think Greg is going to just watch?"

"Hard to say, but that is the plan. His instructions will be to just watch, fully clothed . . . no touching, no jacking, nothing . . . just watch."

"That almost sounds like a punishment."

We laughed. "Well, hopefully not, but it will not be easy for him. Anyway, after our show, the plan is to take you to dinner with us, if you wish. I would like you to, if that is OK with you. Then, again if you are up for it, as I briefed Gloria, I would like you to come back with us for more playtime as a threesome."

"That is quite an elaborate plan, Angie."

"Well, I just hope it works. I want him really excited and unable to relieve himself through dinner. Then, by the time we return home, he should be ready to explode."

"I understand my duty for the first part, but I am unsure about the remainder."

"To be candid, Johnny, this could go many different ways, so after dinner, we will just have to play it by ear."

"OK. This should be fun. I want it to turn out just like you want it tonight."

"Thanks, Johnny. You are a sweet man for agreeing to this. I know it is out of the ordinary. I will certainly thank Gloria, as well."

"I've never done anything like this, either. We've always played in the group, and I've always been with Gloria. But, she seemed to be excited about it, too."

The remainder of the ride home took roughly ten minutes. Greg's car was not in the garage; so far so good.

Johnny and I undressed as casually as if we were married. Our shower easily accommodated both of us and the large, rectangular, waterfall shower-head covered us both. Each of us washed the other, including our sensitive bits. Johnny reacted as expected, but did not pressure me for relief. He even seemed to enjoy shaving my skin slippery smooth around my pussy and ass. That was not his first time performing that service for a woman. He had shaved himself smooth earlier.

"That is one fine cock, my friend," I said, as I stroked his rigid member several times before rinsing him off.

"Thank you. It came with the package."

We laughed. Satisfied that all was as it should be, we toweled off and blow-dried our hair. We brushed our teeth. We always had spare toothbrushes for guests. I checked the time . . . still good margin. We walked to the kitchen.

"Would you like a drink or some pot?" I asked.

"No thanks. Best stay stone sober for this."

"Indeed."

"This is kind of performance art and I really need to be in the moment."

"You are a real trooper with all this, Johnny. Again, thank you."

I heard the garage door open. I turned to Johnny and said, "Please wait in our bathroom. I'll move him to the bedroom, and then on my cue, you can appear in the doorway."

Johnny nodded his head and went to the master bathroom. I took my position opposite the entry door from the garage at the head of the entryway. I made a point of standing up as straight as I could, with my legs shoulder length apart and my hands clasped behind my back. After weeks of experimentation and evaluation before the mirror, this pose, this position best accentuated my hips and my breasts. I could feel my heart rate picking up.

The door opened. Greg was so handsome in his medium gray business suit, still crisp white shirt and solid maroon necktie. A broad, ear-to-ear smile grew rapidly on his face and his eyes brightened when he saw me standing there in front of him in all my glory.

"Wow!" he exclaimed, when he closed the door and stood still admiring what he saw. "That is a helluva birthday present."

"Oh no, my darling, I am not your birthday present."

"Really?" he said, and then slowly took the half dozen steps toward me. I did not move, not even a twitch or fidget. "Then, my gosh, what could be my present?"

"Patience . . . my eager little boy . . . patience."

As he approached me, he reached out – his right hand toward my left breast. I raised my right hand and waggled my index finger. "Ah, ah . . . no touchy . . . not yet . . . at least." He stopped and looked into my eyes with an expression of confusion, like he was asking with his eyes what this was all about. I returned my right hand behind my back. I could actually feel my nipples aching. I did not look, but they had to be erect and hard. I could also feel my crotch getting slippery. "First, Happy Birthday, my darling." He nodded his acknowledgment and scanned my body from arm's length. "Are you ready for your present?"

"Sure," he said, again reaching for my left breast.

"Nope, not yet," I simply responded.

Greg grabbed his crotch. "Damn, Angie, I'm so hard in here it hurts. I want you, now."

"Soon enough, my eager stallion. Soon enough. Please follow me." I turned and led him into the kitchen.

"Nice bum," he said, and I wiggled my hips for him.

"Drop you case on the counter."

"Should I undress?"

"Nope. Stay exactly as you are."

Greg placed his briefcase on the kitchen island and followed me into the bedroom.

"Sit here," I commanded and positioned him in the large stuff chair facing our California King posted and canopied bed. He sat as I told him. He had not even loosened his necktie. "You have always said . . . well not always, but for a long time . . . that you wanted to watch me enjoy sex with another man. You have seen me with other men, but always in our swinger group parties. You have never seen me with just another man. So, that is your surprise gift from me."

"Really?" he answered, still somewhat confused but more upbeat, now.

"Here is your surprise." Right on cue, Johnny appeared still completely naked and to my pleasant surprise, with a nice, rigid and proud erection protruding from his lower abdomen.

"Hey Johnny," Greg said, "in fine form, no less."

"Great to see you, Greg. I hope you enjoy your surprise gift from Angie."

"Oh, I imagine I will."

Johnny waited by the bed. I walked over to Greg, stayed beyond arm's reach, spread my legs wide and squatted about halfway. I inserted my index and middle fingers in my really wet pussy, wiggled them around to get them completely wet and withdrew them. I moved closer, leaned over to dangle and wiggle my breasts, as I moved my wet fingers under his nose. He tried to lick them, but I waggled my raised index finger to gesture no to him. I could see the bulge of erection inside his trousers. So far so good. I wafted my fingers under his nose, again. This time, when he extended his tongue to lick my fingers, I touched my fingertips to his tongue to give him just a little taste.

"I want more," he said.

"I know you do, but for that you shall have to wait." I moved to Johnny, who stood patiently by the bed. His erection was not as rigid as it was when he appeared from the bathroom, but it was still more than adequate for the tasks ahead. Nonetheless, I dropped to my knees and took him in my mouth. His cock responded immediately. With his cock still in my mouth, I turned him sideways, so Greg could readily see me deep throat Johnny several times without gagging.

"Oh wow!" Greg exclaimed. "Good girl."

I continued on Johnny's cock a few more minutes to make sure he was good and ready. I stopped, jumped on the bed, scooted to the middle and turned so my feet were pointed directly at Greg. I raised my head to connect with Greg's eyes. He was smiling broadly. I slowly raised and spread my knees, and drew my feet back toward my hips. I gave my husband a full view of the goodies. I looked to Johnny and said, "OK, cowboy, time to mount up."

Johnny moved effortlessly on the bed and between my widely spread legs. I continued to watch Greg, as Johnny rubbed his cock-head at the entrance to moisten it, and then rubbed it around and on my swollen and aching clit. *Oh my, yes, he is good.* He inserted his cock just a little, and then repeated his clit-rubbing effort. The cycle continued, as he inserted a little more of his cock at each insertion. The rubbing of his smooth cock-head on my clit worked its usual magic. Once he finally inserted to the hilt, I felt like he reached my throat. My legs instinctively wrapped around him and gripped him, as I moaned with pleasure. I tried to play sufficient attention to Johnny efforts, while I periodically checked on Greg. My cuckold husband appeared to still be enjoying the observance of my carnal pleasure and continued to comply with my instructions. Several times I caught him fidgeting, squirming in the chair. His confined erection had to be uncomfortable for him, but the constant irritation also had to be ratcheting up his excitement. Oh wow, is he going to get off like this? Johnny fully stroked into me for several minutes, taking breaks to rub my clit with his slick cock-head. *Oh yes, he is really good with that thing.*

I guided Johnny to the next position with me by simply turning over on my knees with my butt raised. My shoulders and head rested on the bed. I turned my head, so I could hold Greg's eyes. Johnny moved to the side, so Greg could see, and used his fingers to play with the whole area from clit to rosebud. Greg was focused on my presented love box and probably did not notice my constant gaze. Johnny probed, stroked, spread, and even rimmed me a few times. Greg's squirming in the armchair became more continuous, and surprisingly, he kept his arms and hands on the chair's arms. I noticed his hands gripping the fabric and cushion of the chair arms. *Yes, this is working. He is really wound up tight. Is he going to shoot in his pants without any of us touching his cock?*

I wiggled my butt to signal Johnny that I needed him to plug him. He did not need verbal encouragement. Johnny moved behind me, moved his cock up and down against to make sure he had the hole he desired, and gently thrust himself in to full length, producing a guttural groan of pleasure from deep within me. Damn, he feels good in there. Johnny began rhythmically and fully stroking into me. I continued to watch Greg watching me. I reached through my legs to fondle Johnny's swaying ball-sack. I wanted to reach farther back to finger his brown-eye, but I did not want him to ejaculate just yet.

We switched positions, again. This time, I wanted Johnny on his back with his feet toward Greg. I stood, faced Greg for a few seconds, and then turned to straddle Johnny's hips. I squatted down, held Johnny's wet and slippery cock to position it properly, and then settled onto him. I was usually pretty good with this position. I began bobbing my hips on him, taking the full length into me. Johnny was beginning to glisten with beads of sweat. I held his eyes. A worried expression bloomed on his face and he shook his head. I lowered my torso, thinking he had something he wanted to say.

"You're getting me too close. I can no longer hold back. How do you want it?" he whispered to me.

"From behind . . . and then, once you've deposited your cum load in me, I want you to get your head under me and swallow the drippings of my cream pie."

"My pleasure," he answered and smiled.

We shifted positions smoothly. He had said he was close. I positioned my hand, as he penetrated me, again. I moved quickly to fondle his now retracted balls, and then pressed my finger against his anus. Johnny stroked into me harder and with more purpose. He's close. I pressed my finger into him, knowing what that sensation would do for the outcome we both sought. Sure enough, the audible groans and convulsive movements broadcast his climax. He pumped into me several more times, seeking the deposit every last drop of his cum deep in my puss. Once he was satisfied with his achievement, Johnny swiftly withdrew from me. The bed jiggled as he re-positioned himself, and I felt his head between my legs. Once his motion stopped, I figured he was ready to receive. I contracted my abdominal muscles to force out his embedded cum. I could feel it gushing out and presumably into his mouth. Several times, he raised his head to lick my clit and probe my love tunnel for more of his cum. When he was satisfied he got all he was going to get, I felt him move out from underneath me. I flipped over, reached to gently grasp Johnny's head at the ears, and kissed him deeply. I could taste the magnificent mixture of his man-milk and my pussy juice on his lips. I turned back around and sat next to Johnny on the bed.

"What did you think of your birthday present, my darling?" I asked.

"Damn, woman, that was incredible. You made me cum in my pants without even touching myself, and now, I'm hard, again. Is it my turn?" he asked, as he started to rise.

I immediately held up my hand. "Stop!" I commanded. "Nope, not your turn. There is more."

"More?"

"Yes, you are going to sit there and watch Johnny and I get dressed. Then, the three of us are going to dinner at *Le Pétale de Rose*, and then we will come back here for more playtime."

"Really? You expect me to go to dinner like this," Greg said, gesturing to his groin.

I could not see a wet spot, but his erection was clearly visible. "Yes, my darling . . . part of the excitement amplification," I answered.

"Amplification," he protested. "If it gets increased any more, I'll spontaneously combust."

We all laughed. I smiled. "We shall just have to risk it." I nodded for Johnny to get off the bed and to dress. I did the same. Greg remained in the chair and watched us both dress. When I was done, I checked my appearance, and then went to Greg. I reached my hand out, took his hand in mine, and pulled him to me. We hugged and kissed passionately.

"I love you very much," I whispered to him.

"I love you, Angie," he whispered back, "more than you will probably ever know. That was one helluva birthday present."

"I'm glad you liked it. We must thank Gloria and Johnny for supporting my fantasy birthday present to you."

"Absolutely."

"Now, just one more thing before we return to our guest and leave for dinner." Greg nodded his head in agreement. "I want you to reach up in there and grab you some honey to tide you over until we get home."

"Really?"

Greg reached up under my skirt. I spread my legs and squatted slightly to give him sufficient access. His fingers rubbed my pussy, inserted and wiggled several times, and then he withdrew them. He licked his fingers to get a taste without removing all of the essence. "I love you so much. You are one helluva woman and I am blessed to have you in my life."

"Hold that thought," I responded and turned to Johnny. "Sorry, Johnny. I just needed to give him some love."

"Quite alright," he answered.

"Thanks, buddy," Greg said, as he went to Johnny, shook his hand and embraced him. "You are a good and worthy friend."

"I'm honored to be of service."

"Shall we go, gentlemen?"

We took Greg's car with him driving. I insisted Johnny sit in front. I wanted them to talk. I simply listened and respectfully conveyed that it was their conversation. I did not want to participate. Surprisingly for two men, they chatted about what had just happened, Gloria, our last swinger's party and the next one planned for the following weekend.

Dinner was perfect from the exceptionally well-prepared meal of French cuisine to the service and ambiance. In fact, I would say it was near perfect. We laughed and joked about everything. I could not resist running my hand up the inside thigh of both men on either side of me, just to ensure their excitement did not wane during dinner. There was one more phase to my birthday present plan. The three of us shared a very nice *crème brûlée* dessert. I paid the bill with a handsome gratuity.

As we waited for the valet to return with Greg's automobile, Johnny asked, "Do you need me for the next phase, Angie?"

"Well, you have done your part. The answer to your question actually belongs to my husband."

Greg looked at me with a rather puzzled expression. "How so?"

"Well," I said and looked around to establish the absence of any eaves-droppers, "it depends whether you want to experience another of your fantasies."

"Which one?"

I laughed softly. "Does it matter?"

Both men chuckled. Greg answered, "Well, I suppose not. I'm just curious."

"You've told me for several years now that you were curious about playing with a cock."

Greg immediately looked to Johnny, who simply smiled. "Are you OK with this?"

"Actually, Greg, I'm a self-declared and I think demonstrated pansexual."

"What does that mean?"

"It means I do not care what your genital configuration is when it comes to sexual pleasure. I only care about your enthusiasm."

"Interesting."

"So, the choice is yours, my darling," I said. "I'm going to fuck you good. But, if you want to play with a cock, Johnny has agreed to participate . . . if you wish?"

Greg looked to Johnny, again. "Are you sure?"

"My pleasure. Your choice."

Greg smiled broadly. "OK. Let's do it."

The drive home was quite similar to the journey to the restaurant. Greg asked background questions about Johnny's youth and how he learned to enjoy female and male genitalia. It was fascinating to listen to their exchange. I knew many of the details, but it was Greg's questions that proved enlightening. What I did learn about Johnny came in through his revelation that he had played with and continues to play with several transgender friends, as does Gloria. They experienced a fairly broad, spectrum of sexual playmates, including pre-operation and post-surgery individuals, as well as two classic hermaphrodite individuals with confused genitalia.

We barely made it to the kitchen.

Greg asked, "How do you want to proceed?"

"This is your present from me. So, it is your choice. I know you have a good cum load stored up in there," I said and gently grasped his package. "Do you want my puss first or last?"

"Wow! A choice of bounty." He turned to Johnny. "Will you participate if I start with Angie?"

"I will gladly participate as you are comfortable allowing me to participate."

"Well, then, my dear, let's start with pussy."

"Your choice is my command," I replied and led the two men to our bedroom. I began undressing. The men followed.

Not surprisingly, both men were erect, naked before me and ready for action by the time I finished. I went to Greg, knelt before him, and reached my left hand toward Johnny. I took Greg's cock in my mouth.

Before I could grasp Johnny's cock, Greg stopped me. "I'm too close and I want your pussy," Greg announced.

Without a word, I stood, went to the edge of the bed and bent over, presenting my posterior to him. Greg moved behind me and plugged in easily, but did not begin thrusting immediately. I felt Johnny fondling Greg's balls behind me and actually rubbing my clit very effectively. Greg slowly began stroking into me. He was clearly trying to control the onset of his orgasmic assent. I tried to look back. Greg's eyes were closed and his head was arched back. Johnny must have been working Greg's balls and probably his rosebud as well. Then, suddenly, Greg began thrusting into me hard and fast. I just loved the sound of our slapping flesh.

"Oh god, oh god, ooohhh . . . ," he roared and pounded into me deeply. "Aaaahhhh." Greg shook violently. I could feel him shooting a massive load into me. He groaned and growled as he shook, and then just as suddenly, his knees gave way. Greg fell to the carpeted floor, landing with an audible thump. By the time I looked around to see if he was all right, Johnny had knelt down and swallowed him to the hilt, which in turn caused Greg to convulse even more. I did not want to move and I simply watched the two men. Greg's convulsions of pleasure seemed to subside without disappearing, as Johnny continued to work on his cock. Within a minute or so, Greg groaned deeply and began shaking in another rapid orgasm. The second peak was not as sharp, as high, or as violent as the first one; but it proved enough. Greg grabbed Johnny's head to stop him bobbing on his dick. "Enough!" he exclaimed. "Too sensitive."

Johnny smoothly released Greg and moved between my legs. He licked my inner thighs and up to my love tunnel. He was lapping up the remains of my cream pie. He wanted more of Greg's man-milk recently deposited in me. His attention felt so good. As he continued to lick and probe my pussy with his tongue, his fingers worked on my clit – rubbing, stroking and squeezing it gently. He was good . . . really good. My orgasmic climb began much quicker than I expected, and I let it ride. Johnny must have felt my assent. His actions took up an urgency I truly appreciated.

Then, it came. "Yes, yes . . . yes . . . ooohhh aaaww." My climax shook my body and nearly collapsed my knees. I grasped the comforter to keep from falling. As I began to come down, Johnny used his fingers to feel my vaginal contractions. "Well done, Johnny," I said and looked back at him. Greg was still on the floor. "Now, it's your turn," I added and smacked my right butt cheek. "Come fuck me and give me one more load."

Johnny did not need additional encouragement. He knew I was still well lubed and ready. He thrust into me directly and immediately began stroking with surprising urgency. He gripped my hips to hold them in place for his pounding. The slurping and slapping of our union enhanced the sensations. *Damn, I love this stuff.* His orgasm came in short order. He silently pumped his essence into me. When he was finished, he once again knelt behind me to enjoy my cream pie; this time with his own man-milk. Johnny truly enjoyed what he was doing, and I truly enjoyed his effort.

When the three of us had sufficiently recovered from our carnal pleasure, we took a group shower to rinse off the sweat of our exertions and the residue of orgasms. We dried off and moved to the bed collectively.

"You two nearly killed me tonight," Greg announced with a chuckle.

"That's why the French call it *la petite mort* – the little death," Johnny added.

We laughed, touched, hugged and kissed. We settled into our large bed with me between two beautiful men. It had been a good evening. I would know tomorrow, but I felt certain that Greg really enjoyed his birthday present. As slumber began to envelop us, I whispered to Greg, "Happy Birthday, honey."

—

Kathy

(This story is dedicated to Keri Y.)

—

Tommie's boat, or perhaps it was more properly called a yacht or a ship, was one of the largest, most magnificent boats in the Port Saint Lucie harbor. Five of my girls were with me and in an upbeat, anticipatory mood – Anne, Betsy, Caren, Daisy and Ellen. We arrived early, as Tommie had requested. He welcomed us aboard his vessel, introduced us to the crew – a captain, an engineer, the chief steward and his assistant – and showed us to the compartment where we could change and store our belongings. Tommie stood in the hatchway as several of the other women stripped off their clothes without the slightest hesitation or modesty.

"If I may have your attention, ladies," Tommie said, and waited for the giggling and chitchat to stop. "Thank you all for coming and supporting this little event. A word of clarification, if you will allow me." We waited for him to continue. "My guests, who will be arriving shortly, are very special clients of my firm. They are all banker executives from several institutions. I have invited them for an afternoon's entertainment, and y'all are the featured guests. There will be four men and one woman. They are quite aware of what we are about to do, so each of you should feel confident and comfortable. You will not offend any of them. I would like you to give them whatever pleasures they seek, and in case you are curious or concerned, the one woman, whom I have known for many years, prefers pussy, so she will be quite comfortable with whomever takes care of her. Any questions, so far?"

"I don't think so, Tommie. I have briefed all of my girls on the importance of this afternoon for you. We will do you right, trust me."

"I have confidence in all of you. Thank you, Kathy. Now, a few more items of instruction. Please remain covered and no sex on deck, until we are beyond landfall."

"What is landfall?" asked Betsy, one of the naked women.

Tommie smiled. "Sight of land. It will take us about 45 minutes or so for us to make it out to sea beyond sight of land. Then, you are welcome to get naked and do whatever my guests would like you to do. These are good people, so I do not anticipate even the slightest of hiccups this afternoon. However, if any of you might happen to feel uncomfortable or threatened in any way, please call Kathy or me immediately. We will take care of whatever the problem is. Remember, this is a pleasure cruise for everyone, including the working ladies."

The chief steward in the passageway beyond our sight said to Tommie, "Sir, your guests are arriving on dock."

"Thank you, Ross. I will be right up," he said over his shoulder, and then turned back to us. "Show time approaches. Any other questions?" Both Tommie and I look to each of the women. Everyone shook their heads to the negative. "OK. Change your clothes as you wish, abide the rules as I have defined them, and let's have some fun today."

Tommie left. All of us changed out of our street clothes and into nice bikinis. Each of us had a distinct, unique color or pattern, so we could be easily identified. There were some magnificent bodies, all of whom I have sampled and enjoyed. They knew what they were doing and enjoyed it all. I checked everyone, and they followed me. We were all on the primary fantail party area, when Tommie's guests arrived. All of them were in their late 30's or early 40's; all of the bankers were better than average attractive.

"Welcome aboard, everyone. Please allow me to make the introductions. We have Claire, Curt, Damon, Mike and Theo," Tommie said, gesturing toward each person to align the names. No family names were given. I recognized none of Tommie's guests, and we did not need to know them, only make them happy. "And, here we have, Kathy, Ellen, Betsy, Daisy, Caren and Anne," again, gesturing toward each of us. "While this is intended to be an afternoon of fun, pleasure, entertainment and relaxation, I ask you to remain clothed . . . to the legal standard," everyone laughed, "and no sex on deck until we are beyond landfall. After that, your imagination is the limit. The ladies here," he nodded to us, "are for your pleasure, and they truly enjoy what they do." I nodded my head in agreement. "There is plenty of food and drink in the dining room, and the stewards will supply your every desire . . . well, for food and drink. The ladies will handle the pleasures of the flesh. Now, to be direct and frank, please, no excrement. We will clean up any cum, but you will clean up any shit or piss." Everyone laughed, again. "Any questions?" There were none. "Very well, then. Let's get underway." Tommie turned to me. "Kathy, if you would be so kind, please join me on the bridge for our departure."

"As you wish," I answered and followed Tommie up the ladder to the mid-deck, and then up another ladder to the bridge. The captain waited for Tommie.

"Let's get underway, Joe," Tommie ordered.

The captain issued a series of orders to prepare the ship for sea. We could hear and just barely feel the engines starting up. The mooring lines were released. The captain worked the controls and the ship moved slowly away from the dock and into the channel. Tommie sat in a raised chair next to the captain, or rather the captain's station, and Joe moved back and forth across the bridge to ensure his clearances and manage our progress. I stood behind Tommie's chair with my hands on his shoulders. The ship entered the Saint Lucie River channel. We went under the US-1 and A1A bridges, passed Stuart and Sewall's Point, crossed the Inland Waterway and exited into open ocean through Saint Lucie Inlet. The captain headed the vessel due east.

"Well done, Joe."

"Thank you, sir."

"What do you say to a blow-job reward? Kathy, here, is really quite good."

Joe looked somewhat surprised and puzzled, but apparently gained assurance with Tommie's serious expression. "Well, that would be very generous of both of you."

"Excellent. I'll take the helm, and Kathy will give you one of her exceptional blow-jobs. Only thing I ask is you stand here, so I can watch."

Joe moved aside. Tommie stood at the bridge station and assumed control of the ship. I went to my knees in front of Captain Joe, and unzipped his white uniform, nautical shorts. He was wearing briefs, so rather than fumble around with his underwear, I decided to unbuckle the belt on his shorts, and lower both the shorts and his brief. He had a handsome, cut and rigid cock by the time I got him released.

I went to work on his cock, caressing, stroking and pushing him into my throat all the way to the hilt. I grasped his butt-cheeks and pulled him toward me, thrusting his cock past my lips and into my throat, so he got the full sensation. Joe picked up the rhythm, allowing me to move my hands to his balls and butt crack. The conclusion did not take long to achieve. He struggled to remain standing with wobbly legs and a heaving chest, offering audible heavy breathing. In a minute or so, Joe regained his composure and returned his uniform to proper form. I stood and returned to a position behind Tommie's empty chair.

"The evidence of your success and skill are remarkable, my dear Kathy. Well done, darlin'."

I licked my lips, smacked them a few times, and said, "Thank you, Tommie. And, thank you for your deposit, Joe."

Joe leaned forward and kissed my cheek. "I've heard of your reputation, but I had no idea you were so good. Thank you, Kathy, and thank you, sir."

Tommie smiled and nodded his head. "I cherish loyal employees, Joe. Now, if you would be so kind, Joe, please confirm our position beyond landfall and make an announcement to our guests, so the party may begin in earnest."

"Yes sir." Joe checked the radar display, the GPS-annotated navigation chart, made a few measurements, looked astern, and then turned to Tommie. "We are confirmed beyond landfall."

"Excellent. Make the announcement."

Joe flipped a switch on a control panel and picked up the hand microphone. "Attention, please. We are now beyond landfall. Enjoy yourselves."

"Thank you, Joe. Please take the con. Take us east another couple of miles for extra measure, let's say 20 miles out from shore, and then slow to headway to hold our position."

I had no idea what all of that meant, but it sounded very nautical and professional. I leaned forward and whispered in Tommie's right ear. "How about I milk you, now."

Tommie turned his head and kissed me on the lips. "Not just, yet. Let us go below and check on our guests, but first, how about you strip off that bikini and give Joe a good look-see of the woman who just sucked him off with professional élan."

I did as Tommie requested. The air felt good on my skin. I smiled at Joe and did a little pirouette, so he could see my entire body. Joe nodded his head in appreciation and returned to his task. Tommie had stripped off his suit and led me down the ladder. He had a well-maintained body, especially for a near 50-year-old man. No one happened to be on the mid-deck.

On the main deck, everyone in sight was naked. Several couples were just sitting and talking. Betsy was on her knees in front of Damon and tending to his pleasure. Inside the main cabin, Mike sat in a narrow chair with Ellen straddling him and pumping away on his pole, while he fondled both her ample breasts and sucked on her nipples. They remained oblivious to anything beyond their connection. Claire nearly lay in a large, well-cushioned chair, spread before Daisy, who knelt between Claire's exquisite, long legs. The scene was magnificently seductive. Claire's elegant breasts jiggled nicely with very, prominent, erect nipples above small, tight areolas, as her chest convulsed toward her climax. What a sight!   Tommie did not wait to see the conclusion and led me into his master stateroom that occupied most of the port side forward of the main cabin. He closed the hatch behind him.

I grasped his erect cock and stroked him gently a few times.

"You are the best, dear one."

"Thanks, Tommie."

"Would you mind doing all the work this time?"

"It would be my pleasure to top you," I answered and gently pushed him to the bed. I just knew he wanted more than a blow-job. "Do you want it in my pussy or ass?" I always made sure I was ready for either when I serviced clients, since I could never predict what they might want.

"Pussy will be just fine, and thanks for asking."

I coaxed Tommie up to be fully on the bed, fluffed a pillow under his head, spread his legs, and then knelt between his legs fluff him up to full attention. Once I was satisfied with his readiness, I stood over him, so he could get a very good look at the object of his desire. I had all of my pelvic hair removed permanently a few years ago, thus, the view was unobstructed. I kegeled a few times to force out some of my wetness. I managed to deposit a couple of drops on his upper chest.

"Dear God, woman, you are incredible."

"Well, thank you. Clearly, I am ready for you."

"Clearly!"

"So, here we go."

I moved my feet down to straddle his waist. I crouched, adjusted my position, grasped him, gave him a few strokes, and then lowered my pussy to feel his cock head touch my pussy lips. I sort of kissed him with those lips, teased his cock, and felt him rise. He tried to thrust into me, but I withdrew slightly and pushed his hips down.

"Don't move," I commanded. "This is my show."

Tommie nodded his agreement.

I lowered myself to him, again. I held him still and touched his cock-head several times, and took his cock-head in. I twisted slightly to give him a little more sensation, and then withdrew. I repeated the process several times before I lowered myself all the way down on him. I wiggled and flexed my pelvic muscles to grab his shaft, and squeezed him as I raised myself without letting him completely out. I worked on him slowly with purpose to enhance the sensations and his anticipation. I felt the slightest movement to thrust his hips. He was ready for his release. It was time to get serious. I played with him a few more times, and then I moved my feet next to his hips and leaned forward, placing my hands under his arms. I began stroking my hips to rhythmically swallow his full length. As I could feel him swell, I increased the pace, rocking my hips, feeling his rigid shaft moving inside me – that exquisite sensation. I rolled my hips forward to rub my clit on his shaft, as I stroked on him and pound it on his pelvis. The rise to my own peak began. I knew what was coming. The only question remaining in my thoughts was whether I could get him to blow his load before I climaxed the first time. I tried to push the hot waves mounting in my groin aside, and focused my mind and body on his cock within me. I walked the edge of my orgasm until the unmistakable tremors and deep groans of his orgasm unleashed the eruption of my climax. I struggled against my convulsions to continue pumping him, until he raised both hands.

"Stop, stop, stop!" he gurgled.

I did as he commanded. The sensations had probably become too intense in the aftermath of his orgasm. While I did not move my hips on him, I did use my muscles to rhythmically squeeze him like a cow's teat. When I was satisfied he had completed giving me his seed, I rose off him, shuffled my feet forward so that I was squatting over his tight, nearly hairless belly and kegeled my vaginal muscles. This time to squeeze out his man-milk, so he could watch it drip on his abdomen. Once we watched the last drop leave my puss, I shifted my position so that I could slowly lick up the drippings off his skin. He shimmied with the sensations.

"You are one helluva woman, Kathy," he said, and then pulled me up to lay on him. He kissed me passionately, licking my lips for his own taste. "Where did you learn all that?"

"From my brother and sister, and others."

"Amazing," he said. "If I may ask, how long have you been doing this?"

"What? Charging for my services?" Tommie nodded his head. "A couple of years. My sister and I run the show."

Tommie nodded his head once more. "Again, if I may ask, how old are you?"

I rose up off of him and searched his eyes. "Are you asking me as a friend, or as an officer of the court?"

"Oh you are a wise one . . . as a friend and loyal client."

"I am 18, almost 19."

"Dear God above, you must have had one helluva childhood to be so good at such a young age."

I lowered myself back down on him to rest my head in the crook of his neck. "It was a good and worthy childhood," I whispered. "My sister is two years older than me. She started the business, and I joined her as a partner."

"I probably should not ask more, but my curiosity is driving me wild. Would you consent to retaining me as your lawyer, your legal representative and counselor?"

"How much would that cost?"

"One dollar, for you, your sister and your business. I will continue to pay you handsomely for services rendered, like today. All I ask you for is the straight and honest truth."

"I will need to consult with my sister, but I think we can do that. I have always been pretty open about my life."

"We will assume your sister consents, which means our conversations are now covered by attorney-client privilege, which in turn means, I cannot be compelled to divulge any communications between us, even to the police or courts."

"That sounds pretty good, since what we are doing is not exactly in accordance with the law."

"Then, why do you do it?"

"We love sex, plain and simple. We make really good money, doing what we love to do."

"Not many people can say that about what they do in life. So, you were a minor when you started . . . started . . ."

"Hooking," I interjected.

Tommie laughed. "Yes . . . since you got into prostitution."

"Yes, I was actually 16, when Nancy introduced me to the business."

"Amazing. Who is the youngest of the girls onboard?"

"Do you really want to know?"

"Yes. I probably shouldn't, but yes, I do."

"Daisy. She was the one eating at the 'Y' on Claire. She is 15."

"Damn, do her parents know?"

"At least her mother does. I do not know about her father. I've not asked her that. We can ask her, if you wish."

"No. You can and should talk to Nancy about our conversation, but the less who know, the better for all of us."

"OK."

We lay there in quiet for a few minutes. Tommie was stroking my hair, fondling a breast and gently squeezing an erect nipple, while I played with his cock and balls. He was clearly contemplating something, but I did not want to disturb his thoughts. His cock was beginning to respond to my touch.

"We probably should check on our guests," Tommie said softly.

"As you wish."

I sat up, allowing him to stand.

"I'm not dripping or anything, am I?"

I grabbed his cock, leaned forward and licked the head. "Nope, you're fine."

"You are incorrigible."

I laughed. "I try to be." I smiled at him.

Tommie nodded his head for me to follow him. The main deck had become a mass of flesh – eight intertwined and connected bodies – four men and four women. Hand, arms, legs, feet and other body parts were active and doing something.

"Looks like everyone is enjoying themselves," mumbled Tommie. He walked past the flesh pile, out onto the fantail deck.

We found Daisy in a chair, leaning back, nearly reclined, with her legs spread wide. Claire was between Daisy's legs with her face buried in pussy. Daisy smiled and winked at us. Claire would not be distracted from the pleasure she sought. We found two chairs in the shade of the overhang and tried not to disturb Claire and Daisy.

"What can I get you to drink?" Tommie whispered in my ear.

"Diet Coke, please," I whispered back to him.

Tommie went back into the cabin. I sat down facing the two women. Claire appeared to know what she was doing quite well, and Daisy was certainly enjoying Claire's skills. The urge quickly blossomed in my groin. My right hand almost instinctively went to my clit and began rubbing my swollen button. Tommie returned without drinks, saw me masturbating, and sat quietly beside me to watch me and the two, other women. I continued to rub my clit and the all-too-familiar feeling grew quickly. One of the assistant stewards returned with our drinks. I took a quick look at him; he seemed unfazed by the hedonism around him, as he delivered the drinks to the table in front of us and returned to the galley. I continued my rubbing. Even Tommie started stroking his now stiff cock. The up-slope to the peak approached quickly. I could hear Daisy's orgasm, and kept my eyes closed and my thoughts focused on my impending climax. Before I could reach my sure ascent, I felt warm, soft hands on the inside of my thighs. Somewhat startled, I quickly looked to see Claire's broad smile and sparkling eyes moving smoothly toward my puss. I stopped my rubbing, removed my hand, and gave Claire access to my swollen and now throbbing clit. Claire needed no guidance. She wrapped her lips around my clit, licking the head of my clit. She began sucking on me like a small cock and flicking her tongue across the head. The sensations were exquisite. She inserted two fingers into my very slippery and ready puss. Her fingertips pressed forward on my G-spot each time she stroked into me. Claire sucked on me rhythmically. Her tongue expertly attended to my clit. She was really good and truly enjoyed what she was doing; this had to be her pleasure, and I was happy to oblige. Claire made quick work of finishing me off.

"Aaaooohhh," I groaned deeply . . . and, I must have been louder than I thought. By the time I came down from the peak and opened my eyes, Claire was grinning from ear-to-ear, obviously quite pleased with her accomplishment.

Daisy was straddling Tommie, squatting rapidly on his rigid cock. To my amazement, over my left shoulder, the rest of the group was standing in all their glory, applauding the performance they just witnessed. Daisy attained her peak and pressed through the intensity of her orgasm to continue her efforts on Tommie, and she was soon rewarded.

Claire stood, kissed me on the lips, and allowed me to taste my scent, and then went into the main cabin. Daisy instinctively knew I was coming to her. She managed to turn, holding Tommie's cock inside her, so that she was now facing away from Tommie, who in turn placed his hands on both her modest breasts. Once I was positioned between his legs and hers outside his, she unplugged from him, but she remained on him. I moved closer and captured Tommie's cock, as it slipped out of Daisy's pussy. I took him completely in my mouth, sucked out the last few drops of his milk, and licked his entire shaft for all their combined juices. I could smell his cum and hers. I finished on his cock as the distinct trickle of his cum appeared at her hole and bottom of her pussy lips. I began lapping up the combined juices oozing from her puss. I could see and feel her kegeling to push out the content of her puss. As the flow slowed, I probed my tongue into her, to pick up anything else I could taste. I took a few breaks to swallow Tommie, so he would not feel neglected. When I had swallowed everything I could, I stood. Again, the group applauded. I bowed to acknowledge their praise. Daisy stood, and then Tommie.

"Would anyone like to take a swim?" Tommie asked.

A handful of the group or so responded in the affirmative. Tommie went to a bulkhead mounted intercom box on the fantail, instructing Joe to stop the ship for swimming and for the crew to take up lifeguard stations.

Once the boat stopped, several people dove into the ocean, even before the stern swimming platform and ladder had been deployed. Nearly everyone eventually went into the water, floating and frolicking in the water. Even I took a quick dip to cool off.

I was on the fantail deck, not far from Tommie, when Chief Steward Ross appeared.

"Sir, it is 17:15, as you wished to be notified."

"Thank you, Ross." Tommie went to the stern railing and shouted, "Attention, everyone." He waited for the splashing to stop. "It is time to come aboard and head back to port. I agreed to get everyone back ashore by six."

Everyone complied. As soon as everyone was back aboard and the stewards had re-stowed the swimming equipment, Tommie went to the intercom box and ordered Captain Joe to return us to port. The engines were engaged, and we were soon speeding back to Port Saint Lucie.

"Just as we did on the way out, I must ask you to be sufficiently dressed outside the cabin, in public view, once we have made landfall, which should be in about 10-15 minutes, and to refrain from sexual activity on observable decks. You have 45-60 minutes to knock off one more before we dock, so by all means, take advantage of the main cabin and the staterooms below deck."

Naked people turned to enter the cabin, presumably for their last hurrah.

Tommie turned to me. "You are welcome to join them, my dear, if you would like another poke. I need to dress and join Joe on the bridge."

"I'll stay with you, if you don't mind."

"As you wish," he answered and led me through copulating bodies in the main cabin.

I admired his body as long as I could, and then put my bikini back on. Tommie nodded his head, again. I followed him up both ladders to the bridge. By the time we greeted Captain Joe, the skyline of the taller shoreline buildings appeared above the western horizon.

"Joe, please announce landfall to our guests."

"Yes sir." Captain Joe moved the necessary switches and picked up the hand microphone. "We have made landfall."

The return to port was comparatively quick and professionally efficient, without difficulty or obstacles. With the mooring process underway, Tommie thanked Joe for his service and instructed him to secure the vessel once everyone disembarked. Tommie left the bridge. I gave Captain Joe a hug and kiss on the cheek, and then followed Tommie. On the fantail deck, I went to the port side railing, away from dockside. Tommie looked at me, shook his head and motioned for me to stand beside him. I did as he wished, and stood to his left and slightly behind him. My girls formed a line on the port side, still in their bikinis, to give Tommie's guests one last view. The bankers were all dressed. Hugs and kisses were exchanged before they thanked Tommie for the afternoon's entertainment and departed.

Tommie waited for the bankers to clear the dock and turned to my girls. "Thank you very much, ladies. Well done. I think we had a successful cruise. You can dress. Our engagement is concluded. Kathy, if you would join me in my office. . . ."

With the hatch closed, Tommie opened his office safe. He handed me a stack of three, bank-strapped bundles of crisp, new, $20 bills – $6,000, $1,000 for each of us.

"Thank you, Tommie. It was a pleasure doing business with you."

"You are most welcome, Kathy. I'm sure we shall do business, again. Please talk to your sister, as we discussed earlier. If you agree, please call my office and make an appointment, so we can sign the proper papers. You are a good woman, and I am honored to know you."

"Thank you very much."

Tommie held up his right index finger for me to wait. He returned to the safe and handed me another bank-strapped bundle, but this one was new $50 bills – $5,000. "This is a bonus. You are an exceptional young woman with elegant girls. That is for you . . . your choice whether you share it." He opened a desk drawer to retrieve a small satchel. "You should probably put those in here, so they are not so obvious."

I placed the currency bundles in the bag. He closed the bag and handed it to me. I thanked him again, and kissed him on the lips. He smiled. I went across the passageway to put on my street clothes. We joined the girls on the fantail, said our goodbyes and disembarked ourselves. It had been a good afternoon all the way around.

—

Danni

—

I was tired. It had been a long day, made longer by my advancing pregnancy – two months remaining. Some days, the customers at the bank can be a bit prickly. This was one of those days. I just wanted to go home and relax for just a few minutes.

My life had been complicated for too long. My boyfriend and impregnater had proven himself unworthy one too many times, and we had not even reached marriage. With his latest transgressions, I had finally told him to fuck off and get out of my life. I had no intention of listing him as our child's father. I would rather say father unknown than have him in our lives. He was nothing to me. As all that turmoil went down, my father asked me to move back into my childhood home, two months earlier. He had been living alone since my mother's passing three years prior from pancreatic cancer. Home was like a welcome sanctuary, and I was grateful for his offer. Moving back home had been easier than I imagined.

The house was quiet when I entered. I went to the kitchen, retrieved a small can of sparkling water from the refrigerator, and went to my bedroom to change clothes. I needed to get out of my business clothes and put on something much more comfortable. The fizz from the carbonated water felt good to my throat. The process took a half dozen minutes, and then I went to the living room to watch some of my recorded daily programs – nice mindless entertainment.

During the moment of silence before the show returned from the commercials, I heard what I thought was a muffled grunt from the other end of the house. I muted the television to see if I could hear anymore. There it was. I heard it, again. I slowly went to where I thought the sounds had come from, partly concerned about not jumping into something bad, but also to see if I could hear anymore. When I reached Dad's bedroom, the door was not closed, but not fully open either. The sound was clearer. It sounded like he was in some sexual situation. My curiosity compelled me to sneak a peak. As a child, I had seen my parents copulating more than a few times, but Mom was not here, now. I inched forward quietly to see past the partially open door. Dad was sitting on the side of his bed with only a T-shirt on. His eyes were closed. I inched forward a little bit more. I was surprised, perhaps even shocked, to see our neighbor Stan completely naked, on his knees between Dad's spread legs, and bobbing his head on Dad's cock. *Damn!* I had no idea he would accept man-to-man sex. *Clearly, he is. He's enjoying it. Stan has done this before. Wow, I had no idea he was a cocksucker, either.* I also had no idea how long I was watching them.

"That's it, buddy," Dad said without opening his eyes. "I'm close."

Stan was working Dad's cock like he truly loved it . . . enjoyed every thrust onto him, even to the hilt, down his throat. Impressive! *Yes, he has done this before.* I looked back to Dad's eyes and they were locked on me. I smiled. He winked.

"Here you go . . . oh yes . . . aaaahhhhh . . . that it. Suck out that milk . . . all that milk."

Stan swallowed every drop Dad had to offer. There was no spillage. Stan finished, and then he noticed me as well. He actually raised his right hand from between Dad's legs and wiggled his fingers as he smiled.

I had seen enough and figured they did not need an audience to finish up. I went to the kitchen and sat down at the table. In a few minutes, they both came to the kitchen – dressed, this time, well at least in shorts and T-shirts.

"Great to see you, Danni," Stan said.

Dad sat down at the table with me.

"Great to see you, Stan. I hope y'all had fun."

"Oh, we did," Dad interjected.

"Yes, we did. Gotta go. See y'all around."

"Bye, Stan," I said.

I waited until I heard the front door open and close. I looked at Dad. "How long have y'all been doing that?"

"Oh, a couple of weeks."

"How did it start?"

"Well . . . kinda hard to say. I suppose we had been hinting around for a few weeks. I was bemoaning my extended lack of sex, and he kept hinting he could help. Finally, I asked him directly if he wanted to suck my cock."

"Really? That was pretty bold."

"He was pretty brave. After we crossed the line, he confessed that he was very worried I might have some homophobic reaction. We eventually got past that."

"I had no idea you were into men."

"Well, sweetie neither did I. I suppose that first time I was curious. It had been so long since I had a good blow-job, I wanted to know how he would do."

"How did he do?"

Dad smiled. "Really good, actually. He is an enthusiastic cocksucker."

"Well, how about that! I had no idea. He's always been a low-key, friendly guy."

"Indeed. I had no idea either. Surprises around every corner."

"How long has he been into cock?"

"Since he was about eight years old."

"Wow! Have you done him?"

"No! No interest. I'm not into cock or cum. I just wanted a good blow-job."

"Have you fucked him?"

Dad stared at me for several seconds without any communicative expression. "Well . . . yes."

"I'll be damned. Dad . . . why?"

"I haven't had any since well before Mom was diagnosed."

"So, you're OK fucking a man?"

"Sure, why not? He's good. Ass is ass. I get off. He loves it. Everybody is happy. I'm sorry you saw that."

"Why?" I asked.

"Well, apparently, you are offended by man-sex."

"Nope, not offended at all. Just surprised . . . I didn't expect it from you, or from Stan, for that matter."

"I don't need your approval," Dad said.

"No, you don't." *Well, now, do I take the next obvious step? Oh yeah, why the hell not. No one will get hurt.* "Would you like my help?"

He looked deeply into my eyes, and I did not blink. "What exactly are you asking?"

"Well . . . I haven't been getting much sex either, lately."

"You're pregnant."

"Yes, I am. Does that mean I don't deserve sexual pleasure?"

"Are you actually asking me to fuck you?" Dad said rather directly and pointedly.

"Yeah, I guess so. But, if you don't want to, can I at least suck you off? I miss the taste of man-milk."

"Damn, Danni. I had no idea you were so horny."

"You never asked."

"You would actually do your old man?"

"Sure. It's not like you can get me pregnant." We both laughed. "You are not going to hurt me, or coerce me into doing something I do not want to do. Plus, once the baby is born, you can help with taking care of her. After all, you are retired and a stay-at-home dad."

"Now, there is that."

"Would you like me to show you?" I asked.

"Really?"

"Sure. Why not? I can show you I'm serious."

"If you want . . . ," he answered rather meekly.

I moved to his side of the table. He turned his chair to face me. I knelt in front of him. "You're sure you're OK with this?" I asked. He nodded his head as I looked into his eyes. *He's actually a little scared. Well, Dad so am I. Neither of us have ever done this.* I unfastened his shorts and opened them. He was already hard and sprang to attention when his cock was released from the confines of his shorts. I had seen my father's flaccid penis many times during my youth, but I had never seen it erect and swollen to full glory, and I certainly never touched it. Now, I held his magnificent specimen in my hand, feeling the thin, velvety soft skin move so freely over the hard shaft underneath. What's more, his cock-head was much larger than I remembered it. I moistened his cock-head with my mouth to feel the smooth curves and glorious shape. *My oh my, is this a magnificent cock or what?* I began working on his cock. He was thicker than other cocks I have had in my mouth. It took me longer than usual or expected to relax my throat and get my lips down to his balls. I kept up a regular pace alternating hand strokes, deep throat thrusts, and tongue caresses of his cock-head. I had not even reached the fondling-his-balls stage, or fingering his brown-eye, when he exploded into my mouth. I kept going on him, swallowing as fast as I could. *Wow! That is a surprisingly big cum load, especially after depositing a load in Stan's mouth an hour or so ago.* I continued extracting every last drop from him. *Nice! He sure does taste good. I have missed this delightful elixir for all these years. Maybe he will become a regular supplier.* No more pearls for consumption could be licked up and his rod had softened a little.

"That was fun," I said.

"It was breathtaking," he responded. Dad reached, grasped my head and leaned forward to kiss me on the lips. "I had no idea you were so good with dicks."

"Well, you never asked. I doubt the topic would have ever come up, if I had not seen you enjoying Stan munching on your pole."

Dad chuckled a little. "Yes, but that just happened."

I flopped his dick back and forth a few times. "Like this just happened."

"You got that right." He paused, looking into my eyes. He patted his knee, gesturing for me to sit on his knee. I did. "All those years your Mom was sick were sexless for us. I even stopped masturbating during the last six months of caring for her. I was just too tired. Stan was kind of hinting around, not really saying or asking anything directly. I was so desperate for anything that when he suggested he could help, I just whipped out my dick. Before I could blink, he was on his knees and swallowing my dick, and I let him. It felt so good. I think I must have cum a quart that first time. He nearly choked on it, there was so much." We both laughed at the image. "Do you want to do this, again?"

"Right now?"

Dad laughed. "No. I'm good, but I'm not that good. I mean tomorrow, the day after, and the day after that."

"I've not reached any limit, yet; so, I would say, yes, I do . . . for as long as you will give it to me."

"So, you don't have a problem doing your father?"

"Do you have a problem doing your daughter?"

Dad laughed, again. "Good point. I guess not."

"Then, neither do I."

"Can I lick you off . . ."

Before he could finish his sentence, I stood, pulled down my shorts, hopped up on the table next to him and spread my legs wide.

"My, aren't you the eager beaver." He turned his chair, buried his face, and went to work on my pussy. He was not the best muncher I had experienced, but then again, he was probably out of shape . . . had not tasted pussy in a long time. He inserted two fingers in my wet slit and began working my G-spot, as he sucked on and licked my clit. *Oh yes, that is good enough.* To my surprise, rocketing to the peak took less time than usual for me. He wanted to keep going, but my clit was so sensitive after my climax that it was almost painful. I stopped him. This time, I reached down, grabbed his head and leaned forward to kiss him deeply . . . with tongue this time.

We continued to exchange oral pleasure for several days at least once or twice a day, and sometimes more often. Then, one morning, I noticed him still asleep with the top sheet and comforter thrown back, and some very attractive morning wood. It was too much to resist. I carefully stood on the bed, straddled him, and lowered myself onto him, guiding his cock into me. He woke up as he entered me and smiled. I stroked on him for several minutes, but my distended belly exceeded the capacity of my legs. Holding him inside me, I turned to face away from him and gently moved us to a doggy position, which was easier for me. Dad knew exactly what was expected of him. He waited until I was settled in position, and then he began thrusting into me. He varied his position numerous times, clearly attempting to give me more stimulation than just penetration. I reached between my legs to fondle his balls, press on the base and pushed a finger against his rosebud. He groaned and pumped his seed deep into me. Incredibly, he kept going and kept himself hard, obviously wanting to get me off, if he could. My orgasm proved more difficult than usual. I was starting to get uncomfortable and my big belly made almost any position harder. He tried so hard.

I finally stopped him. "My legs are starting to give out, Dad. Sorry. I know you are working to get me off, too."

"Why don't you lay on your back at the edge of the bed and let me see if I can lick you off."

"Are you sure? My pussy still full of your cum."

"Not to worry, my darling daughter."

I moved as he suggested. He grabbed a couple of tissues. As he mopped up, I squeezed out what I could for him. The taste of him would probably still be there, but he wiped up most of it, at least to his satisfaction. He soon buried his face in my pussy and worked my swollen clit really well – sucking, licking and rubbing. To my pleasant surprise, my orgasm came quickly and rolled through like waves of hot lava. As I descended from the peak, he licked all of me and even probed my love tunnel with his tongue. He was really good with his tongue.

"Whew!" I exclaimed. I raised my head to capture his eyes. "That was impressive. You know, Dad, I have never been fucked so lovingly since I began fucking at 12 years old."

He smiled. "I'm glad you enjoyed it. I certainly did. Someday, you will have to tell me about that."

"Sure. But first, I'm thirsty. Let's get some orange juice."

We went to the kitchen naked. Dad went to the refrigerator to retrieve the jug of orange juice and a couple of glasses. I sat at the table. He poured two tall glasses, and then sat across from me at the modest square table. The cold orange juice felt and tasted really good.

"Are you really sure you are OK with what we are doing?" he asked.

I had to chuckle . . . *is he having buyer's remorse?* "Yes, Dad. I think it is great. I'm just sorry we missed out on all those years."

"The laws says . . ."

"Fuck the law!" I interjected, more sharply than I intended. "How can what we just did be wrong. I meant what I said in the bedroom. I have never been fucked so lovingly, and I really meant it."

"Thank you for that, Danni. But, I feel compelled to say, the law calls what we just did incest – a very serious crime. I do not want to feel guilty of a crime."

"Then don't. I don't. I feel great. The law is wrong. The law does not recognize, accept or understand the love we share. Pleasure is pleasure," I said and chuckled softly, "kinda like you said, an ass is an ass. You haven't fucked me in the ass, yet, but you will, and I am willing to bet a dollar to donuts that my ass will probably feel quite like Stan's ass, or any other ass you've fucked. You have not forced me to do anything I did not want to do. You did not hurt me. I understand why the law must exist, but the law should change and improve. How can it possibly be wrong . . . what we just did . . . and we will do many more times, as long as you want to."

"Oh, I want to. I have missed sex, which is probably one of many reasons I accepted Stan's attention so easily. Your Mom was never really into sex. Oh sure, she was sexual in the early days. After all, we created your older sister and you. But, once your sister and you were born, it was like something flipped a switch in her. You and I have done more in the last few days than your Mom and I did for the last 25 years of her life. I really missed it, Danni."

"Well, I love it. So, you can have as much as you want. I just hope you do not tire of me, or I wear you out."

This time he laughed. "It is so exciting fucking you. I am just amazed that you turned out so sexual. I had no idea such a treasure trove was so close. I'm so glad things worked out like they did and you moved back home."

"Me too, Dad. After the baby is born and I heal up, I really want to show you my kinky side."

"Your kinky side? As if doing your dear old dad is not kinky enough."

We both laughed heartily. "Yeah, my friends will freak when I tell them what I have discovered."

"Whoa, be careful now. We may not agree with the law and we may defy the law, but the more people who know about what we are doing, the more risk we take that some overly zealous police officer or prosecutor could ruin our lives."

"I understand all that, Dad. But, as you will soon learn, I have friends that are far more out there than we are. It's incredible believe me. I know men and women who have been doing parents, siblings, grandparents, neighbors, and one guy a little bit younger than me, who has been fucking his great-grand-mother since he was 12 years old. In fact, that guy has been doing his mother and grandmother for years. The women in his life have been sucking on him since before he can remember."

"Wow! That is so hard to believe. I had no idea."

"Most folks don't. Getting to know some of these people has helped me learn."

"I had no idea," he repeated.

I giggled a little at the thought. "Knowing some of my friends and now experiencing your magnificent cock, I'll bet some of my friends are going to want some of your cock, too."

"Will you share?"

I smiled broadly. "Of course I will. I will proudly share. You may not know how great your cock is, but to me, it is the perfect combination of length, thickness and shape. I cannot imagine a more perfect cock. I really want to show you off to my friends, and I know there are a few of my guy-friends who are going to want some, too."

"As long as the men don't expect me to suck their cocks, eat their cum, or take their cocks in my ass, they can have all they want."

"They will have no complaints, of that I am certain."

"How about I make us some breakfast," Dad said. "And, you can tell me about how you got started."

"Sure. You want me to help?"

Dad held up his hand. "Not necessary." He stood. His cock was in a semi-aroused state. I really wanted to go after it, again, but I left him alone. I was hungry. "You just sit there and relax, and tell me the story."

"OK. Are you sure? You might not want to hear some of this."

He stopped mid-stride and spun around, appendages flying. "Did anyone hurt you?"

Damn, it is so nice seeing him completely naked and comfortable being naked in front of me. "No, no! No one hurt me, or forced me to do anything." He nodded his head, turned and set about his task. "Dede taught me how to masturbate when I was seven years old."

"Your sister Dede?"

"Yes. I saw her masturbating one night, and I begged her to show me. She eventually did. It felt so good. I actually got to see her climax a few times and talked to her about what an orgasm was. It took a few years to finally experience one . . . well, at least the early version."

"Have you done each other?"

"No. We never did. My best friend Becky showed me how to give and receive oral . . . at least with a female. I soon learned that Becky was doing her

Dad. It took me a lot of persistence, but I finally got Becky's Dad to fuck me. He was very gentle, since he knew it was my first time."

"Did he do Dede, too?"

"No, she did not want to, although it was offered more than once. Now that I think of it, I don't know when or with whom she started fucking. I'll have to ask her. She's never been quite as . . . how shall I say this . . . enthusiastic about sex as I am. Heck, Becky and I did her Dad together a few times. She and her Dad are still intimate to this day."

"Amazing! I am in awe."

"Just part of a healthy sex life, Dad. Heck, if you want to do Becky, with or without me, I'm fairly certain that can be arranged. Becky and I are still great friends, still intimate on occasion, and I know she would love to play with your beautiful cock."

Dad laughed. "I already have a lot to adjust to with all this."

"You're doing a really good job at that adjustment, Dad."

"Thanks, Danni. All of this is rather overwhelming. Your Mom passing three years ago was traumatic. She was a good woman . . . just not very sexual. I have gone from nothing but masturbation a few weeks ago to enjoying blow-jobs from a man and now fucking my youngest daughter. It may not seem like much to you, but it is mind-blowing to me."

My father completed his preparations, served up two plates of eggs, bacon, fried potatoes and whole-wheat toast, and refilled our orange juice glasses. "You've always been a great cook, Dad. Thanks for this," I said, glancing at the plate before me.

"My pleasure, Danni. Thank you for being such a good daughter."

I swallowed my mouthful, chuckled at his words, and patted my round belly. "Not that good, Dad."

We both laughed hard. *I really need to thank Stan when I see him next. This would have probably never happened if he had not been on his knees blowing Dad.* The future seemed ever so much brighter and more stable, now. The possibilities for the future were enormous. The future felt good.

—

Joanne

—

The weekly Wednesday afternoon bridge card games gave us time to catch up on the neighborhood gossip. This week, it was my turn to host, and the participants this session included Diana, who was usually at the weekly games, along with this week's attendees, Susan and Elizabeth, who preferred Liz. I was the only one with a toddler child. Jessica was taking her afternoon nap. Diana and I usually talked of sex these days, but we all knew Liz was the least comfortable with sex talk. She was far more conventional and traditional than the rest of us, so we curtailed many of our usual topics when she attended.

The talk this day focused on children, school, teachers and the latest attempt by our community board of education to cut costs and remain within the revenue target. These were not particularly stimulating discussions, but they were necessary. Susan had two children – a boy 13 years old, and a girl 10 years old. Liz had three girls – 9, 11 and 15 years old. They were my canaries in the mine for what lay ahead for our children in public school. Diana had no children and doubted that she and Brian would ever mutually decide to have children. She acknowledged that her available window was closing, but she showed little concern.

The opening and closing of the front door announced the arrival of our seven-year-old Ryan.

"Hi, Mom," he said and kissed my lips. "Good afternoon, ladies."

Each of the women returned his greeting.

"Everything OK at school, dear?" I asked.

"Yep. Sure. Missus Brown gave me another gold star for my drawing today."

"Good for you, sweetie."

The ladies offered their congratulations, as well.

Ryan put his backpack on the floor, quietly unbuttoned my blouse and pulled the right side back. My soft, sports bra enabled him to easily extract my right breast. The cool air felt good. I tried to act as if nothing untoward was happening. Diana knew all too well; she just smiled. Liz & Susan displayed various forms of shocked expressions. Ryan held my right breast in both his hands for several seconds, as if he was admiring the unique mound of flesh. I could feel my nipple rising and hardening, partly from the cool air and partly from anticipation. Ryan began to knead my flesh, squeezing my breast gently until he saw drops of milk appear from my nipple. He applied his mouth and started his rhythmic suckling, holding my breast in both his hands and continuing to massage the teat that gave him what he sought. His eyes were closed, as he focused on his activity. I looked at each of the ladies. Diana gave me a wink with her smile, which I returned. Liz averted her eyes with obvious signs of embarrassment and discomfort. Susan could not take her eyes off Ryan at my breast. Ryan was a good, strong sucker. He had also picked up the trait of occasionally and gently biting my nipple with his teeth while he drew milk from my breast. It was not a hard bite, more like an awareness bite – I'm here. The sensation of his little nibbles worked like mild electric shocks to my groin. How he picked up that nuance, I have no idea. I certainly did not teach him to do that, but I definitely appreciated the added stimulation.

The card game stopped. Not a word was said. Only the occasional slurping sound of Ryan's suckling could be heard.

The telltale sensations of pleasure began to well up from my crotch. I knew what was coming. I actually tried to resist those unique feelings. I closed my eyes in my struggle, and then took a quick glance to Diana – it's going to get me. She smiled. I closed my eyes again and pretended to look down at the top of Ryan's head. His hands continued unabated, gently pushing and squeezing my breast.

I heard Liz huff, get up from the table and leave the room. I could not let her see my eyes or my face; it would only add to her . . . what . . . had to be her sense of revulsion. I could feel Diana's smile. I did not have to see her eyes. She knew what was coming. The hot rush of the crashing wave sent convulsions through my whole body. I tried desperately to suppress the physical and audible manifestations of my orgasmic climax without complete success. As the peak subsided, Ryan stopped, pulled away leaving my breast exposed, and looked into my eyes. He smiled, as though he knew what he had just done for his mother. He kissed my lips, and then returned to my breast. He must have satisfied himself that he had drained my right breast after a minute or so. Ryan sat up without taking his eyes off my breast, and then careful returned my teat to the confines of my bra, made sure I was properly positioned for comfort, and then buttoned up my blouse to my cleavage.

"Thanks, Mom," Ryan said, and kissed my lips again. He left the family room and went upstairs to his room.

I finally looked at Diana, who was still smiling from ear to ear. Susan's expression remained frozen in awe, as if she could not believe what she had just witnessed. I gave her a meager smile. Susan remained frozen. I looked around for Liz. She was nowhere in sight. Everyone waited a sufficient time for Ryan to reach his room.

"Well done, Joanne," said Diana softly.

Susan finally released her awe-struck expression. "Isn't he a little old for breastfeeding?"

"Well, I don't think of it as breastfeeding, since he clearly does not need my breast-milk for nourishment. I think it is more like comfort and reassurance to him."

"Did you have an orgasm while he was sucking on you?"

"Yes, she did," answered Diana, almost jubilantly.

"That never happened for me when I breast fed my babies."

"That particular aspect just started for me a few months ago, maybe a year."

"You should see her when she is not fighting to hold it in," Diana added.

Susan snapped her head to Diana. Her expression turned stern. "You've seen this before?"

"Easy, Susan. Yes . . . a couple of weeks ago . . . out by the pool."

Susan snapped back to me with a more severe expression on her face and in her eyes. "So, this has become sexual for you!" she nearly spat. "This is verging on incestuous."

I put both of my hands on the table. I held Susan's eyes. Diana rapidly looked from one to the other, waiting to see what happened next. I took a long, cleansing breath. I started to respond, but no words came out, and I needed another long, deep breath to relax and dampen my anger.

"I am sorry you feel . . ."

Liz passed down the hallway, past the entryway to the family room. "I have to go," she said strongly, without looking into the room.

"Liz, please, come here. Let's talk about this," I pleaded.

The front door opened, but did not shut. I expected to hear the door slam shut in defiance. Instead, we could only hear the muted click of the door latch. Another long pause passed before Liz appeared in the entryway. "I don't know what there is to talk about. What you just did is wrong . . . verging on criminal," she said with surprising calm.

"Liz!" protested Diana.

"Are you going to fuck him next?" Liz growled. Her words stabbed all the more, since she rarely used profanity, and that was the first time I had heard her use the word 'fuck' . . . and it was not in a good way.

"Liz!" protested Diana, again.

Once more, I had to take several deep breaths, as Liz waited for my response.

"You're right, Liz. Perhaps there is nothing to talk about. I do not have to justify how we raise our children to you or anyone else. You choose to . . . you choose . . . to see something nasty, when all there was in that encounter with my son was love."

"You should have cut him off before he was one," she responded.

"So you say. Where is that written in stone?"

"Are you going to be feeding him your tit when he is 13 . . . or 20?"

"Is there something wrong with that?"

"You can't be serious, Joanne," Susan said.

"Where does it stop?"

"I don't know."

"There ya go," spat Liz.

Diana held up her hand. "Stop!" she demanded. "You are each entitled to object and make your own decisions on how best to raise your children, but how dare you condemn Joanne for loving her children, for giving so much of herself to her children."

"You agree with this?" Liz said and waved her arm toward the card table. "You condone this . . . this . . . this incestuous conduct?"

"My God, Liz! Damn you! This is absolutely nothing of the kind," Diana reacted.

"I think you had better go," I said, looking at Liz.

She did not say another word and left.

"I'd better go, too," said Susan.

"I'm sorry you feel this way, Susan. I can only hope both of you can calm down when you've had time to think things through."

"Perhaps," she responded. "Maybe you should rethink your position." Susan did not look back as she left.

Diana grasped my hand and looked into my eyes. "Don't let them change you, Joanne. The love you share with your children is a beautiful and magnificent thing."

"Apparently not."

"Believe in yourself."

"I do, but I've never had anyone react like that."

"Forget them."

"I can't. They probably represent the majority out there."

"Fuck them! What you have with your children is very special. Hell, I can't imagine how they would have reacted if the saw or even knew what we did that afternoon." Diana winked at me.

We both laughed hard.

"I need to go check on, Ryan, in case he heard any of that. I do not want him, or either of my children, contaminated with that corrosive, antiquated thinking."

"OK. I'll see ya later. Stick to your guns, Joanne. Don't let the bitches get to you."

"Thanks, Diana. You are a good friend."

I waited for the door to close behind her, and then I went upstairs to check on my son. The afternoon's reaction cast a dark cloud over what I had always thought was an ordered and worthy life. I needed to talk to Peter about what happened, but first Ryan was most immediately important and Jessica would be up soon.

———

Max

(This story is dedicated to Ginger E.)

——

Gina and Mike had invited us to dinner at their country home, a modest but comfortable home. The house sat back on their five plus acre property next to a good size, dammed pond with plenty of large, mature, elm trees for shade from the afternoon summer sun. Janis and I always enjoyed the parties and dinners at their home.

When we arrived, we joined them with a nice glass of wine. Gina was finishing her *sous-chef* activities, while Mike was preparing the grill. It would be traditional American barbecue fare this evening – steaks, whole potatoes and green salad. As was usually the case with the four of us, Mike and I went outside for the grilling and airplane talk, while the ladies remained inside with their girl talk. There was not much for me to do other than watch Mike perform his manly duties.

The wine flowed freely. By the time we sat down at the patio table, we were all well lubricated. We laughed and joked about everything. The meal was exceptional, as always. Mike and I cleared the table and rinsed the dishes. I sat back down with the ladies. This evening played out like many such get-togethers at each other's home, until Mike changed the script without the slightest hint.

Mike stripped off his clothes, standing there before us stark naked with a stiffening but not fully erect cock and announced. "I'm gettin' in the hot tub." He went to the good size, aboveground, hot tub, uncovered it, and turned on the pumps. Steam rose from the exposed water. He had preheated the water.

The remaining three of us looked at each other without words, as if to say, now what do we do? To my pleasant surprise, Janis pushed back her chair, stood and stripped off all her clothes without the slightest hesitation. It was quite uncommon for her. She usually was not bashful or modest about exposing her ample breasts, but it was rare for her to remove her panties, or her bikini bottom at a nude beach. Yet, there she was in all her beautiful glory. Janis followed Mike into the warm, bubbling water.

I look to Gina. "Do you want to join them?"

"Sure," she answered. Instead of removing her clothes on the patio, Gina went inside.

I removed my clothes and laid them over my chair. I did not need a reason or an excuse to get naked, but I was always cautious about offending anyone with my immodesty. The water was quite warm. I sat on the edge of the tub opposite Janis and Mike. He had his arms resting on the edge. Janis was sitting right next to him, and I imagined she had his cock in her hand, although I could not see through the bubbles. I lowered myself into the hot water.

"Feels good," I proclaimed.

Mike was unusually not talkative and the expression on his face suggested Janis was working his cock well. Gina returned in a one-piece swimsuit. I was disappointed, but that was her choice entirely. She sat down on the edge of the tub next to me.

"Oh, come on, Gina," Mike said, "what's with the suit. Get naked like the rest of us."

"No thanks."

"We're all friends here," Mike continued to press her.

I patted her leg and said softly, "It's OK. No pressure."

Then, Janis stood up. "You're the only one not naked."

My oh my, I sure do love lookin' at that body. I chose not to say anything.

"Well," said Mike, "at least show 'em your magnificent tits." Janis jiggled her breasts. "Come on, Gina, join the party."

"I'm here, aren't I? I'm in the water, aren't I?" Gina protested.

"Yeah, but you're still dressed. We're not."

"That's OK."

"We're all good," I said. "Let's just enjoy this comparatively cool summer evening and good friendship."

"Come on, Gina," Mike persisted. "At least pull your top down."

To my surprise, Gina pulled down part of her suit top, exposing her left breast. Almost instinctively I reached up and gently caressed her bare breast. She looked down at me as I fondled her breast. Without thinking, I partially stood and took her erect nipple in my mouth. I began rhythmically sucking on her nipple and caressing it with my tongue.

Gina softly said, "No," and put her hands on my shoulders to signal her disapproval.

I stopped immediately and turned to sit beside her on the edge of the tub. Mike was also sitting on the edge of the tub with Janis between his spread knees and bobbing her head on his cock.

"Oh yes," Mike groaned. Janis was really working on him.

Without a prompt and to my pleasant surprise, Gina descended into the water and moved smoothly between my legs. I spread my legs for her. She took me into her mouth with easy grace, and worked my cock with clear expertise and pleasure. When I looked up from the top of Gina's head moving rhythmically on me, Janis was bent over the edge of the hot tub and Mike was behind her and obviously working to plug into my wife. He was apparently not achieving a good insertion, but he was certainly persistent. The combination of Gina's skill and the sight that captivated me rocketed me to an amazingly swift and intense orgasm. Gina swallowed every drop I had to offer and she made sure she got it all. When she was satisfied, Gina stood and kissed me passionately. She had great lips and tongue, and I could taste my juice on her lips.

As Gina moved to sit next to me, Mike helped Janis out of the hot tub and bent her, again, over the edge of the outside of the hot tub. Janis looked directly at me and held my eyes, as Mike pressed his efforts to enter her. It was exciting to be watching them. I wanted to see him thrust into her and deposit his load in her. He apparently gave up his attempts in front of an audience. Mike grabbed Janis by the hand and nearly dragged her into the house, apparently to focus on their coupling.

"I guess they didn't want us watching," I said.

"Apparently not," answered Gina.

I looked to Gina. "Please allow me to be so bold, may I lick you off?"

She smiled, at least, and said, "No. It's OK."

"You got me off . . . quite well, I must say, and I would be honored to get you off in return."

"Thank you for that, but it's not necessary."

"Are you sure?"

"Yes. Thanks. It's that time of the month for me." Gina got out of the tub.

I joined her. "That doesn't bother me."

"I know, but it bothers me. I just can't relax like that."

"Do you want to go watch them?" I asked, changing the subject slightly.

"No. That would probably not help Mike. It looked like he was having trouble getting hard enough to fuck her. Probably too much wine, but you never know."

"Perhaps so."

"You are welcome to go in and join them, if you wish," Gina said softly. "I don't mind."

"That's OK. I'll stay with you. Do you want to sit down?"

Gina nodded her head and returned to the chairs at the table. I chose to remain naked, which did not seem to bother her in the slightest. We talked about her recent graphic arts projects and her plans for making a sustainable business. Her skills with Adobe Photoshop and their related application improved with each task she took on with her computer. She was not ready to call herself an artist, but that is the descriptor that seemed most appropriate.

I had no idea how long Gina and I talked, but it was engaging and worthwhile. Janis and Mike appeared from inside the house, both still naked and both with smiles on their faces. Mike's cock was limp and still wet in appearance, which probably meant it was satisfied.

"Looks like y'all had a good time," I said.

"Yes, indeed," responded Mike. "Always a pleasure." Janis just nodded her concurrence.

"What time is it?" asked Janis.

None of us had a watch. Gina found her cell phone under some clothes. "Almost eleven," Gina announced.

"We best be getting home," Janis said. "Sago will probably be wondering where we disappeared to."

We all stood, hugged and kissed. Janis grabbed her clothes with no attempt to put them on, so I did the same. We would drive home naked, which was always an extra treat. I loved to see Janis's breasts jiggle with each bump in the road. We thanked them for the great company, delicious meal and extracurricular activities. I opened the passenger door for Janis. She grabbed my shirt from my arm and put it on the seat.

Janis whispered to me, "I've got a nice cream pie for you when we get home."

"Nice," I said.

We waved to Gina and Mike, as we started down the long driveway to the rural road. There was little risk on our drive home, since it was all country roads with about half of it still gravel. I decided to contain my eagerness and let Janis talk when she was ready. It only took a mile or so.

"I know you want to hear what happened."

"Sure, you know me."

"Mike tried a few times at the hot tub, but he never got hard enough to get in . . . probably too much wine. After all, he's performed in front of you before. Anyway, we went to their guest room bed. It still took me a while to get him hard, but he eventually got there. To my surprise, he worked pretty hard with his dick to get me off, but I never quite made it when he shot his load in me. He said he hadn't cum in a couple of weeks, so it should be a nice one for you. Most of it has probably dripped out, but there should be enough for you to enjoy."

"Do you want to stop now, so I can finish you off?"

"No. Let's get home, so we can enjoy ourselves. Doing it in the car or on the roadside just isn't as exciting as it once was."

"OK."

"Did you and Gina fuck, too?"

"No. She said she was on the rag, so I never got close to her pussy."

"Did you get to play at all?"

"Nope. Just talked . . . well, you may not have seen it since you were sucking Mike, but Gina sucked me off in short order."

"I'm sorry, sweetheart. I'll do my best to make it up to you. At least you got to experience one of her famous blow-jobs."

"Thanks honey."

A few minutes later, we arrived home. I shut the garage door before we got out . . . no need to embarrass the neighbors. We tried to let Sago out. She had to be ready to pee for the night. Sago was poking her nose into Janis's crotch. She wanted some of Mike's man-milk she smelled. Janis let her lick the inside of her thighs a little, and then I made her go outside. By the time, I reached the bedroom with Sago, Janis had the covers and top sheet pulled back. She was laying on her back with her knees raised and spread wide; she was quite ready. Sago thought the invitation was for her. We laughed and got Sago settled onto her bed.

I smiled broadly and jumped to my task without words. My tongue probed her pussy. Sure enough, I could taste her and the distinct flavor of cum – Mike's man-milk. I mixed my lapping up her juices, enjoying her delicious cream pie, and sucking and tongue flicking her clit to heighten her pleasure. Janis responded well. Her moans and writhing body movements signaled her rise to climax. I inserted two fingers to work her G-Spot, as I continued my attention on her clit. I began thrusting my fingers into her, rubbing her G-Spot with each inward thrust. Janis was indeed ready. She started her unmistakable ascend to the peak she sought in comparatively short order. All of her muscles began to twitch, and then shake. Her arched back and her moans came from deep within her and became almost a primordial growl. I pressed my efforts to extend her peak, as long as she would allow me. Janis grasped my head and pushed me away from her clit – too sensitive. Her convulsions of pleasure continued and slowly began to subside. I could feel the rhythmic contractions of her vaginal muscles – a sure sign it was a good orgasm for her.

When I could no longer feel her carnal convulsions, I slowly removed my fingers from her, but I did not move. I just wanted to enjoy the smell of her satisfied pussy and feel the warmth of her pleasure on my face. Janis's chest heaved rapidly, her breasts jiggling with each exhalation, as she fought to recover after her exertion. Her respiratory rate gradually slowed. She took one last deep, cleansing breath, and then raised her head to look into my eyes still peering over her bare mound.

"Oh my, that was a good one, honey," she pronounced. "Well done."

"Thanks. Truly my pleasure."

"You've always enjoyed munching the puss. I'm such a lucky woman."

"And, I am a blessed man to be here," I said and gave her clit a good swipe with my tongue, which sent shudders through her body.

"OK, you devilish little boy. I hope you're ready. I need a good fucking, now."

"You already had a good fucking tonight."

"I need another one. Stop wasting time. Poke that dangly thing in me and go to town."

Surprisingly for me, I needed little effort to get hard. I moved my hips closer to hers. I rubbed the head of my cock on her still sensitive clit, intermittently lubricating my cock-head with her plentiful juices at the opening. Each time I hit her clit she twitched, again. Then, in one smooth, slippery stroke I went all the way into her, causing her to gasp.

"Oh yes," she muttered, "fuck me good. Fuck me really good."

I figured she was no longer interested in subtlety or finesse; she did indeed want a nice hard fucking. I immediately began pounding into her. The slapping of our flesh was so pronounced and audible, adding to the sensations for me . . . and probably for her. I loved to watch her breasts jiggle with each impact.

"Yes . . . yes, yes," she mumbled.

I could feel the beads of sweat building, and then descending down my torso. I shifted my position, as I continued to stroke into her, in an effort to rub her clit as much as I could. That was apparently all she needed. Her head arched back, again, and her body shook uncontrollably as orgasm enveloped her. I persisted in giving her as much as I could. As she began to recover, I stopped.

"No, no, keep going. You've not shot, yet, and I want to feel your orgasm." She smiled and grabbed my hips, clearly gesturing for me to continue my exertion. "Who knows, maybe I can get off, again." She raised her head and shoulders to kiss me.

I returned to my effort. Janis did her part. She twisted her torso so that she could reach under her legs and between mine to stroke my balls, pulling on them slightly as I stroked. When that was not enough to push me up the mountain, Janis resorted to what she knew was a surefire trigger.

Janis felt for my rosebud, found it and gently and rhythmically pressed my button. When that did not immediately send me up the peak, she said, "Do you want to take me in the ass? I prepared before we left for Mike and Gina's."

The mere suggestion was apparently enough. I felt the characteristic sensation of my ascent. I scooted my knees forward, grasped her hips as if to hold them firmly and began to rapidly thrust into her. "Aaaawwww," I groaned, as I began pumping into her. I had no idea what I had left, but whatever was there went deep into her. I held her tightly to me until I came down from my peak.

I literally collapsed and fell away from Janis. This time it was my chest that was heaving, gasping for air. Janis moved to straddle my face with her pussy just above my mouth. She was trying to feed me my cum from her pussy, if there was any in her. I could see her contracting her abdominal muscles, trying to push out whatever was inside her. Between breaths I licked her lips. Sure enough, eventually, I got a few drops. I was pleasantly surprised there was any in there. I had never been a big cummer.

Janis got off of me and lay down, rolled toward me, and placed her top leg over mine. She rested her head on my shoulder with the arm wrapped around her. Her breasts and erect nipples always felt good on my chest. "We always have such great sex after we've been with others."

"That we do, my darling," I acknowledged somewhat breathlessly.

"You worked hard, Max."

"All to pleasure you, my dear."

"And, you did that in spades. We should both sleep well tonight."

"You got that right." I kissed her passionately. "I love you very much."

"I love you."

"Do you want to clean up before we head to never-never-land?"

"No. I'll wash the sheets in the morning, and who knows, maybe we'll knock off another one in the morning with your usual morning woody."

I smiled and kissed her again. We repositioned and cuddled, again, under the covers this time. I switched off the lights. Sleep claimed us swiftly.

Cato

(This story is dedicated to a family in Australia
that shall remain anonymous
for reasons that will become all too apparent.)

———

The family compound sat comfortably in the middle of 40 hectares (100 acres) of mature and healthy forest. The family had owned the land since the colonial days. Over the years, the compound evolved as buildings were added to accommodate the growing family. Five main homes arranged in a 'U' orientation housed four generations of the family. A large, well maintained swimming pool occupied the middle of the 'U' along with exterior tables and chairs to seat the whole family plus some. Several cottages provided comfortable privacy for guests and transient extended family members. While as many of the trees as possible were retained around the buildings, several large plots had been fully cleared and fertile ground cultivated to grow a broad range of fruits and vegetables as well as sufficient grains and grass to support a dozen milk cows and goats. They also raised pigs, chickens and even a few turkeys imported from the United States. The farm was productive beyond self-sufficiency. The family sold their excess in the local farmer's market, earning sufficient income to support the family.

I knew much of the detail from Caleb, my best friend and classmate in school, since we had both started school together. We had been mates through primary and into secondary school. Caleb had stayed at my house and met my family many times. Yet, every time the discussion turned to visiting his farm and meeting his family, the subject was changed. I had met his sister who was two years older and his brother who was two years younger than Caleb. I had also met his parents at various school events but never at their home.

At lunch this particular day, Caleb said, "My Mum wants to talk to us after school today."

"What about?"

"About you spending the weekend with us on the farm."

"Really?"

"Yes, really. Can you stay? She will drive you home after we talk."

"Sure. I don't know why not. I will call my Mum to tell her I will be a little late."

"Excellent."

"So, I'll finally get to hear and see what is so secretive about your farm and family?"

"Mum wants to make sure you understand the rules."

"What rules?"

"She will tell you. It is not my place"

"We've done some rather personal things together, Caleb," I reminded my friend.

"Yes, we have, but have you told your Mum and Dad what we've done?"

"Oh God, no."

"Well, that is exactly what my Mum is concerned about."

"I don't think I understand."

"You will. Now, it's almost time for afternoon classes. Why don't you call your Mum before class starts."

"Good idea."

We deposited our disposables in the rubbish bin and went to the common telephone for students. Caleb stood by me and heard my part of the conversation.

When I hung up, I said, "She said it was alright."

"Smashing. Let's get to class. Don't want to be late."

It was more difficult than usual for me to concentrate on our studies. My thoughts diverted to what I might hear from Caleb's mother. The clock seemed to creep along, but the end of the school day arrived. Mrs. G. was waiting for us when we walked out to the pick-up area.

"Ay Mum," Caleb said loudly, as he opened the passenger door.

"G'day Mrs. G.," I said, opening the rear door.

"Good afternoon boys." Mrs. G. waited until the doors closed and she heard two clicks from our seat belts. She drove away to make room for other parents behind them. "How would Tommy's Café be for our chat?"

Caleb looked over his shoulder to see my head nod concurrence. "That should work, Mum."

The drive only took ten minutes and our conversation was all about the school day. Mrs. G. parked and we found a nice corner table, away from the few patrons in the establishment. Caleb and I sat across from his Mom. A waiter attended to us promptly. Mrs. G. ordered a pot of tea and biscuits, while Caleb and I asked for sodas. The waiter returned with our drinks.

"Let me jump right to it," said Mrs. G. "I wish this particular conversation did not have to play out this way, Cato, but I am a realist in our society." I nodded my head. "I understand you are now producing . . ."

"Producing?" I asked.

"Semen."

I felt myself fidgeting and flush. I must have turned beet red.

"I am not trying to embarrass you, Cato. I was only trying to speak frankly. I also understand you and Caleb have traded cum."

I looked immediately to Caleb, who simply smiled and shrugged his shoulder. "Yes, we have," I confessed.

"Thank you for sharing that with me, Cato. Our family is rather unique. We are very open, at least within the family, about sex and anatomy. We keep our family life private, which is why we do not often invite people to visit. Caleb has been after me for several years. You are best mates, and I respect that. However, to be blunt and direct, it only takes one slip of the tongue to spoil our privacy. For reasons we can talk about later, if you wish, society is not tolerant of our lifestyle and it is very unforgiving of our alleged violations of societal norms. You and your family have been most generous with Caleb, and it is time to welcome you into our family. However, as Caleb respected your family's rules, we expect you to respect ours. So, let me stop there and ask if you have any questions?"

"I am not sure what all this is about. Caleb has told me about your farm, and I suppose I assumed it was like any other farm in this area of the country."

"Well, it is . . . to an extent, but I must know . . . my whole family must know that you will respect our privacy. What you see, hear, feel, taste, smell when you are will us must remain private. We are not ashamed of who we are, but we are also realists to know the society in which we live. Does that make sense?"

"I think so. But, I do not know what you are concerned about here?"

"Caleb trusts you, so I shall trust you. Before I explain our concern, I must say we are taking a rather serious risk in even talking about this with you. We should be talking to your parents."

"That probably would not work," I said, interrupting her.

"Yes, therein lies the problem. I do not want our way of living to come between you and Caleb, and the friendship the two of you enjoy, which is precisely why we are having this discussion. If you can accept our conditions, you will be exposed to things your parents would likely not approve. As a minor child, which you are, as is Caleb, that exposure would betray your parents' authority under the law. We have no interest whatsoever in becoming crosswise with the law. I hope you see our dilemma."

"I think I do."

"I need your assurance that you will respect our privacy," Mrs. G. said, staring rather sternly at me.

I looked into her eyes and felt the seriousness. "I promise."

"Very well, then. We have four generations of our family and some of our extended family living at our compound. We will soon have the first of our fifth generation appear in a few months. My parents and two of my grandparents live on the farm; one of my sisters and my only brother also live at the farm. My older sister visits from time to time. I was raised . . . Caleb and his sisters are being raised with nudity and exposure to sex. You are 13 years old, like Caleb, and you are past puberty, so biologically you are an adult, although the law says you will not be an adult under the law until your 18th birthday. We are proud of who we are and how we live, but we do not flaunt our lifestyle with anyone, and we expect every visitor to respect our choices. Now, the important part . . . no one, and I do mean no one, should ever force or coerce you into doing anything you do not wish to do. It is your choice entirely if you want to remove your clothes – no requirement, no pressure. It will be your choice entirely whether you wish to participate in any sexual conduct, and by that I mean any touching for pleasure. Always, no means no, period, full stop. Lastly, our family cannot and will not get between you and your family. You must respect your family and whatever restrictions your parents may have applied. Do you understand all this?"

"Yes ma'am."

"We will be honest with you. We will trust you to be honest with us."

"Yes ma'am."

Mrs. G. held my eyes, glanced at Caleb, and said, "Please don't disappoint us, Cato."

"I won't Mrs. G."

"Do you have any questions for me or Caleb?"

I glanced at Caleb beside me. He did not react and just waited for me. I looked back to Mrs. G. "I probably have questions I do not know how to ask."

"Well, you are welcome to ask any question of anyone in our family, as long as you respect our privacy and our rules."

"Thank you Mrs. G. I will not let you down."

"I trust you won't, Cato. Thank you. Now, finish your drinks. Let's take you home, so I can ask your parents for their permission for you to spend the weekend with us."

"Excellent. I'm all for that."

When we arrived at my home, my Mom and siblings – two older sisters and my younger brother – were home. Dad was not expected home for another hour or so. Mom and Mrs. G. had a nice, short chat and permission was granted. True to her word, Mrs. G. did not mention the conversation or the conditions of my visit, and I was perfectly fine with that reality. I exchanged the books and school materials in my backpack for a change of clothes, a couple pairs of undies, and my few toiletries.

The drive to the G. farm took another 45 minutes, since they lived in the country beyond the other side of town. It was a gorgeous drive, and to my surprise, my family had passed by the entrance to their property many times on our way to the state park and beaches to the north. Mrs. G. turned off the main, paved roadway onto a rather windy, gravel path. She stopped. Caleb jumped out to retrieve the post for the compound from the large roadside post box. Mrs. G drove down the pathway through a comparatively thick part of the forest and a rather thick hedgerow that was too straight to be naturally occurring. The thick, continuous hedge appeared to be a more natural form of a fence. On the other side, there were the compound's buildings, just as Caleb described them. Mrs. G. drove to the left corner house of the 'U' and parted in an adjoining, covered carport.

The interior of their ranch-style home was spacious, well kept and homey. We followed Mrs. G. into the kitchen. Mr. G. was stark naked, chopping fresh vegetables probably for the evening meal. I had never seen him without clothes before and I could not take my eyes off his long, flaccid cock and no hair around his cock or balls.

"Welcome to our home and the farm, Cato."

"Thank you, Mr. G. It's great to finally be here." I tried to look away, but apparently I was not successful.

"It's OK. I experience that response a lot, I'm afraid," Mr. G. said and chuckled.

"It's true," Mrs. G. added and turned to her husband. "Do you need any help at the moment?"

"Nope. I have this under control. Go get comfortable."

"Come on, Cato. Let's do the same," Caleb said, and then he grabbed my hand and led me down the hallway to his room. Once inside his room, he closed the door, but did not lock it. "Do want to take your clothes off?"

"I guess so. Sure."

Caleb immediately began undressing. He partially folded his clothes and placed them on the back of a wooden, straight back chair. I folded my clothes and placed on a small chest of drawers. I felt my dick reacting, but tried not to think about it. Caleb smiled and said, "My Dad has a really nice cock, ay."

That did it. Whatever control I thought I might have had vanished in an instant, as the image of Mr. G.'s magnificent member returned front and center to my thoughts.

"There's my mate," Caleb said, staring at my spontaneous erection. "Let me take care of that for you. It will help." I hesitated, not knowing how to respond. He did not wait for consent.

Caleb dropped to his knees in front of me and took my cock in his mouth. It felt so good – the wet, warmth of his mouth. He had only stroked onto me a half dozen times or so, when the hot, electric jolts shook my body. He slowed his motion, and then stopped. As he withdrew, he licked the tip several times, which sent more shudders through my body.

Caleb licked his lips. "Yummy, yummy. That was good."

"Do you want me to do you?"

"Not necessary. I just want to relief a little of the pressure, just in case you might feel embarrassed in front of my family with a hard on . . . not that they care. It happens all the time . . . even to us."

"I've never been naked in front of people before . . . well, other than you, Caleb."

"I know, which is why I wanted to help you and tell you not to worry about stiffies."

"Thanks mate."

"Indeed. What are mates for, right? Anyway, we need to get out there. You can do me later, if you wish."

"Sure."

I followed Caleb back out to the large room that was the kitchen on one end, the living room on the opposite end and the large dining table in the middle. For the first time, I saw Mrs. G. without clothes. She maintained a pin-up level body, despite birthing three children and no signs of stretch marks. Like Mr. G., she had no detectible pubic hair. The most intriguing part of her anatomy was her puffy, mounded, pink areolas on modest-sized, less than perky breasts with prominent erect nipples.

"Are you boys ready for supper?" asked Mr. G.

"Yes sir," I answered.

"Caleb," Mrs. G. said, "call your sister and brother to dinner." Caleb left to retrieve his siblings. I placed my hands in front of my groin. "It's OK, Cato. Your youthful vigor will come in handy around here. Would you like me to help you with that?"

I felt my whole body flush. "No thank you, Ma'am. It's just a little embarrassing."

"I can only assure you there is nothing to be embarrassed about . . . an erection is a normal and natural male response. They are not uncommon around the farm."

Caleb returned with Nate and Missy, who were introduced to me. Nate was 11 years old and showed no signs of pubic hair. Missy was 15 years old with nice perky breasts and puffy areolas like her Momma. She wore small white panties, which was a curiosity in this household.

The meal was all homegrown on the family farm – a vegetable medley salad, baked chicken, baked potatoes, butter and fresh milk. The conversation centered solely on school and there was even genuine curiosity about my experience. Missy was not particularly talkative. She finished her supper and excused herself from the table. *She seems a little angry. I wonder what the problem is? What is she angry about? She is a very attractive girl and anger does not suit her.*

When everyone had finished dinner, Caleb and I cleared the table. Caleb started washing the dishes, putting leftovers in the refrigerator, and cleaning up. I helped without asking why. By the time we finished cleaning up, Mr. & Mrs. G. had moved to another room.

"Let's go," Caleb said. "I'd like to introduce you to my great-grand-parents."

"OK."

We went to the adjacent house that was the base of the 'U' distribution. Caleb stopped before we reached the full, surrounding porch. "A couple of things you should know before I introduce you. Great-Granddad S. does not approve of cocksuckers like us."

"Really. That seems strange. Your family is very open."

"Yes, odd. Granddad D. is also not into cock. So, we just don't mention things like that around them and we don't ask them to play with their cocks.

"OK."

"Also, Great-Gran'mum S. has the biggest clit any of us have ever seen. We are always showing it off, and she does not mind. Actually, I think she enjoys showing it to people. Let me ask her if we can touch and suck on it a little. Sometimes, she doesn't feel like clit play."

"Are you sure? She's never met me."

"You are with me. Just let me ask her first."

"OK. Hey, Caleb, before we go inside, I was wondering . . . your sister seemed angry at dinner. Is there a problem I need to be aware of with her?"

"No. I don't think so. It is just that time of the month for her."

"Oh! That's why she was wearing knickers?"

"Yeah. She's also probably horny and no one wants to have a poke at her when she's bleeding."

"I would," I proclaimed, although I immediately questioned my spontaneous words.

"Well, then, I'll ask her for you."

"I don't want to embarrass her. I've never fucked a girl, so I don't know what I'm doing."

"It's OK. It's just messy. We can throw a tarpaulin down and wash it off afterward. Heck, if you do it, perhaps I'll take a poke at her, too."

"Have you fucked your sister?" I asked with surprised curiosity.

"Yes, and my Mum."

"Really?" Caleb nodded his head. "Wow! That's incredible."

"Not so incredible . . . just natural for us."

"Damn, that's amazing. I can't imagine fucking my Mum."

"That's only because you did not grow up with sex openly in your family, which is the primary reason my Mum was so concerned about questioning you before you came here."

"Sure. I understand."

"Are you ready to meet my great-grandparents now? You can ask more questions later."

"Sure."

They stepped onto the porch and approached the front door. Caleb knocked but did not wait for a response. I followed Caleb inside. Mr. & Mrs. S. were sitting in adjacent, large, leather covered, lounge chairs, watching a television program of some sort. They were both clearly older. Their skin was more saggy and wrinkled than the others. I felt my dick stiffen, again, but I tried to ignore the reality. Mr. S. sat with his legs open. His uncut cock just lay there, surrounded by graying pubic hair. Mrs. S sat cross-legged. Her breasts were deflated with her nipples at the bottom of the arc of her breasts. She had short, grey hair and a broad smile that bloomed when we walked in.

"Well, now," Mrs. S. said, "who is this young buck you have with you, Caleb?"

"Gran'mum, Gran'da, this is my best mate from school, Cato."

Mr. S. extended his right hand. Caleb shook hands. "Nice to meet you, boy."

"Nice to meet you, Mr. S."

Mrs. S. extended her hand to me . . . not for my hand but to grasp my dick. She wrapped her hand around me and pulled gently toward her. Then, she released it and held it between her thumb and index finger. Mrs. S. inspected like it some laboratory specimen. "Very nice." She released me. "A pleasure to meet Caleb's best mate, Cato."

"Thank you, ma'am."

"What can I do for you, Caleb? Well, actually, I can probably guess. You want to show your best mate my famous clitoris."

I looked at Caleb. He just smiled at me, and then said to Grandma S., "I guess I am getting too predictable."

"That's quite alright, Caleb." She turned on the adjacent reading light, scooted her pelvis toward the front edge of her chair, and spread her legs wide placing her knees over the chair's arms. *Damn, I can't believe how easy this is for an old woman.* "Go ahead, boys, have a close look."

I followed Caleb's lead. I knelt down with him between her widely spread legs. "Wow!" I started to say that's the size of a small cock, but I caught myself not wanting to offend Mr. S. I glanced over to Grandpa S. He was watching us with a smile of his face. *I guess he approves.* I could feel my rock hard cock throbbing.

"You can touch it, if you wish," Mrs. S. said.

I looked back to Mr. S., who gestured with his head to go ahead. I looked at Caleb, who made essentially the same gesture. *This is incredible. I can't believe Caleb's whole family is this open and devoid of modesty.* I reached out and touched the soft skin partially covering her clit. *Damn, it feels like a small cock – soft skin that moves over a hard shaft beneath the skin. Even the tip looks like a cock head poking out of foreskin.*

"Here . . . like this," Caleb said. He gently grasped each side of her clit shaft with his thumb and index finger, and began to rhythmically stroke her, just like he was doing a small cock.

"Oh, yes," Mrs. S. gushed, "that's my boy. You know just how to stroke it." She leaned her head back and closed her eyes to enjoy the sensations.

I watched Caleb work her clit. He inserted two fingers and began stroking into her love tunnel, and then intermixed sucking on her clit and flicking his tongue on the tip. After several minutes, Caleb looked at me and gestured, as if to say, do you want to try some? I nodded my head and smiled. Mrs. S. did not move as we switched places. I replicated Caleb's efforts.

"That's it," Mrs. S. murmured without raising her head or opening her eyes, "you're doing real good, my boy. Just keep going . . . just like that. Momma's goin'ta heaven real soon."

Her hips began to pulsate, almost like she was fucking. I kept doing what she seemed to enjoy. Confirmation came several minutes later when all of her muscles began to twitch and shake.

Mrs. S. groaned, "Oohhh yyyeesss." Her breathing became shallow and rapid, while her entire body continued to shutter. "Aaaahhhh." As the tremors subsided, Mrs. S. held up her hands, but did not push me away. "Enough," she said clearly.

I stopped and withdrew from her. Caleb and I remained kneeling in front of her.

"I know Caleb has learned since infancy how to eat the kitty, but Cato, you surprise me. You are to young to know about a woman's pleasure."

"Who taught you?" asked Mr. S.

I looked to Grandpa S. and answered, "Caleb taught me, sir."

"Apparently, you learned well, lad. The missus doesn't climax like that often."

"Quite so," added Mrs. S.

"Thank you for allowing me to do that, ma'am."

"The pleasure was mine, Cato. You are welcome to visit any time you wish." She glanced at my erection. "Would you like me to take care of that for you?"

I was a bit surprised and hesitated.

"We'd better get back to the house, Gran'mum," Caleb responded.

We said our good-byes and left his grandparents' home.

When stepped outside, it was dusk. "That was incredible," I pronounced.

"I thought you would like that. She does have an impressive clit, doesn't she?"

"That's an understatement," I answered. "Have you fucked her?"

"Yes, as a matter of fact, I have . . . more than once, actually."

"This is all so much for me to absorb. I've always known your family was different, but I just had no idea. All this is amazing and yet scary."

"I've grown up with bodies and sex since as far back as I can remember, and my parents and sister tell me it was from birth for all of us."

"Why?"

"Well, to my understanding, it is because my family believes bodies and sex are natural and normal. But, I suppose we really should have asked Gran'mum and Gran'da. Maybe we can ask Mum and Dad later. Now, we really should go inside."

"Sure."

I followed Caleb into the house. Most of the lights had been switched off and the quiet of night occupied the common rooms. Missy was in her room, sitting at her desk with headphones on and probably listening to her favorite music while she did something on her computer. Nate was not in his room.

The light on in his parents' room indicated the door was open and they were not asleep. I assumed Caleb wanted to inform his parents that we were back home. Caleb did not speak and stopped at the door. I looked in and was shocked. Mrs. G was lying on the bed with her legs straight up and spread wide. Mr. G. was between her legs with his arms straight and just under her shoulders, as his hips thrust into her. I could see the shaft of his shiny rigid cock on each outward stroke. More shocking, Nate was between his father's legs, fondling his scrotum and testicles, while he watched the union of his parents close-up. Mrs. G. noticed us, smiled and gave us a little wave. I stepped back away from the door, feeling embarrassment that we walked in on a moment of intimacy.

I knew my parents still enjoyed sex. I could hear them from time to time, but I had never seen them doing it. I had seen my parents naked more than a few times, but never having sex.

"It's OK," Caleb whispered to me. "We watch our parents all the time. They don't mind."

"Really?"

"Yeah. We don't have to watch," Caleb said and started to move away.

"OK. If they don't mind, I'd like to watch. I'm fascinated."

Mr. and Mrs. G. shifted positions several times as we watched. When Mr. G. pulled his knees forward beside Mrs. G.'s hips, it gave Nate even better access. I was captivated by Nate's caressing of his father's balls as they swung like pendulums with each thrust. Mrs. G. was the first to climax, as her extended legs began to shake and wobble like those inflatable tube men used for advertising. She groaned and arched her head back, enjoying the orgasmic waves washing over her. Mr. G. redoubled his efforts to extend her orgasm and picked up his thrusting pace. His climax came within minutes with his hips slapping against her flesh in audible claps, as he pumped his juice into her.

Mr. G. rolled off of Mrs. G., away from us, and lifted his near leg over his youngest son, still between his legs. His chest was heaving from his exertion. His cock was not quite as stiff as it was and it was now covered with the combination of their juices. Another shock came when Nate immediately moved to his father and began licking his cock like a big ice cream stick.

"We have an audience," Mrs. G. said softly.

Mr. G. raised his head while his youngest son cleaned up his cock. "Ay boys."

Mrs. G. looked back to us. "Either or both of you boys wanna have a go?" she asked. "It's all warmed up and happy for you, if you wish."

Before we could answer, Nate jumped to his Mom, inserted his dick and began thrusting his hips. She caressed his hair with both hands and allowed him to continue. Mrs. G. waved us forward. Caleb slowly stepped forward. I followed him. This is mind-blowing . . . being so close to an 11-year-old boy fucking his mother. Nate was feverishly pounding away into his mother; the slapping of flesh confirmed each inward stroke and gushy, slurping sounds accentuating each outward stroke. Mrs. G. cupped her ample left breast. Caleb knew the signal and did not need words. He climbed on the bed and went directly to work, attending to her left breast and nipple. Nate's conclusion, whatever it was, did not take long to achieve. His whole body stiffened, and I heard a soft, almost inaudible grunt. Nate kissed his mother on the lips, withdrew from her and returned to his father's now flaccid but still impressive cock to finish his clean-up task. Caleb did not hesitate. As soon as Nate moved away, Caleb took his younger brother's place and began humping his mother without hesitation. Mrs. G. looked at me, grasped her left breast, again, smiled and nodded her head. I knew what she was suggesting and moved next to her. I fondled Mrs. G.'s left breast to feel the soft, fleshiness of her tit. I swirled by tongue around her erect nipple like Caleb had showed me. Mrs. G. stroked my hair and caressed my head, as I sucked on and tongued her nipple. She seemed to be appreciative of my effort, but it was hard to think of her with a tittie in my face and mouth. I occasionally glanced to see Caleb's cock thrusting into Mrs. G. *I know this is wrong, but it feels so right.* Then, I recognized the characteristic snorting of Caleb's orgasm, as he shot his load into her as deep as he could. He too kissed his mother on the lips when he was done.

"Thanks Mom," Caleb said softly.

"My pleasure Son." Mrs. G. looked directly into my eyes. "It's your turn, Cato, if you want to fuck me."

I stopped sucking, but held her breast in both hands. "Is it OK?" I whispered.

"Yes," she answered, "as long as you want to feel it."

Caleb and I switched places. There was already cum oozing out of her pink slit. I could feel my cock throbbing so hard it was almost painful. I looked down at my swollen cock-head, aimed it at the cream-filled opening at the bottom of her slit, and smoothly slipped it into her. It was warm, almost hot, and very slippery and smooth. *This feels so good all by itself, and this is my first time.* I began thrusting into Mrs. G.'s love-tunnel. *That feels even better.* Her skin was so soft and velvety. I looked up, as I continued stroking, to see her smiling broadly and watching me. The sensations proved too much for my inexperience. The peak came sharply. I grabbed her hips and thrust hard into her, as the hot waves and bolts of my electric orgasm shot through my body. Then, without thinking, I leaned forward and kissed Mrs. G. on the lips.

She grasped my head at the back of my neck and head, and kissed me more passionately, poking her tongue into my mouth and dancing with my tongue. The sensations and emotions were overwhelming and proved more than I could handle. Tears formed and descended my cheeks. Mrs. G. released me and I sat back cross-legged between her still spread and raised knees. *What are those tears? Am I feeling guilty for having done this, for having witnessed what I have today?*

"Who wants Momma's cream pie?" Mrs. G. asked with a light and airy voice.

Again, Nate was the first to move without words and planted his face between his mother's legs, presumably licking up the combined deposits of all of us. While Nate worked on Mrs. G., she looked past her youngest son to hold my eyes.

"I hope this was not too much for you on your first visit," she said.

"I've never done anything like this. I certainly understand your words this afternoon better."

"Do you want to talk about it?" she asked, as Nate continued his task between her legs.

"I don't know." I lowered my eyes.

"What is bothering you, Cato?" Mrs. G. asked.

Mr. G. raised up on his left elbow, looking at me.

"Isn't all this incest?" I asked, shocking myself with the question. "I'm sorry. That slipped out."

It was verging on surreal. *Here I am, sitting naked in front of Caleb's parents with his younger brother still lapping up the undoubtedly still flowing juice.*

"It's OK, Cato," Mrs. G. answered. "It is an understandable concern given society's definition of normal. Yes, according to the law, sexual relations between immediate family members is incest; but, let me ask you. Was anyone forced or coerced to do anything they did not want to do?" I shook my head. "Was anyone hurt or injured?" I shook my head, again. "Then, why is it wrong?"

"I don't know. I was just taught that it was."

"Yes, exactly. You were taught society's normal. There are good reasons for the law, but there are also inappropriate reasons, as well. Pregnancy between immediate family members can produce malformed children. Our entire family takes precautions to ensure pregnancy does not happen between related family members. We love each other. We love the pleasure of sex, as a celebration of life, if you will. We have raised our family . . . all our children . . . with that same respect for and appreciation for sensual pleasure."

Nate apparently finished licking up as much as he was going to get. He took a seated position next to me. Caleb sat on the other side of me. Mrs. G. raised herself, crossed her legs without the slightest sign of modesty, and sat in front me. Even Mr. G. took a seated position on the bed next to Mrs. G.

"This is why I asked you all those questions, so carefully this afternoon. Most people, including your parents, I suspect, would not approve of the way we choose to live our lives. What we are doing . . . what you experienced to-night . . . is not wrong. Yes, it is against the law, but the law is wrong in that it is too broad and indiscriminant. Did any of this feel wrong to you, Cato?"

"Well, no, it felt very good. Please don't misinterpret my concern. I am most grateful that you have welcomed me into your family . . . that you have allowed me to share in your pleasure. It is just that I have so much to sort out in my mind, like why does society react so strongly to something that feels so good, so right, so appropriate? I don't know the answer, but I think it is important for me to understand. I have so much to learn from you."

"And, you are free to learn as much as you wish, as long as you respect our privacy and our choices."

"I will," I said as earnestly as I could.

"Excellent. Then, we shall have no problems. Now, the hour is advancing. We all need to be off to slumber," said Mrs. G. "Perhaps, we can pick up the conversation tomorrow. It is important for you . . . and for us."

"Sure. That would be nice."

"Very well, then. Thank you all for this evening's pleasure," Mrs. G. said. "See you in the morning."

With that, Nate, Caleb and I got off the bed and left the bedroom. Nate went to his room. Caleb and I went to his room. I had so many questions to ask Caleb, but I knew we also needed to get to sleep. My mind churned over this evening's events, but sleep soon claimed me.

—

THE END

of

Volume II

J. Laux Perren
Author

J. Laux was born in Toulouse, France. She immigrated with her parents to the United States before her school years and still resides in New York City – a metropolitan city she truly enjoys. J. Laux spent all of her school years in the city and proudly graduated from Columbia University with a Bachelor of Arts degree in Sociology. She is fascinated by the human condition and experience.

DUCLERC